Tea at
Gunter's

Tea at Gunter's

Pamela Haines

**INNER
CIRCLE**

First published in this edition in
Great Britain in 1991 by
Inner Circle Books of London W1

The quotation on p.71 from the poem 'Juliet' by Hilaire
Belloc (*Sonnets & Verse*) is reproduced by kind permission
of Gerald Duckworth

British Library Cataloguing in Publication Data
Haines, Pamela *1929 –*
  Tea at Gunter's.
  I. Title
  823.914 [F]

  ISBN 1-85018-089-X

Printed and bound in Great Britain by
Billing & Sons Ltd, Worcester

for Tony

Chapter 1

'There he is!' my mother cries, standing in the doorway, 'there's Uncle Gervase!' Joyfully, triumphantly almost: '*Impossible* to arrive before Gervase!'

It's 1937: Coronation Year: and perhaps, who knows, perhaps while we are here, Princess Elizabeth and Princess Margaret Rose may come in? My mother has already asked:

'Would you, Lucy, be able to behave, know *how* to behave, if their grandmother were to bring them?'

But now she can think only of reaching as swiftly as possible the corner table where Uncle Gervase waits for us. I try to keep up with her but, clumsy-winged (she would fly if she could), she pushes ahead of me: striding, she is pulling out of shape the skirt of her beige suit: her fawn velours hat, pushed up by her thick hair, is slightly askew. She trembles with a sort of joyous excitement.

Gervase has already seen her: leaping up to greet us, shaking, smiling, his twitching limbs seeming to knock into, over, everything:

'Winifred! Look—this is awfully *good* of you, you know—'

There is a flurry. He has backed into a waitress. No, but really—this is the most frightful ... 'Look, I'll—' He rushes round to pull out chairs for us: 'Winifred. Lucy.'

But several people have turned round. Staring hard, while pretending not to.

'How dare they,' my mother will say afterwards. 'How *dare* they!' Later, she will add, 'Of course one gets a very vulgar sort of person everywhere nowadays. Even, alas, in Gunter's.'

She's sitting down now, hitching up the skirt of her suit; her pouchy face comes to life as the conversation begins: aged six (seven, seventeen) I am scarcely noticed as they talk jerkily, in stops and starts, about Patmore where she and Uncle Gervase grew up together in the golden days.

For this, we have come all the way from Bratherton in Yorkshire —there and back in the day. It's my first visit to Gunter's (although

I

my mother comes every year). I'm only here because Uncle Gervase has asked to see me: I haven't wanted to come. And already, after only a few moments, I'm forgotten—like the food. How can any sandwiches, cakes, éclairs, meringues even, hope to compete with this absorbed journey into the past?

'What did they talk about, then?' my father will ask me afterwards. Then angrily: 'I know—don't tell me. Patmore. Bloody *Patmore* . . .'

But Patmore is a convent now; has been since 1925. Gervase, its former owner, lives in a cottage in the grounds. Only in his forties, he looks sixty; loud-voiced, as jerky and unco-ordinated as a schoolboy when he moves, victim of violent headaches, disconcerting memory lapses, he cannot concentrate on any one subject for long. (My mother must hold him to this one, Patmore, Patmore, Patmore.)

Once upon a time though, he was beautiful. Until sometime in 1917, when the change began which was to turn him gradually into the eccentric we are taking tea with today.

'Don't pity the dead, Lucy,' my mother says. 'Pity those who *didn't* die. Who were never the same again . . .'

Now, in his cottage, Uncle Gervase reads a lot, writes a little, possibly, and helps in the garden certainly; the convent girls, although they laugh at him, are friendly. And he is an absolute brick when help is needed with a Christmas play, a bazaar, a garden fête.

Outside Gunter's, it's hot, sultry, scorching even. August. But my mother always comes up at this time, for sentimental reasons. She'd be loth to change to a more fashionable date. (Surely we cannot be expecting the Princesses?)

Now, she's making some rude remark about my father. Some moan of despair. 'Peter is so this, so *that* . . .' The tea party is nearly over. I have behaved badly, and will be told off on the journey home.

Before we leave though, Uncle Gervase will tell us a joke. Each year he brings us one, or even two: his mind, tenacious of little else, is tenacious of these. He gets them from the girls at the convent; (it's not always clear which has pleased him most : that they've told him, or that he's been able to remember).

Oh, those jokes.

2

'There was this chap on an—on an omnibus (it's rather a *good* one this—I got it yesterday) and he—he won't pay his fare. The conductor, don't you know, is in an awful bate, "Come on," he says, "who do you think you are? Pay up—like everyone else." But this makes the chap *tremendously* indignant. "Look *here*," he says, "you can't speak like that to me—I'd like you to know, my man, that I was brought up at *Eton*." "Oh no," says the conductor, jolly quick: "Oh no you wasn't. You was eaten—and brought up ..." '

*　　*　　*

Even in dreams (particularly in dreams), I never go back now.

Gunter's is gone anyway. I was in London yesterday and, stupidly, looked for it. Standing where it should have been: wondering if I'd mistaken the number; asking a man just turned out of Chesterfield Street:

'Gunter's? It's gone. Been gone *years* now—'

I'd purposed only the swiftest of controlled glances; yet now I'm desperate with loss: victim of that irrational demand that nothing ever, anywhere, shall change in our absence.

The man is saying, comfortingly:

'A nice little teashop, Gunter's—people still ask after it ...'

As I am asking?

'*Everyone*,' my mother is saying, 'but everyone has heard of Gunter's. Anyone who is anyone—and who has memories. Impossible not to have heard of it, Lucy!'

But who is this?

'... Leeds to London and back, just for a cup of tea. It'd be sad—if it weren't so daft.

'I'd *forgot*. It's the company. Tea and memories—and Gervase. Worth every bloody mile to you, Winifred, that is ...'

Ghosts at Gunter's, help me.

*　　*　　*

3

If, that first time, I hadn't much wanted to go, my mother had wanted even less to take me. Nothing about me pleased her in those days; and except that Gervase had asked to see me (and how could she refuse such a request?) she would gladly have left me at home.

'I think you're to be looked over. Shown off. Compared. God knows—' said my father, putting me to bed that night; his manner with me unusually short.

But, after a bit, I'd realised that it meant a visit to London, and grew over-excited. This she liked least of all: for distracted by her half-hearted promise to try and visit the Tower, I scarcely listened to what she said.

('Please listen, Lucy. What shall I *do* with you, why *ever* did I say that I'd take you?')

But it was her warnings that in the end aroused my curiosity. 'Lucy. However Uncle Gervase behaves, whatever he does—you are on no account to make any remarks. *Whatsoever*. And above all—do not stare . .'.

I spoke to my father about it, when he took me out for my Saturday treat—ice and pop in a café near the market place in Bratherton. But he'd seemed cagey. 'Ask her,' he said. 'I wouldn't know, I've not met him.'

A few facts had sunk in: I knew that although he was called Uncle he wasn't her brother; she'd had brothers, twins, who'd died ('I did tell you, Lucy.'): Gervase was her stepbrother.

'He and I share no *blood*, you see.'

On the journey, she repeated the warnings. Sitting opposite me, her carefully pressed suit already beginning to crease, her velours hat pulled down, her usually shiny face thickly powdered. 'Above all, don't stare, Lucy.' She looked unfamiliar, and as the train approached King's Cross, agitated too. ('I wonder, really, why I brought you?') Hunched up in her corner seat, she drummed her fingers nervously: 'Your voice is like the Leeds slums,' she told me. 'And with your front teeth missing . . .'

She had made me curious though. The reality was pure disappointment. I don't know what I'd expected (performing dog, red-nosed clown, falsetto-voiced midget?) but here was just a very tall, elderly man, knobbly, with sparse white hair and a high colour; skin drawn tight over his cheekbones, his chin jutting out as he spoke:

'But—it's *you*, Winifred!' he exclaimed, staring at me very hard. 'Really—awfully *like*, don't you think?'

The flurry of our entry was over and we were all sat down: remembering not to stare back, I smiled nervously—mouth closed to hide my missing teeth.

My mother said quickly: 'I'm afraid I've no idea what I looked like at that age, Gervase. I—'

As if making a discovery, 'It was Easter,' he interrupted in a very loud voice, 'You came to Patmore at *Easter*, Winifred. And—and just a week after, you lost both your front teeth. I remember exchanging them for two lead sepoys—from my army, you know. You were most fearfully keen to have them, I remember. They stood by your table in the night nursery—'

'Yes,' said my mother, colouring. Her face had gone very soft. 'Yes.' Then in a crisper voice:

'She's Peter's *build* of course, Gervase. On the small side. His features, too. And the hair—his father obviously. *Fortunately*, it's a shade of red which *just* misses vulgarity.'

They paid me no more attention after that. They were talking about Patmore: my mother, looking at once happy and yet unhappy; Uncle Gervase, gesticulating, excitedly diving for more memories.

Unnoticed, I ate all the sandwiches then several iced sponge fingers. Finally, bored, I announced very loudly that I'd far rather have gone to see where the Princes were murdered.

There was no response; so, desperate, I fired off a stream of questions—some of them landing in the pauses of their absorbed conversation. 'Why's his hair so white? Has he got some children at home? *Why* can't you share your blood with him? Why's he pulling at his tie like that? What *happened* to him in the Great War?'

Suddenly taking notice, my mother said angrily: 'The child is over-excited, Gervase.' She made some remark about my father. 'Peter *stimulates* her too much,' I heard her say. 'Entertains her with a deal of quite unsuitable information.'

But Uncle Gervase, addressing me directly, said it didn't matter at all: he repeated this several times, his smile curiously sweet, but like the rest of him, very jerky. As he spoke his wrists shot forward from his shirt cuffs, as if propelled.

5

'All those remarks,' said my mother wearily, in the train going home: rubbing her forehead with her knuckles as she always did when tired. 'And when I had *particularly asked*—'

'He took seven lumps of sugar,' I told her; remembering with pride that I'd been better at handling the tongs.

She sighed heavily. 'Nervous people have this craving for sugar, Lucy. He's neurasthenic, you know. He had a most terrifying time in the Great War. Suffered horribly—'

Like my father, then? But she interrupted me at once:

'Oh that! That was just *physical*. Gervase's is in the mind—he will *never* recover, Lucy.'

She didn't speak much after that, except to say, just as we were nearing home:

'Gunter's has gone off, I think—a little. In its day, I'm not sure I didn't prefer *Rumpelmeyers* . . .'

The next year Uncle Gervase provided, if not excitement, at least some of the embarrassment my mother had promised.

I was wearing a new dress. Royal blue velvet, with a cream lace collar and matching velvet buttons, it had been bought for the occasion, and had cost I suspect more than she could spare. It was very uncomfortable in the heat. She was pleased when Gervase praised it, but then as I grew restless, pulling, wiggling the top button which had grown loose, she told me irritably not to fidget. A moment later the button dropped off onto my plate—catching as it fell the edge of a chocolate éclair.

Uncle Gervase, leaning forward, picked it up at once. Then, to my horror, he stood up and holding it in the air began to recite, to sing almost:

'Lucy had some buttons—'

A waitress stopped in her tracks, then moved swiftly on again. His voice was loud, quavery: I was sure everyone around would be forced to look:

'Lucy had some buttons
Spherical was their shape.
And every time that Lucy laughed
A button would escape . . .'

6

'That's all I can think of,' he said suddenly, sitting down again, nervously—as if he'd just realised where he was.

My mother wiped some cream off the edge of the button and put it in her handbag.

'I've been wondering,' she said, 'about visiting Patmore?'

Uncle Gervase made clucking noises. 'Winifred. If you *could*—'

'If only I felt,' she went on, 'if Lucy perhaps—the *schooling*, Gervase. Peter, you see, insists that the Council school is adequate ... his salary, of course ... the most we can pray for now is a scholarship to grammar school.' Her face, always soft, crumpled almost, when she was with him, looked collapsed now: 'Gervase, I *think*—'

'Look here,' he said, 'I could speak to Reverend Mother, or—or to Sister Xavier. No—but I'd like awfully to do that.' Warming to his theme: 'It *is* rather a special case.' His hand shook so much that I was afraid he would miss the cup, knock it sideways. 'It would be rather splendid, if ...'

But my mother, her voice sounding thick, panicky, said: 'It's not possible—even with arrangements. Peter would never—and there'd be expenses ... It's not possible at all, Gervase—'

Her distress distressed him. He looked this way and that, knocking against the table with his knees, rearranging himself, agitatedly putting another lump of sugar in his tea.

Then he was inspired:

'I heard a *very* good one, Winifred. About Mussolini and the Pope. I had it, you know, from Bishop Turner—he was at Patmore for—for Confirmations. It appears you see, that Musso ...'

But the topic was too painful—even though she duly laughed when, a trifle mangled, the point of the story was reached. It was 1938. There might be, probably would be, a War, and she didn't want to think about it.

The next year, she could think of nothing else.

We wouldn't of course be coming up again, wouldn't be able to, for the duration. 'What will *become* of us all?' she asked. 'What shall I *do*?' I thought that she was going to cry, sitting there in Gunter's.

In the train going home she did weep. She was coughing too, flushed, and I became afraid that her asthma would pounce before we reached home.

Then suddenly, the train rattling through the darkness, she said, in a very calm voice:

'A hawfinch came and nested in the orchard, that summer, Lucy. Late spring, early summer, 1914. It was in a cherry tree, if I remember rightly. Its song was odd—a sort of sharp, *biting* sound, Lucy. Tom (he'd have been your real uncle), Tom could imitate it to perfection—but some boys stole the eggs, and we never saw the birds again. It was the only sad thing to happen that summer. Until August.' She turned her head to the window, pulled up the blind: 'You've no idea, Lucy. No idea at all—what it was like for us. *Everything* came to an end then. The lamps went out, all over Europe.'

In the darkness a train sped by, its windows flashing brightly. She said sadly, 'I shall not see them lit again in my lifetime.'

I thought they were her own words. She frightened me with her images of a whole continent plunged into primitive darkness and chaos, and for the rest of the journey I sat eyes tight shut. Falling after a while into genuine sleep.

I woke to find we were nearly there; we were alone in the coach. My mother looked at me. Her face was blotchy, agitated:

'There was this song,' she said, ' "What shall we be when we aren't what we are?",' her voice had thickened again. 'Peace came too late, Lucy,' she said, 'We'd thought it would never end and when peace came, it was too late. For *me*, it was too late.'

'Oh *Lucy*,' she said—she had never appealed to me before.

'What shall we be,' she asked, the tears streaming down her face, 'what shall we be, Lucy, when we aren't what we are?'

Chapter 2

In the event, she'd a very easy War. Her asthma barred her from doing anything very active; and except for a few months at the beginning, we had no evacuees. She passed the time somehow, without doing anything very much—yet always appearing slightly exhausted.

I sometimes wondered how she did pass the time. It wasn't with housework certainly; she loathed cooking, and all the cleaning was done by Mrs Pickering, a tiny birdlike woman from the other end of the town, who worshipped her and fussed over her regularly. Nor was it in social life; she hadn't really any friends—close or casual—and always spoke disparagingly of 'people who gossiped their lives away.' Next door to us, Frank Tucker and his crippled wife Nora were visited formally, once a month, as if by the lady of the manor. (In my first term at the grammar school, when I'd overheard two girls in the cloakroom talking about her I learnt that she was known locally as 'the Duchess of Bratherton'. Thinking of, and remembering their 'Ho, ho, ho, she says,' I had wept all the way home).

Then, there were what I thought of as her 'religious bouts'. She'd been brought up as a Catholic—in a half-hearted way was bringing me up as one too—but for most of the year there was little evidence that she had a religion. Then, every six months or so, there would be a sudden revival, usually without warning. Accusing herself of having been very slack religiously, she would get up each weekday morning for Mass; her 'Garden of the Soul', crammed to bursting point with parchment markers, holy pictures, and black-edged memorial cards, followed her about the house; and yet again, she would begin the Nine First Fridays: frequently, too, there would be an elaborate novena for some mysterious Cause. On Thursdays and Sundays she would drag me along to Benediction, where occupying the front row of the church in feudal manner she would sing the 'O Salutaris' and 'Tantum ergo' loudly in her rich wobbly contralto. (The opening and closing hymns, from the Westminster Hymnal, she would disdain. 'We never sang those at Patmore').

9

Then as suddenly as it had begun, the bout would be over. She would have a migraine, or there would be a change in the weather, bringing on an attack of her asthma; or Father Casey would say something in his sermon. 'We, of course, had our *own* chaplain. Father Ainslie. One would *never* have heard that kind of sentiment...'

Another mood, one which I remember strongly and which would affect her for days at a time, was a kind of restless boredom; she'd stride about, to and fro (and she was big: with high heels, would have been taller than my father) like some giant tethered animal, possessed by a vast, undirected energy which days later, departing, would leave her worn out and languid.

In this she was quite unlike my father. He, too, was often restless, so that when he was at home—admittedly as little as possible—the whole house would feel full of his suppressed, conserved energy. A banked-down fire. Waiting, waiting, waiting. My mother's I thought of as self-destructive; his was self-preserving. And whether he was out drinking, playing snooker, singing choral works or letting rip his favourite music-hall songs, he brought with him always this sense of terrific, coiled-up vitality. As one of his friends said (for he was very popular—outside the house): 'Let's ask Peter Taylor, we say. If anyone does, he'll make a go of the evening, will Peter.'

The backdrop for all this was their unhappy marriage. As a child I'd thought quite simply that all families were like ours; later, equally simply, I'd wondered why ever they stayed together. Perhaps, I thought sometimes, the battlefield—strewn as it was with dead hopes—was a scene they needed? If so, it couldn't have been for the sake of the heat or the noise, for most of the time a quiet coldness prevailed (although every now and then there would be a sortie when, shocking me, one or other would draw ammunition from their considerable arsenal).

An only child—my brother had died four years before I was born—I stood unhappily in the middle; I don't recall consciously being used as a weapon—certainly not by my father. On the other hand if there *was* a war, then my mother could be said in one sense to have won it: for when in 1937 I'd gone to Gunter's for that first tea, I'd been my father's child. By 1945, when we went back there again, I was hers—and hers alone.

I still didn't please her, though; the difference now was that I tried—I cared. I minded passionately that, from happiness, she should have come to this misery; and whenever I saw her, soft, tremulous, eager, sitting opposite Uncle Gervase, then I would grow soft too: thinking how she had been exiled from Paradise; vowing that one day, somehow, I would make her happy again.

But although so completely hers, there were some small pockets of rebellion—private areas not amenable to her influence. My friendship with Elizabeth Horsfall for instance, whom she disliked (that my father thought highly of her, admired her vivacity, only made matters worse). 'She's so *vulgar*, Lucy,' she would say.

Another cause for her concern and complaint was something which seemed to me the most natural thing in the world: my Yorkshire accent. Elizabeth had one, my father had one, everyone about me seemed to have one; and although I'd realised vaguely that my mother spoke differently, I'd never consciously noticed it. Her voice was just—my mother's voice. Not that my accent was particularly marked: merely twenty-odd years ahead of the fashion— but my short 'a's' irritated her, and at intervals over the years she'd threatened me with speech lessons. Then in 1948 she brought up the subject yet again, as part of a more general worry: my future.

Elizabeth and I had just left school. She'd gone, immediately, decisively, into receptionist work at the King's Head, a country hotel several miles out of Bratherton. But for myself, I hadn't a single idea of what I'd like to do. Unattractively timid by nature, I trusted vaguely that something would come along, without very much hope that I'd like it when it did. My mother on the contrary, was full of ambitions for me, most of which she presented as already achieved (she was always rather better on destinations than journeys), but which after a short period of enthusiasm would be discarded. We ended up with shorthand and typing which had been one of the first, obvious suggestions. There was a good, sound place in Leeds, which my father could afford; but this she sniffed at:

'You'll get nowhere from there, Lucy. It wouldn't widen your contacts at all.'

Instead she began to talk, longingly and hopelessly, about another and quite different secretarial college: the White Rose.

Only a few miles away, in Harrogate (near the Pump Rooms), the White Rose Secretarial College offered on its syllabus—as well as shorthand, typing and book-keeping—flower arrangement, history of art, etiquette (including, I'd once heard, the correct way to eat globe artichokes) and French conversation. The fees were enormous.

'Thank God we've not the money,' said my father, reading the prospectus. 'All the ruddy place does is keep poor little rich girls out of mischief.'

He was probably right. I knew the place of course. Although I'd never actually met anyone who'd been there, the name cropped up regularly enough in the local papers. '... is to be presented this summer ... recently completed a course at the White Rose ... hopes to be accepted at the White Rose this autumn ...'

Some of these girls my mother dismissed at once: 'Clogs to clogs in three generations—that family has risen *much* too quickly!' or 'Her parents are in trade, Lucy,' or 'Why *do* people think money can buy breeding?' But the place itself held for her an aura. Corridors of possibilities. At the very least, it would place me in contact with people who hadn't been to a grammar school, weren't short of money and, in the main, didn't have accents. And from such a beginning what might I not achieve?

'You'll maybe let me know then—when you've decided,' said my father sarcastically.

He was quite safe. There wasn't the money for it, and that was that. And secretly I was glad.

It didn't stop my mother talking about it however. That summer, walking through Hyde Park on our way to Gunter's, she harked back to the subject continually, irritably, in between telling me off for waddling. 'You look like a duck,' she said crossly, as I walked, hips thrust forward in an attempt to make my short summer dress nearer to the New Look which I could see everywhere about me.

But once inside Gunter's—all was forgotten; as usual I might as well have not been there. It was Uncle Gervase who paid me attention—asking me solicitously what I was going to do with myself now that I'd left school?

I murmured something about shorthand, typing—

He turned suddenly to my mother:

'Look, Winifred—about this White Star place.' He stirred his tea wildly, the spoon clattering against the cup, 'the—the one you mentioned in your letter. I've been wondering ... Are the fees awfully high?'

'Oh, *there!*' cried my mother, as if to dismiss it at once; contemptuously almost: 'Oh, *there!* Ninety, perhaps a hundred pounds a term. Quite absurd ...'

She looked down at her hands. He was silent for a moment, then,

'Would you—could you, do you think—' He hesitated, his face twitching. Then nervously, in a rush: 'Look—do you think you could let *me* pay, Winifred?'

My mother's face creased. I thought for a moment that she was going to cry, but she concentrated instead on pulling down her hat—pushed up continually by her thick hair. Her mouth still working, she said:

'It's—I ... I couldn't, Gervase. It's—' Then in a choking voice: 'Darling—you *can't. Gervase!*'

I looked away, not being able to bear it for her. At the next table a couple—son in khaki and new Sam Browne, mother in a tulle hat—were arguing fiercely, their anger barely concealed. I fixed my attention onto them. But Uncle Gervase, turning to me again suddenly, asked: smiling encouragingly, bushy eyebrows raised: 'What do *you* think, Lucy? Should you—should you like to go there?'

But before I could speak, my mother said for me: 'Of *course* she would, Gervase. It's the sort of chance, you see—you know, I'd thought ...' To my horror, I saw that tears were running slowly down her cheeks, driving a pathway through the pale powder.

'Look here, it's the *convent*, you know. It appears they're doing frightfully well. They want to expand. Buy some more Patmore land,' trying to reassure her, he waved his arms about, his bony wrists shooting back and forth as he gestured. 'My—my solicitor's arranging a sale. Very favourably I shouldn't wonder. And my own living expenses at the cottage—they're not great at all.' He paused, his chin jutting forward, 'Look, I'd like awfully to do this, Winifred —'

'Besides,' he added, when she didn't answer; his head nodding vigorously: 'who else is there in the family—now?'

This reference to her family had an immediate effect on my mother: blowing her nose loudly, she said that of course we'd accept. Then Uncle Gervase, as if relieved of some burden began talking at once in a rapid, staccato manner. Little sentences, unconnected, fragmentary. Several times he asked me about the White Rose—or White Star as he called it, but without waiting for an answer. He even tried a joke—

My mother smiled palely throughout; she seemed overcome still, unable to look directly at him, every now and then blinking rapidly to keep back the tears.

Tea over, he became even more excited. Asking us, eagerly, if we couldn't both, just this once, stay on? His club could find a hotel; book dinner; telegraph . . .

'We could all go to a theatre. There's a—a show the Americans have put on. I hear it's rather jolly. *Oklahoma* I believe they call it. And by all accounts, the convent girls—'

He looked from one to the other of us, his face suffused with excitement: 'What do you say? Winifred? Lucy?'

But my mother, flustered, explained that we couldn't possibly. There was no question of it: 'You see, Peter could—if he were to get *angry*, Gervase, he might—could *stop* all this!'

She was crying again. Flustered himself now, Uncle Gervase put us in a taxi, and insisted on coming with us. When we got out at King's Cross, he underpaid the driver by mistake and then greatly embarrassed, overtipped him grossly, the coins spilling in a shower on the taxi step. As he waved us goodbye, my mother was openly crying, and I thought too that I saw tears in his eyes.

But only about an hour out of London, she livened suddenly, her distress giving way to an almost manic gaiety.

'I can't believe it!' she kept saying, arranging the fingers of her gloves, pulling and smoothing them . . .' Her voice shook: 'Such *generosity*, Lucy!'

She was full of wild, extravagant ideas; wondrous things which would come to pass: 'As soon as you have the diploma, you must go to London,' she exclaimed, filling me with fear.

She chattered on, my lack of enthusiasm unnoticed. She became subdued only when she remembered that my father would have to be told. 'He wouldn't accept money from Gervase, you understand that, Lucy?'

After some thought however, she came up with an idea. 'An

inspiration.' 'It can be a legacy,' she said. 'That's it, Lucy—a legacy! Perfectly reasonable—and *just* possible. A distant cousin, I should think. Some Patmore connection he doesn't know of.' She warmed to her plot. 'It could come by second post, while he's out—I have the name of the family solicitors put away somewhere.

She leant forward, chin cupped in her hand, eyes shining. 'Lucy, darling—it's going to be *all right!*'

But I didn't in the slightest want to go to the White Rose: and now that it was a possibility, I felt terrified.

As soon as I woke next morning, I decided to try and disinfect my news by telling it to Elizabeth. I'd heard my father leave the house early: one of his occasional day's fishing—an act of kindness to Frank Tucker.

I went in to my mother: she was lying in bed, Pugin our ageing cat curled up at her feet. She had a severe headache; 'too much excitement, Lucy.'

But she seemed cheerful enough. Consoled that she was happy, I kept quiet about where I was going.

The Horsfall home was only about five minutes' walk away, on the main road out of Bratherton. I took my bicycle though, because usually Elizabeth and I decided to go off somewhere, to escape her mother.

The front door was open. There was no sign of anyone about so I went through to the kitchen, where I found Mrs Horsfall. Sleeves rolled up, she was making pastry. She lifted a floury hand at me then pushing past, she called up the stairs loudly: 'Here's Lucy come, Elizabeth!'

I tried then to go straight on up, but her bulky uncorseted figure, with its crown of dark frizzy hair, blocked the doorway.

'Put the kettle on, love,' she said. 'And sit you down. She's not out of her bed yet.'

I took a chair reluctantly: the warm kitchen was full of the heavy smell which always hung about Mrs Horsfall. Strong, sour. For years now I hadn't been able to eat a biscuit in their house,

15

because once I'd seen her offer the tin round with the lid tucked under her arm and had been sure afterwards I could taste her mixed with the ginger.

Nowadays, quite irrationally, I'd come to connect this smell with the vague but forceful views she held on nature cure, food reform and the healthy life generally. Not that she had any views which weren't forceful—recently I'd been hearing a great deal of them: ever since she'd taken to having what she called 'little talks' with me. Although these could be on any topic and often were, their purpose was always the same—to find out what Elizabeth was up to; that she never seemed to learn anything from me didn't discourage her at all. But today, she began by enquiring politely after my mother, whom I knew she disliked. 'Very nice—a trip to London,' she said, raising her eyebrows. Then with hardly a pause she went on:

'Lucy, this hotel job, now. I'm not sure it'll do at all. Twice-cooked food and odd hours. *Very* odd hours.' She shook some flour over the board: 'She'll not have been bothering with Nature's call, that's for certain—she'll be full of *impurities*. Everything upset. But she'll not listen to me, Lucy. It really fashes me. Yesterday, I said to her: "You're to come into Harrogate next week, Miss, the Royal Baths. We'll have you irrigated—" '

Elizabeth walked in. 'Heck,' she said angrily. 'If it's not boys—it's bowels.'

She crossed over to where the kettle, boiling now, was spitting over the range. 'Wotcher, Lu,' she said, pulling a face behind her mother's back. When she'd made the tea she offered round the biscuit tin, scooping up a handful for herself first.

'*Lucy* doesn't clog herself up with sweet things,' commented Mrs Horsfall. Elizabeth took no notice. Gulping down her tea, she mouthed at me: 'I've met a smashing boy ...' Then out loud she said:

'Lu and me are going down by the river, Mam.'

This seemed to please Mrs Horsfall, who was always telling us that fresh air was free. As we went to get ready, she called after us that we weren't to sit in any stuffy cafés. '*She'll* be lucky,' muttered Elizabeth.

A few minutes later we left. Pedalling along the wide road with its Georgian houses, on through the traffic, past the turning leading up to the town, then freewheeling down the steep leaf-shaded hill to the river.

Bratherton in the summer was a very busy place. An old market town, it was full of history: sightseers came by the charabanc load to visit the 14th-century castle, perched on the sandstone cliff, or to see the hermit's cave which later had become a murderer's refuge. They strolled thickly along the riverside buying china souvenirs and pink rock, or walked through the beechwoods to see the famous well—gazing wonderingly at the collection of hats, shoes, gloves, parasols, teddy-bears, even animal corpses, which over the years had been turned to stone by the lime water which dripped non-stop from the rocks above.

But nowadays neither Elizabeth nor I bothered with the sights. In season, we always made straight for the riverside, with its bustle, its cafés, souvenir shops, rowing boats, punts, canoes. Elizabeth particularly loved it there. Last summer and the summer before, whenever we'd the money we had hired one of the punts, then she'd made me take the pole, while she kept a keen look out for likely boys in rowing boats, who seeing how badly we were doing, might offer us a tow.

Today, as soon as we reached the river, she stopped at a milk bar and although we'd only just been drinking tea ordered buns and strawberry ices. There were no boys in the café, but as she stood at the counter she kept turning round and looking at the path beyond the striped awning. I knew that if any did come in, they would notice her even though she was wearing old clothes and no make up, for as she'd told me so many times: she had the one thing that really mattered; the thing without which all the cosmetics and clothes in the world were useless. 'I've got sex appeal, Lu.'

Of me, she despaired. For about three years now she'd been trying to teach me basic techniques. 'I know it's easy for me, Lu—only with that hair—heck, *you* shouldn't have to *try* even.' But I never did anything right. I couldn't sway my hips, I couldn't wink convincingly; worst of all, when I *did* get noticed, I never knew the right thing to say. 'I give up, I really do,' she would say, after a

17

morning's work had yielded only two soldiers—both of them asking *her* to go out.

Leader and led, that was the arrangement: and had been always; right from the far-off days of 1939 when, just evacuated from Hull, she'd arrived at the Council school in the middle of the Christmas term. With her high colour, her large features (Mrs Horsfall's, refined by dilution with Mr Horsfall's mousey ones), her mop of frizzy hair, and her big new front teeth, she'd been instantly noticed; and within two weeks—pushing out of place a blonde, chubby girl with Shirley Temple ringlets—she'd become queen of the playground.

She chose me twice for Nuts in May; but although I'd been already over three years at the school I didn't dare to speak to her, until one dark December afternoon when, after putting up my hand during percussion, I walked along the corridor to the lavatories, and saw her looking through the boys' coat pockets.

She looked startled for a moment. Then, in her breathy voice, she said 'Want to know what I found in Billy Holroyd's?'

I nodded. 'Dried cow muck and a dead frog,' she said, pulling a face. Down the corridor, the thin chiming of the triangles came through the closed door. She leant back against the coats and took out a length of Spanish; breaking off a piece for me: 'You got a brother?' she asked.

I explained; and she said, 'I'm an only too.'

She chewed with her mouth open, her big teeth black with liquorice. After a moment she said: 'I've noticed you lots—you're a Roman candle, aren't you?'

'What?' I thought it must be something to do with my hair.

'R.C., silly. I heard you tell Brent. You ought to go to your own school,' she said; then looping the Spanish onto a coat hook, she folded her hands piously : '*Our* church, the services are champion. "Dearly beloved brethren, is it not a sin to get behind a fat man and prick him with a pin?" ' She took the liquorice down and knotted it round her fingers. 'That's a joke,' she said.

She seemed to be waiting. I tried desperately to think of something, anything, funny to do with religion, but all I could remember was a joke about Mass, which I hadn't really understood: it was Uncle Gervase's, and he and my mother had laughed over it that last summer.

'In our church we have a priest, and he says "Dominic, have the biscuits come?" then the little boy what's helping says "yes, and the spirits too" ...'

She didn't laugh, and I said feebly:

'It's a Latin joke.'

'Don't be daft,' she said. 'Jokes are in *English*.' She gave me a push towards the lavatory: 'Get on in and throw your water.'

She waited outside, drumming on the door and singing in a nasal voice, 'Whistle while you work, Mussolini is a twerp, Hitler's barmy, so's his army ...'

But our absence together had been noted, and that afternoon we had to stay in late, copying out with our scratchy pens a list of the kings of England. The friendship had begun; and in its odd way survived that school and then, after we both got scholarships, the grammar school too. This summer was the first time we'd been separated.

Now, walking over with the buns and ices, she sat down at one of the tables not far from the entrance. I could see straightaway that she wanted to talk about her new boyfriend: she'd been shouting hints as we wove our way in and out of the traffic.

'He's called Andrew, Lu. And he's been left school three years. His figure's smashing. You can see everyone looking jealous like. But he's to go in the Army next month, that's the awful part.' She bit hungrily into the sugary bun. 'And his kisses, Lu. Heck—I can't think why we thought anything to those ones at the pictures. He says his are French ones ...' She giggled and stuck her tongue out.

I didn't understand. But as we always shared our information—Elizabeth providing the greater part (and virtually all of the experience)—I wasn't worried. Almost all we knew, we'd discovered for ourselves: my mother, telling me nothing, had managed to escape even the formal revelations, the 'little talks' which Elizabeth had complained of in the Horsfall home. ('You should have *seen* her face, Lu. And she'd not got it right either. I mean, I don't think like she'd ever really *looked* at me dad—if you get me ...')

But: '*You* wouldn't know,' was all she said today. 'That Brian—' Last Christmas her cousin Brian, a redhead like me but more carrotty, had leapt from behind a door in the Horsfall home, giving me a pleasurable fright which I hadn't done anything about repeating since. 'That Brian. He was born yesterday.'

Two boys carrying a pile of sandwiches walked past and settled themselves at the next table. She looked them over:

'Let's get us milk shakes, Lu,' she said, jumping up, 'Give us a bob.'

As she came back, carrying the glasses of frothy yellow liquid, passing purposely a little too near the boys' table, she asked: 'You any news, Lu?'

When I told her, she stood quite still, holding the drinks: 'Get away,' she said. 'You never—' She stared hard at me. 'Heck, Lu— you can't!'

'Of course I mightn't get a place,' I said. (It was a hopeful thought which had just come to me.)

'All those posh girls,' she said. 'Still—if your mam's got the money . . . Remember Brenda Kitchin, Lu? She'd a cousin was at the White Rose—very rich they were—she said the woman who runs it's ever so awful. Sort of a dragon.' She paused. 'Heck, Lu. Next thing—you'll be talking "laike thet".'

For a while we chatted about the White Rose; then, losing interest, she began to talk instead about the hotel, in a very loud voice. She'd pushed her chair round so that she could see the boys without turning—now she was carefully watching them watching us.

Soon, she moved back to the subject of Andrew.

'There's a dance on next month,' she said. 'I'm bringing him. Want to go?'

She told me a lot about his family then, and what she and he did on their outings.

'What's your mother think of him?' I asked, unable to imagine anyone Mrs Horsfall would approve of.

'Pardon?' she said, absentmindedly. 'Oh—not so bad. She reckons he looks clean-living. That's a compliment and all from her, Lu.'

The boys got up to go, banging noisily against our table. When they'd left we talked for a while. Then Elizabeth grew restless.

'I'd best go,' she said. 'I've to meet Andrew.' I had shopping to do, I told her: in the morning, that was. Realising as I said it, that the town would be crowded by now.

'Daft,' she said. 'If I'd thought, I'd have got a blind for you.'

Pushing our bikes, we walked up the hill. Suddenly exasperated:

'Those boys in the café,' she complained, panting: 'You never tried, Lu.' She shouted against a passing lorry: 'You have to *practise*! I've told you till I'm sick. I mean, heck—boys *go* for red hair.' She was just in front of me now; over her shoulder, she called:

'Look at Rita Hayworth—how'd you think *she* got on, eh?'

Chapter 3

Back home, I found my mother asleep; I made some lunch for her and put it on a tray. The rest of Saturday yawned before me: I thought vaguely of going back to the river, but there didn't seem much point. Upstairs in my bedroom, the air was stifling even with the windows open, and after a while I wandered downstairs.

In the sitting-room the curtains weren't drawn yet; it smelled fusty and even when I let in the afternoon light, revealing Pugin in one of the armchairs, it felt oppressive still. Cluttered, it had, not the orderly fussiness of a Victorian interior but the random ugliness of a junk room. There were large awkward-shaped chairs covered in faded cretonne, a brown sofa with sagging springs, a corner cupboard whose door didn't shut; and above the fireplace, a hotch-potch of ornaments—an ashtray made from a Great War cartridge base, a Portobello jug, Old Bill in Staffordshire pottery, a chipped 'Present from Whitby'; but, belonging to my father, these had at least been put there intentionally, unlike the furniture, which was accidental: pieces meant to be temporary which it was unlikely we'd ever change now. More than any other room in our untidy, uncomfortable house, this one symbolised for me the unhappy state of affairs. My mother never dreamt of improving it: treating it always, as she did her whole life in Bratherton, as an outrage beneath her dignity to try and remedy; while my father spent as little time in it as possible—sometimes when he was alone, strumming on the piano, but mostly treating it like a station waiting-room, shabbiness and grubbiness taken for granted while he waited. (For what?)

I decided I would spend the afternoon with the Memory Box; Pugin, through half-closed eyes, watched me as I took it out. Once a chocolate box—its faded yellow bow still clung to the worn maroon velveteen—the Memory Box was the home of all my mother's Patmore photographs and relics. 'Your *heritage*,' she had called it when I was a child: showing it to me only on special occasions.

The jumble inside was divided into two compartments (hard and soft chocolates?) but without any system, so that once a year at least: 'We really must make an album of all this, Lucy,' my mother would say. But so far she hadn't even begun. It was the element of surprise she liked, I think, and an album would have made too predictable viewing.

Today it was the prospectus of St Mary's Convent, glossy and impressive, which lay on top: on its cover, above the direction to apply to Sr Xavier, a sunlit photograph of Patmore, while inside, livening up the details of School Certificate, piano, hockey and home-grown vegetables, was a stirring account of the house's history, and more photographs—the panelled dining-room, the wide oak stair-case, the gallery and (marked with an x) the priest's hiding hole. I'd often looked longingly at this prospectus, especially in my first term at grammar school; my imaginings of boarding-school life, a sort of stew of L. T. Meade and Angela Brazil, were confused and romantic in the extreme, but for a while the idea of going there had possessed me completely—reaching its height during a phase, very short, when I managed to convince myself that Gervase was my real father.

'The money just isn't available' explained my mother, blinking rapidly as she did when upset; adding bitterly, 'Even were they to grant a special rate, it would be impossible.' And the craze of course had passed, so that today I only gave the brochure a quick glance, before going on to the photograph underneath.

'Winifred—Patmore, 1910'. My mother, in ankle-length white broderie anglaise standing on the lawn, eyes screwed up against the sun; the house behind her looking less formal than in the prospectus: a door open, a curtain flapping, a hat lying on the stone seat.

My second favourite of them all, this picture showed off her hair: abundant, and so intensely fair as to be almost white. She'd kept a cutting of it from that time which showed the texture and some, but only a little of the brilliance. Now, although still very thick and not grey at all, it was a dull, dusty colour, but then it must have been her main asset: for all the photographs show a jolly—even a generous face—but not a pretty one. It was, I think, the old story of a gift so great in one direction as to make any other lack irrelevant. Only last week, with a shock almost of recognition, I saw sitting in a restaurant, a girl with hair of just this same radiance surrounding

23

just such a pouchy heavy-featured face and indifferent skin; but laughing and talking, she was saved, just as my mother must have been, by animation and excitement.

She told me that she had her father's looks, together with her mother's build; but there were no pictures of him in the Box, and only one of my grandmother: a heavily-corseted, matriarchal figure, sewing in a garden chair, staring at the camera through pince-nez, disapprovingly. 'She *looks* so unkind,' I'd remarked once; but my mother had replied: 'Nonsense! She could be very gay indeed—there were *lots* and lots of happy times, Lucy. It's just that you have to remember what she had been through.'

Then she would tell me about it, all over again.

It appeared that at thirty, and more or less as a last resort, my grandmother had married a frustrated would-be journalist with a minor post in the Home Office. Although she didn't realise it he was then already halfway to becoming an alcoholic, and only two years after their marriage he lost his job. Several years of discomfort and terror followed, in cheap rooms and boarding-houses, with my uncles, twin-boys, and my mother. Between bouts, my grandfather was charming, but inevitably the bouts grew more frequent and the charm more scarce, and when my mother was about three or four, he died of cirrhosis.

Two years later—to everyone's surprise, and her own too, I think—my grandmother met, and married, Robert Tinsdale: a comfortably off, middle-aged widower, Roman Catholic, head of an old recusant family, owner of Patmore, and father of an eleven-year-old boy, Gervase. Her worries seemed over, and with an eagerness bordering on fanaticism she embraced the whole way of life—not only changing her religion, but also instilling into her children a belief that the only worthwhile life was that lived by the minor landed Catholic gentry.

'Of course, strictly speaking,' my mother admitted once, 'we haven't any Tinsdale *blood*. But I was so young when I went there, the twins too, Tom and Bertie, we all took the name. From the very beginning it was our *home*, Lucy.'

She reminisced often, the present invariably and inevitably coming off badly beside the past. 'When I look at this pokey house! We had so much space, Lucy—the long landing at Patmore: you could put ten of ours here into that. And those big oak chests that used to stand there—the linen, Lucy, the linen was always herb-smelling. How I miss the flowers! *All* the flowers. So much purple, I love purple . . . The vine on the west wall was very, very old, Lucy. I only hope the nuns are looking after it properly. And the ornamental hedges—they need upkeep too. Gervase says that during this last War the nuns grew vegetables almost *everywhere* . . .'

But sometimes her memory would let her down; and then frantically, with an upset out of all proportion, she would search for the missing detail. Once it was a plaster frieze with hunting scenes on it. 'I *nearly* see it, Lucy. But the flowers, the way the leaves went—that's gone. I've not been bringing it back enough. I think it's *lost*.' Why not ask Uncle Gervase? I suggested. Or we could go back and look? But her voice thick with emotion, she said that no, she could never do that : 'I could *never* go back. Perhaps, possibly—if you had been to school there, *possibly*.'

It had all been perfect: every day a holiday (in spite of a governess); every relationship unmarred by conflict. Robert Tinsdale ('Papa'), bluff and easygoing, was thrilled with his new family; Gervase, apparently, was equally delighted. And the sun had shone, every day, all day.

They'd played games. Her favourite one had featured the priest's hiding hole : from her description, even if safe the hole didn't sound at all comfortable, but evidently playing in it, with permission, had been one of the highlights of her childhood.

'The hole really had been used, Lucy. A Jesuit, Gervase said. I *wish* I could show you some of the family papers—Gervase used to explain all the history part to us, the background—the *terrible* tortures, Lucy. He said some of the priests were so frightened then, they used to have nightmares that they were being disembowelled, and wake up screaming. And he said that sometimes guests at houses like Patmore were really *informers*—they'd pretend to want to go to confession, then they'd betray the priest. It was a *terrible* time, Lucy—for families like ours.'

Gervase had played the favourite game, 'even when he was quite big, and already at Stonyhurst. Tom and Bertie would be two Jesuits on the run, and he would be the priest hunter. I was the lady of the house. But he'd tell me what to say, because of my being the youngest. I had to raise the alarm and get the boys hidden. Then Gervase would come along—knocking on the panelling and making noises like splintering wood, calling out for them to surrender. Sometimes he'd let them escape, but sometimes not. We never knew beforehand how the game was going to turn out ...'

I reached out for the next picture. My arm jerked and the Memory Box, turning over suddenly, scattered letters, photographs, newspaper cuttings about the carpet. I bent to pick them up, and it seemed to me then all at once that every picture was of Gervase. I had never realized there were so many. Gervase playing croquet, Gervase at Oxford, Gervase in a Stonyhurst group, Gervase playing tennis, Gervase in Elizabethan costume, Gervase on horseback, Gervase in Italy, Gervase, Gervase, Gervase ...

'He was so beautiful, Lucy. If you could only have *seen* him then!' But I was never able to reconcile this Gervase of the photographs with the twitching uncle of tea at Gunter's; the sea change had been too great. 'His looks, Lucy, were the sort that made one feel protective—as if he might *break*. And yet he was the strong one; I always thought of him as the strong one. He was a brother *first* of course. But *later*—well, it was quite a different story, Lucy ...'

He'd first begun to take notice of her, other than as his little stepsister, when she was about fourteen and he was twenty. ('I've been the *only* woman in his life, Lucy. His mother, you know, died in childbirth; and with my mother, he was always a little stiff— Although they got *on* perfectly, of course.') Evidently Gervase had never taken any real interest in girls before: this particular venture was highly approved of, and that he should have chosen my mother delighted Robert Tinsdale and made my grandmother overjoyed; marriage, taken for granted, became just a matter of time. Gervase was happy to wait. A year or so later he came down from Oxford, having had a book of poems published privately, and began preparing to take over, gradually, the running of Patmore. His intention was to lead a life of beneficent leisure. The date: 1913.

But it's to the following summer my favourite photograph belongs. In it, my mother leans back against a tree ('Gervase took this one, Lucy. We'd all been chasing round the orchard like children ...'), her ribboned tucked dress looking improbable for a game of tig, her hand over her mouth as if surprised.

July 1914. Gervase has written on the back:

'To Winifred—"A man who would woo a fair maid
Should prentice himself to the trade,
And study all day
In a methodical way ..."
(With apologies to W. S. Gilbert)'

Underneath, my mother had scribbled, 'last days of happiness'. 'Everything about that spring and summer was perfect, Lucy. Perfect. Even rain, I don't remember *any*—the strawberries, the plums, the roses, they all came on early. We had picnics, Lucy, and expeditions, and days by the sea. And in May there was London, and Rumpelmeyers and Gunter's (those ices, Lucy!)—then we went to "the Passing Show" at the Palace. Tom, who was quite a clown, used to do a *wonderful* Basil Hallam, Lucy. "Oh Hades, the ladies, all leave their wooden huts ..." I can see Basil Hallam now, Lucy. "I'm Gilbert the Filbert ..." And with Elsie Janis—"You're here and I'm here and the whole wide world is a little cosy corner, for you and me ..." We had the gramophone record—we loved our gramophone. We had Gervase Elwes too (that *other* Gervase, Lucy). He sang—I think they were songs by *Shakespeare*, Lucy ...'

Within a month of that picture, Gervase had enlisted; and the twins, who were to have gone up to Oxford that autumn, followed soon after. By the early summer of 1915 all three were in France. Tom and Bertie, known to me only from the photographs as two gawky, dark-haired boys, were both killed the following September, within a few hours of each other, at the Battle of Loos. 'Tom's body was never found, but when they sent Bertie's kit back—the people in charge, they can't have been thinking—*everything* was there, Lucy. Even his blood-stained breeches. We should have burnt them, of course, but old Simon, the head gardener, buried them for us, in the field behind the orchard. Where St Mary's have their hockey pitch.'

She was reticent otherwise about these brothers: they featured often, it was true, in reminiscences about the nigh perfect past, but less as real people than as bit players in the drama of Winifred and Gervase. That she had felt deeply at the time, I'm certain; but now, they were no longer central to the action.

By the time of their death, Patmore had already become a convalescent home for officers. Then in the summer of 1916, Gervase,

B

who so far had led a charmed life, was wounded in the shoulder on the first day of the Somme; later in the year he came home on extended sick leave. 'I should have married him then, Lucy. Hurried marriages like that, in wartime, they weren't frowned on, and I was eighteen after all.' But she hadn't done so. 'He *would* wait, Lucy. He wanted desperately to be able to settle down—for everything to be peaceful again. And Mother agreed with him—at the *time*.'

He went back to France. But his run of luck was over. Wounded badly in the chest, he contracted pneumonia from exposure; one lung was permanently damaged; and when eventually he reappeared at Patmore, there were other, even greater worries.

'He was *impossible*, Lucy—quite impossible. *So* unlike himself! He would fly into these *incredible* rages; then after, he'd be full of remorse—but *just* as difficult. Some days, he wouldn't speak to me at all.'

His removal to a special recovery hospital puzzled her: 'They called it shell shock. A sort of neurasthenia. It was something quite new to us at that time. *I* thought, Lucy, that he didn't love me any more . . .'

Spring 1918. In the Box, there wasn't a single photograph or souvenir to commemorate this next part of her story. Yet the facts were simple enough. My father was wounded at Cambrai; his leg turned septic, and after a lengthy stay in hospital he was sent to convalesce at Patmore. About the next three months however, my mother would say nothing—I'd had to piece the story together bit by bit from odd remarks—but by midsummer, she had broken her engagement to Gervase.

Novelty, I think, was the real culprit; novelty, and also being admired at a time when she felt unappreciated. That my father had been good-looking then—as indeed he still was—I knew from the photographs in my grandparents' front room; but to my mother, his dark vivid colouring must have seemed in unusual contrast with the delicate almost fragile beauty of Gervase; and governess-educated as she was, she must have found his background exciting and different too.

He'd been brought up in Leeds where his father kept a small grocery shop—although the family came originally from the Dales —and after leaving Leeds Modern had been clerk in a firm of insurance brokers for two years before joining up, going into the army under age. His Yorkshire accent had entranced her. 'She'd have me lay it on thick, then, just for the fun of it,' he'd told me once, in an unguarded moment. However little either of them had told me, those spring months in a flower-scented Patmore had an aura about them of barely suppressed physical excitement—at once explaining and excusing what I realised (from various fragments of quarrels, bitter asides, innuendoes) they both thought of now as a misplaced idyll.

Gervase, not surprisingly, took the news very hard. Whether it was this shock that accounted for his failure ever to recover fully or whether he would never have done so anyway, is an unknown. But whatever the real cause, the Gervase of the Memory Box had gone for ever: leaving behind him guilt, and a question mark, which my mother would answer according to her mood.

'I *know* I could have cured him' she would say. 'They mostly *did* get better, Lucy.' But then another time: 'It would have been a *tragic* marriage. He would *never* have recovered, you know.'

It was my grandmother however, who reacted most strongly to the news. Robert Tinsdale had had a stroke a little time previously and understandably she was worried about this, as well as upset for Gervase, but the real sense of outrage seems to have been caused by something quite other: the threat to her whole way of life. My father, whom she'd thought charming enough when he was a patient and she was Lady Bountiful, as a prospective son-in-law was intolerable. No background, no breeding, with a distinct northern accent and no proper education: a clerk with no prospects. It was only the War which had made him an officer, a 'temporary gentleman'. Worst of all, she'd complained, he wasn't a Catholic (although even had he been a duly Mariolatrous, sound Fish on Friday man, he still wouldn't have done, since it was only the once persecuted recusant families who were the thing). 'If she could just have kept *calm*,' my mother said once. 'If we could even have *discussed* it a little—I was still under age after all—then, perhaps ... who knows?' But semi-hysterical, all her hopes and plans dashed, my grandmother proceeded to threaten her in the most hackneyed terms. 'You'll be cut off,' she said. 'None of us will have anything to do with you!' Robert Tinsdale was too ill to be told. But had he been able to have an opinion, my grandmother said, it would have echoed hers (an unlikely thought, but since he never spoke again one that couldn't be disproved).

She wasn't the only one to behave dramatically however. My mother, who had been good, happy, acquiescent all her life, now, with a grand gesture of defiance left Patmore for Leeds, to live with my father's family. If she was expecting a summons back within the week, she must have been surprised. No word came at all.

She stayed in Leeds six months altogether; and inevitably, there were difficulties. She conceded to me once, grudgingly, that they'd been kind to her, but that was as far as she would go. Yet my grandparents must have been at the least slightly puzzled by this sudden courtship. My father was barely twenty, and as he hadn't made her pregnant, what was the hurry about? I don't think either, that she found them sufficiently shocked at her disinheritance—I doubt for instance that they behaved as if they were harbouring a runaway princess.

They had troubles of their own, anyway. Arnold, their eldest son, was a sergeant in France, and another son, Norman, had been killed earlier that year. Then, only a few weeks after my mother's arrival, their only daughter, Ethel, died in the first epidemic of Spanish 'flu. A jolly girl, with buck teeth and a friendly smile, she'd got on extraordinarily well with my mother. How the relationship would have turned out eventually—I don't know, but it evidently meant a great deal to her then; and she would still sigh occasionally: 'If Ethel had only lived, Lucy'—although it was perhaps not so much to miss her as to mourn the loss of an ally: 'I *know* she would have taken my side, Lucy.'

They were married in October, on my father's last leave before the Armistice; then in the New Year when my father was demobbed and, luckily, got his old job back, they went to live in furnished rooms in Leeds. Here, I think, reality finally succeeded romance. My grandmother, her bluff called, had shown it to be genuine: my mother's letters were sent back unopened and other than a few lines of formal permission, the wedding not acknowledged. And from Gervase—not a word. She had been truly cut off.

It was this time too, I think, saw the beginnings of that restless boredom I now knew so well. She had nothing to do all day except housework (although what little there was she probably found highly complicated). Possibly she'd have handled very competently a large and loyal household staff, for that after all was what she'd been brought up to. (And later she was to inspire great devotion in Mrs Pickering who, slipping into the rôle almost of ladies' maid, coped happily year in and year out with the trail of disorder, and the kitchen confusion inseparable from my mother's attempts at cooking. 'She's not been brought up to it, like, you know.')

Three years later, and her in-laws had begun hinting about children. 'It was all I was good for,' my mother would say bitterly. 'To give them a grandchild.' Then in 1924, my brother was born; she had an excuse to get in touch with Patmore, and this time her mother replied—it was a cool, dismissive note (still kept in the Memory Box) with muted congratulations, and a little news. Robert Tinsdale was dead; Gervase was still not back to normal ('Please do not *attempt* to see him, Winifred.') and it was doubtful whether he would ever be able to run the estate properly—a convent was very interested, and they were thinking of selling up. That was all.

The brief interlude of my brother's life was celebrated in the Memory Box, only by a couple of photographs, showing a large fair-haired toddler in rompers standing on the lawn; it is summertime so that the pictures must have been taken shortly after my parents' move to Bratherton, in the spring of 1926. One July evening in the following year, Michael climbed out of his cot and, in his night clothes, rode his small red tricycle down the back path. The gate wasn't properly fastened, and he went outside—pedalling directly into the path of a lorry.

It had been my father, not my mother, who'd supplied the details. She'd been tight-lipped on the subject. He'd described it matter of factly, as if shock had detached it from any emotion, and as a result I had never thought it to be real in any personal sense—it might have been the tragedy of some other, unknown family.

My mother hadn't wanted another child. What the real pattern of those first seven or eight years of marriage had been I don't know; but in one of the few remarks I remember her making (usually she would say: 'you can't expect me to discuss *that* time, Lucy,') she'd said of Michael's birth: 'all that pain and suffering—for nothing. And it was no help to the marriage. No help at all.' It was a difficult, forceps delivery, there were severe complications, and she'd been told that she was most unlikely to conceive again—so what her feelings were when expecting me, I can only guess. But afterwards they were quite clear: she didn't want me.

Two months before I was born, her mother had died suddenly of a heart attack, and this loss, cutting off still more links with Patmore and removing finally any possibility of reconciliation, must have had a profound effect on her. After my birth she almost certainly suffered from a post-natal depression which, undiagnosed and untreated as so often happened at that time, dragged on for years; apathy alternating with the now familiar, restless boredom.

One of my earliest and clearest memories is of being in the same room with her: she was sitting in the armchair while I had some wooden bricks on the carpet. I remember that she didn't speak to me, or seem to move at all; the room was growing dark, but she'd put no light on. Then I must have bumped into her, or jolted her in some way because she said suddenly and angrily, and absurdly loudly even allowing for childish memory, something like: 'Who asked *you* to come in here?'

Most of the affection, attention, stimulation I received in those first years, came in fact from my father. Frank, who had just moved in next door, told me once: 'It was some sight your Dad pushing the pram. But I didn't laugh—no one laughed. He'd bath you round at ours. Nora were alive then and you'd sit on her knee.' I think too that he did quite a lot of the cleaning in the house—Mrs Pickering didn't appear till I was seven or eight—and as he was working quite hard for his firm at the time, he must have been very tied: especially as it was the social side of his job he enjoyed most. Later, it was always he who played with me at weekends; and in the evenings I would wait for him to come and put me to bed. Even when in my first year at the council school, I had a small birthday party, it was my father who managed it entirely, sitting at the piano in a homemade paper hat, cigarette in mouth, playing, singing, 'Lookie, lookie, here comes cookie'. 'The music goes round and round', 'Who's afraid of the big bad wolf?'.

My mother did, however, do two positive things in those early years. She'd already scored a great success with her in-laws by giving them a grand-daughter (Uncle Arnold, married just after the War, had had three boys); now, unwittingly, she scored another. She insisted that I be christened Lucy, after Gervase's mother who had died in childbirth. The Taylors, delighted, assumed at once that it must be after my grandfather's sister, Aunt Lucy Thornthwaite—whom my mother might have heard speak of, but whose existence she'd certainly forgotten. Aunt Lucy was very flattered. A formidable widow, she lived over at Holmfirth. Her husband had been decorated in the Afghan War, and on our twice-yearly visits the medals would be brought out of their glass case and the story retold. Although what I remember about her was her vigorous black moustache, which seemed to grow longer and thicker each visit. 'And how's my little namesake?' she'd say invariably, planting a bristly kiss.

My mother's other positive action was to insert a notice of my birth in *The Times*—I was already several months old when she did it (in a sudden burst of energy), but Gervase (and she had been hoping for this surely?) happened to see it, and that same day, from his cottage in the grounds of St Mary's Convent, he sat down and wrote her a long, rambling letter.

This too, she kept in the Box. Its writing, thin, feathery, uncertain, is only just recognisable, so altered is it from that on the early photographs; the thought is confused too—reminiscences merge with suggestions so that the sense isn't always clear. But there is no recrimination, no self pity—he merely wants, very much, to see her again.

'Do you ever by chance come up to London? If so, couldn't we meet, possibly? What about Gunter's in Berkeley Square—or has that gone?' And if she does come, could the meeting be in August? An odd time, but it suits him—he is often up staying at his Club then. Does she remember, he wonders, the time ('*before* Armageddon'), one August the twelfth, when they had all been at Gunter's, his father too—and she had teased them for not being out on the grouse moors? Was that a *true* memory, or a false one? She must say. 'I seem unable as it were, to feel a certainty about—' Then through the word 'anything' he's drawn a line. An accidental jerk, or deliberate?

That summer my mother roused herself and went up to Gunter's, for the first of those annual reunions which soon were to become the central event of her year. Back home again however, she was no better. My existence, even though it had been the direct cause of her seeing Gervase again, continued to be a nuisance to her. Her asthma, which she had had only hints of before, dated really from the time of that first tea—but the rest of her ill health, the migraines, the debility, the languor, she blamed on my birth.

Those first seven or eight years though, I wasn't at all unhappy. I had an ally, full time. My father had wanted a daughter; and told me so, frequently. Even my first, reluctant visit to Gunter's seemed to make no difference to the pattern. Instinctively I didn't discuss it with him before or after: he rarely mentioned Patmore anyway, and the days of my mother's obsessive reminiscing had not yet begun.

But about this time he began telling me of his war experiences—doing so not occasionally, but incessantly, as if he'd reached some stage when he *had* to talk. On a simple level, my knowledge was soon considerable—almost encyclopaedic: long before I'd heard of 1066, and even before I knew my fairy stories properly, I had a head full of howitzers, mark sevens, French heavies, Jack Robinsons. I was his strange but willing audience—so willing, that I think sometimes he forgot it was a child he was talking to; often I was frightened: rats, shot at for sport, sleek and well fed on army food and corpses, flitted disgustingly through my dreams, while a live one, glimpsed once, streaking, fleshy and plump-tailed over a gravestone, set me to a high-pitched screaming.

Other times, he would talk as if I weren't there at all: usually when he'd been drinking. He confessed once to a feeling of overwhelming wickedness: 'There were four of us went in together—all clerks in the office. All pals. I was the only one came back.' But this was beyond me: 'Weren't you glad then?' I kept saying, 'weren't you *glad* they didn't kill you?'

It was his religious attitudes, however, that had perhaps the most lasting effect on me. He'd been brought up as a Methodist (yet another nail in his coffin at Patmore) but sometime during the War he'd lost it all, practice and beliefs. He'd raised no objections to being married in a Catholic church; and the fact that I was being reared as a Catholic—one of the few things my mother had insisted on—was to him a matter of indifference, almost of irrelevancy. Later, I went through the forms mechanically, even making my first confession and communion. But his attitude prevailed, so that even now, close as I was to my mother I kept it up only to please her.

The change of allegiance from a father- to a mother-centred world was gradual but, once it had begun, inevitable. I never saw it

34

happening. I remember only that my mother began to talk—that she seemed suddenly to be always talking, and that Patmore, Patmore, Patmore was what it was all about.

My father, she belittled regularly. 'Of course,' she would say, vigorously brushing my hair, 'Peter was there for only half of the Somme. *Gervase* was in right at the terrible beginning,' or 'Really the things Peter has told you, Lucy! He's *so* insensitive. Of course— Gervase was a *poet* . . .'

There was no real fight for possession. At the first signs of a struggle—not weakly but out of pride I think—my father must have stood back. Now, we weren't friends at all: it seemed I had taken sides, had made a choice, and that I couldn't remember doing so consciously was no help whatsoever.

Whenever I thought about the situation now, it was with a sullen, half-hearted sort of anger. But that was seldom. Worrying for and about my mother was a full-time occupation.

Gathering up from the carpet and the sofa all her scattered memories—the letters, the photographs, the cuttings—I pushed them back into the Box, shuffling and pressing to make them fit. When I'd done this, I thought, I would go up and see if she was awake.

The front door banged suddenly, and I sat up, guiltily.

Pugin got down from the armchair and as the door opened and my father came in, he padded over to him, rubbing his head and ears against his trouser leg.

By now I was standing at the cupboard, flipping through an old magazine I'd hurriedly snatched up. My father shook Pugin off.

'My God, it's hot,' he said, still in the doorway, mopping his brow.

I asked: 'How was the fishing?'

'Frank felt dizzy. He drank a couple of pints too fast in the heat. We called it a day.'

Neither of us moved. I glanced across at him: he was standing very squarely, not looking at me at all but at some point beyond. His face, always tanned in summer, was flushed; his dark hair, thick, greying slightly now, damped down by the heat.

He was still a very attractive man (Elizabeth, and three others in my class who'd seen him, thought him smashing). Now, my recent session with the Memory Box had prompted me to play an old game. Screwing up my eyes, I stared hard: trying to catch a glimpse of the young officer of Patmore, Spring 1918. I was successful. Through my half-closed eyes I saw a man thirty years younger . . .

'What's up?' He moved suddenly. 'Something wrong with your eyes?'

'Nothing—no. The sun—'

'I wish to God you'd get something to do. Mooching about the house all day. Have you been out at all?'

'Yes.' I heard my voice sounding sullen. 'I did the shopping—'

'How's Winifred?'

I said that she was asleep. He shrugged his shoulders: 'I'll not disturb her then. I'll have a bath and be off.' He turned: 'London go all right?'

I nodded; feeling sick at the thought of the White Rose. But he had already turned to go out:

'Why don't you get yourself a boy-friend?' he said from the doorway, pulling hard on the knob, narrowly missing Pugin.

Shaken—his coming, and his going, had upset me—I put the magazine back, closed the cupboard docr with difficulty, then took down a book from the shelf above.

Gervase's poems. (Mauve binding, handmade deckle-edged paper—a few pages foxed; fading silk ribbon markers, and a curious smell or scent—redolent I supposed, of Patmore.) Inside: nothing to startle.

'When dusk with milky wings unfurl'd
The crimson of the sunset reaves . . .'

or

'. . . my travail o'er
Were I, benumbed, to rest by Stygian shores . . .'

Once, several years ago, dreaming of him as a father I'd tried to make something of them, but now I seldom opened them. Not that there was anything there to tax the understanding; even from the little I knew, they didn't seem to me very good.

'Hushed now the reedy stream's lament
The owl's nocturnal call, the nightingale ...'

or, a change of tone, this:

'Now you see her, now you don't!
That's my girl playing hide and seek.
There's a cloud about her. Whitest gold ...'

'He adored my hair. Lucy,' said my mother. Upstairs, secreted
away, she kept a second copy, which she read often.

'It's a very great experience, Lucy. Being loved by a poet.'

Standing at the sink a little later, filling a kettle to make tea for
her, I thought: I shall have to go to the White Rose.

Although on the surface she often made me impatient, I was
bound to her, enchained by my pity. If she wanted the White Rose, I
must want it too; for, my mind full of the Memory Box, I thought:
trailing clouds of borrowed glory, hadn't I come into this world to
make her happy?

Chapter 4

Two weeks later, I was called to the White Rose for an interview. The principal, Miss Metcalfe (the 'dragon' described by Elizabeth) was abroad and I saw only her assistant, Miss Laycock. A small, faded woman, nearly as shy as I was, she invoked Miss Metcalfe constantly; beginning and ending each sentence with 'Miss Metcalfe says,' or 'Miss Metcalfe thinks'. But to my surprise, she told me that I was accepted, 'subject to confirmation.' I hadn't thought it would be so simple; and my mother, who would have liked to be invited along to the interview ('I would have *liked*, Lucy, to have been able to explain some of the background') seemed disappointed almost that there hadn't been more to it. 'I suspect of course,' she said afterwards, 'that if one can pay the fees, one is admitted. As simply as that. But then, up here,' she wrinkled her nose, 'it's *brass* that talks.'

She took this opportunity to make one of her attacks on my accent. She'd heard, she said, of a Miss Lister who taught voice production in Harrogate, 'A drama teacher, I believe—there are excellent reports of her anyway.' She was going to write to Gervase about it. 'If this Miss Lister could even get you to *hear* yourself, Lucy!'

But all these horrors lay several weeks ahead, and in the meantime I had to fill in the days: an old problem, made more difficult this year by Elizabeth's having started work. As a family we'd never gone in much for holidays and the War when it came provided the perfect excuse. Before that my mother had taken me a couple of times to some great-aunts in Wiltshire, sisters of her mother, where I'd been discussed a great deal, and disapproved of even more. (Small wonder that I'd forgotten the details: the only relic an unreasonable dislike of the soft, rich landscape.)

This holiday, my idleness irritated her. Girls in *her* day ... Why for instance didn't I go out and sketch? Hadn't I once been rather keen? she asked, speaking of something she herself had killed many years ago; when, sitting in the kitchen I'd drawn huge, crude imaginary monsters, crayoning them in violent reds and purples. 'They're unnecessary,' she'd said of them angrily, muttering once or twice 'Peter is behind this'; and bringing me home instead a Toytown colouring book. I'd soon lost interest: regaining it only for a little while around thirteen, when I fell in love with the art teacher.

Now, to please her, I went off for long bicycle rides in the warm afternoons, taking a book in the basket: all childhood favourites (I wasn't a great reader outside of school) and all in old editions which had belonged originally to Gervase, and then to my mother. *The Red Fairy Book, Three Men in a Boat, The Prisoner of Zenda.* Their fly leaves inscribed in fading ink: 'Gervase Tinsdale from his loving godfather, September 1900.' 'Gervase Tinsdale, Patmore 1899.' Sometimes a Latin tag: 'Est multi fabula plena joci. Ovid,' in the Jerome K. Jerome, 'Decet verecundem esse adolescentem. Plautus,' in the Anthony Hope. I read and re-read them all, the musty smell of their pages an evocation of Patmore. But that summer, although I was seventeen now, it was the fairy tales which I took most often. The beauty of their shape, their blend of excitement and security, the way in which impossible odds were overcome, was a combination I found irresistible, consoling, apt.

I heard nothing from Elizabeth. I didn't want to bother her, because I supposed she was spending all her free time with Andrew. Once or twice, I wondered vaguely about the dance she'd mentioned.

Then, with only a week or so to go before the White Rose term, she rang me late one evening, shouting excitedly down the phone, 'It's tomorrow, that dance, Lu! Long dresses and all.' And then, as if I'd been refusing invitations for weeks, 'Your last chance to meet Andrew, Lu!'

What it was in aid of or who was giving it, I never found out. But it began at seven-thirty and was thoroughly respectable with only orange squash to drink. The hall was very shabby. It had been a rainy day and the warm damp brought out the smell of San Izal on the dusty unpolished floor. Together with a lot of other girls, I sat on a bench at the side.

My appearance was giving me little confidence. As usual, I'd had nothing suitable to wear and earlier in the day had had to borrow a dress from Elizabeth. It was very frilly, in worn blue taffeta, and when I'd come down, ready to set off, my mother who hadn't been keen I should go in the first place had said disapprovingly, 'Lucy, that dress *shrieks* Elizabeth Horsfall.' There was a quantity of bead embroidery round the neck which was beginning to come away, but Elizabeth wouldn't let me remove it. 'You've just not an idea,' she said despairingly, 'what boys really go for, Lu.'

She herself was dressed in tight-fitting red sateen with an outsize bow on her bottom. Looking radiant, clasped tightly by an adoring Andrew, she sailed past me continually. I sat on; my bead embroidery didn't seem to be giving me any advantage—unfair or otherwise. Once or twice Elizabeth pulled a face at me as she passed, but on the whole she seemed to be disowning me.

At last a Paul Jones was announced.

We twirled round to 'A life on the ocean wave'. Whenever the music stopped there were two or three girls to one boy and each time I was jostled out of the way. Until on the last gallop round, I noticed a boy skip deliberately to one side, to land exactly opposite me.

'Alan Holdsworth,' he said, leading me at once into a waltz. 'And I've been wanting to ask you all evening.'

He had dark hair smoothed down shinily, and thick horn-rimmed glasses, and as he danced he pumped my left arm up and down, up and down. He was rather shy, he explained. 'But I'm grand when I get going.' He was training to be a salesman in shoes: 'I'll have to get over this shyness though.' He'd been with the Koylis, for his army service, 'But even that didn't help, really.'

I warmed to him at once. We danced together the next number, and then the next and the next—Elizabeth frowning and winking at me every time we passed. Later in the evening, I met her in the dimly lit ladies room at the back of the hall.

'Well done,' she said. 'He's no Gregory Peck, Lu, but at least he's in trousers.' She peered into the fly-blown glass. 'I thought you were *never*. Sitting there like a sunk Yorkshire pud.' She rubbed at her nose with a grubby powder puff. Sounds of 'The lady is a tramp' were coming from the dance floor.

'Oh, heck, Lu,' she said. 'I'm going to die when Andrew goes. Isn't he wonderful, Lu? Don't you think he's smashing?'

Back in the hall, both boys were waiting for us. The four-man band struck up 'Jealousy', and Elizabeth, the red sateen bow askew now, set off at once. Alan, tangoing with surprising competence, asked did I go often to the pictures? It appeared that we'd seen and liked most of the same films. *Brief Encounter* was coming to Harrogate, he said: would I like to see that? We made a date to go together, in a fortnight's time.

At ten-thirty, Mr Horsfall came to collect us. Elizabeth wasn't at all pleased; Andrew, she told me, lived in quite the other direction.

'Next thing, they'll be looking to see I've my knickers on. It's *her*,' she said. '*She* sent him.'

The White Rose was in a small crescent, two floors up above a shop selling homemade chocolates. That first morning, the sight of the violet and rose creams, the truffles, the chocolate ginger and the brazils nauseated me, as I hurried breakfastless and apprehensive through the side door with its White Rose emblem, and then up the dark narrow stairway into the school itself.

No one saw me arrive; and remembering where the cloakroom was I went and hid in there, pretending to fiddle with my hair while girls came in and out noisily. I looked carefully at their clothes, uncertain of my own. Predictably, there'd been a last-minute rush to get me ready, my mother's enthusiasm not stretching to the practical aspects, her mind already leaping ahead to the time when the course would be over and, superbly qualified, I would begin my real life. She was never anyway very helpful over dress—although generous enough with her coupons when she hadn't mislaid them. With this, as with so many other things in life for her, if one couldn't have the best then the matter was of no more interest. 'Of course even the worst clothing can't disguise breeding, Lucy. But I find it very hard to accept the sort of ill-made rubbish foisted on us nowadays.' The inevitable rayon, which she still called 'art silk', came in for her special scorn, as did the Utility label, and nylon from parachutes. 'Quality was something I just took for granted, Lucy. I had a whole drawerful of gloves, as a girl. All *real*. Leather, silk, cotton, full-length kid. I remember especially a pair of grey doeskin ones—I wore them for tea at Gunter's, that last visit before the Great War.'

I would determine then, to return her one day to the world of real silks, real skins; but at the same time I was impatient; rationed from the moment I'd taken any interest in clothes I felt starved of glamour, the New Look my particular worry. In the spring, inspired by the velvet rings—first three, then four—which Princess Margaret had added to her coat, I'd sewn a horrid multicoloured frill round the bottom of an old summer dress; but the shape had been wrong, and Princess Margaret had by then become bouffant-skirted.

'Eighteen coupons for a New Look suit,' said my mother. 'And the most flimsy material. What's wrong with a tailor-made?' But money had been short also, and we were too proud to ask my father. ('This legacy, now, Winifred? It'd better cover the lot.') The end product had been depressing: a still serviceable school blouse topping an old Gor-Ray pleated skirt, but a sensible enough choice as it turned out.

Most of the girls seemed to know each other already, and there were cries of recognition. All of them seemed self-possessed (a familiar first-day illusion I've had several times since, as if an inner eye shuts out the lost-looking, the pale, the nervous). A few minutes later a bell rang loudly and, some of the girls exclaiming 'Gosh, is this it?' we all crowded into the typing room.

For the price asked, I'd imagined an array of gleaming new machines, but each desk held only a very old upright, docketed with a student's name, so that a noisy giggling search began at once. Miss Laycock scurrying in, begged us almost frantically to be a little quieter. 'Miss *Metcalfe* is coming!'

When the principal made her entrance a few moments later, the silence was immediate. Saying loudly, 'Good morning, Ladies!' she walked up on to the dais, and from there looked down on us all, searchingly. I'd found to my dismay that I had a central front row desk; and afraid to look about me, I tried to gaze at her with what I hoped was an alert yet humble expression. She hadn't turned out to be at all what I'd pictured—which for no particular reason had been someone rather spiky. She was big, like my mother, but more solid; and she seemed to be uniformly bust all the way down. Dressed in navy blue with touches of white, her thick legs stockinged in dark brown lisle, the whole tree trunk was topped by a Roman emperor's face, and tightly curled, greying hair.

Her voice was penetrating. When after a nervous silence someone tittered at the back, she remarked coldly, 'I had hoped, Ladies, that you would have left your giggles with your gym tunics.' Then almost immediately, she launched into what must have been the set speech for every first day of the Course:

'Here at the White Rose,' she began, her hands folded in front of her, 'here at the White Rose, we are dedicated to one task, and one task only. The making of reliable, responsible, resourceful secretaries. Secretaries capable of filling posts anywhere in the world. Indeed,' and here she paused for effect, 'indeed, were I to tell you where some of my former students have been, you would all be out with your atlases at once!' 'She looked around her. 'Reliable, responsible, resourceful,' she repeated. 'These are the "three 'R's' " of the White Rose.'

Her voice boomed on: speaking of rich opportunities, of satisfactions, wide horizons, devotion to work, integrity, absolute discretion. My eyes glazed with over-attention; my mind wandered.

'And in conclusion,' I heard her say at last, as I returned with a jerk, 'I would like to draw your attention to a few minor points. The first being *clothes*. Exaggerated fashion has *no* place in the business world. I hope I shall not have to say this again. For office wear, I would suggest a blouse, a skirt, a cardigan—a tailor made perhaps; I should like also to suggest a tie, but here perhaps I am not *completely* up to date.' She smiled stiffly. 'And lastly, Ladies, language. The use of colloquialisms and slang can only debase our glorious inheritance, the English tongue, so that we shall not, on any occasion, use them here. The Americans may have won the War, but we are still a free nation!' Two girls laughed nervously. 'We shall never, for instance, speak of a "boss', but always of an "employer", never of a "job", but always of a "post". We shall *never*, even amongst ourselves, substitute "OK" for "all right" . . .'

It was over at last; and calling 'hard work, hard work, Ladies, is the secret' as she went, she left us to Miss Laycock, and our first typing lesson. Open manuals at the ready, keys and clumsy fingers hidden by a guard we began a supervised assault on our uprights.

When at midday we were released, I heard all about me, often in reassuring Yorkshire accents, a buzz of complaints.

'This place might as well be school . . .'

'But it *says*—no uniform!'

'There's a terrible list of rules in the corridor—'

'An even worse one in the la-ta. Have you seen *that?*'

In the afternoon we were introduced to shorthand, Miss Metcalfe's particular, consuming interest, ('A skill, Ladies, which will repay every moment spent. We shall be spending *many*.') and to book-keeping.

It seemed a long time till four o'clock, and by the time I reached home, I was exhausted. My mother was waiting, avid for detail, leaning forward, hand cupping her chin. She'd made a large tea, which was unusual for her. Edgily hungry I wolfed down cake, disappointing her with my non-committal answers.

She didn't want to hear about the work.

'The girls, Lucy. What were the girls like? Who did you go to lunch with?'

'With Marjorie,' I said.

'But Marjorie *who?*'

I didn't know, and hadn't asked. In any case, she hadn't been at all what my mother, falsely, imagined as the typical White Rose student. In the next desk to mine, she'd kept looking across at me appealingly during the typing lesson; I'd noticed her hands particularly, clumsy and red with cold even in the airless centrally heated room. She'd been having trouble centring her machine: pushing hopelessly at all the knobs, looking quietly desperate. At lunch, she'd been one of the last to go, and we'd drifted out together. Over egg and tomato sandwiches, she told me that horses were her real life. It was her parents who'd insisted she did a secretarial training first. 'I'll never stick it,' she said miserably, her eyes filling with tears.

'She's something to do with horses,' I told my mother.

'Racing, you mean? There *is* the Littlejohn family. He owns those racing stables. *Their* daughter would be of a White Rose age . . .'

But she couldn't make much of it really; and I couldn't help her. Nevertheless something that I'd said must have satisfied her for very soon after she announced happily that she'd planned a special first night of term supper. 'A ragout of beef. I've already made it, Lucy. And I've saved some farm eggs to make a custard.'

With a fatalism born of experience, I watched her evening collapse. The custard curdled and no additions of precious yolk were able to save it; my father, who was in a hurry to go out, irritated her by smoking throughout the meal; he also assumed, justified by previous experience, that the stew was whalemeat.

'If you gave up even five minutes to eating it,' she said, her brow twitching angrily, 'you'd realise it was beef.'

'I've learnt the hard way. How do you think I manage,' he asked, pressing his cigarette butt on to the plate, 'except I try not to taste any of it?'

Spooning up our grainy custard neither my mother nor I mentioned the White Rose. Possibly he'd forgotten. When I'd come down that morning he had already left, and he'd been out the two evenings before. But she was too angry, and I was too proud, to remind him of it now.

Chapter 5

I hadn't told my mother about Alan, and when I did, she wasn't at all pleased. She'd hoped, she said, I was going to concentrate on the White Rose and not gad about; there would be time enough for that in London. 'And heaven knows, Lucy, what type you attracted in that dreadful dress.'

She insisted on meeting him first, but there were several Holdsworths in the Bratherton directory, and before I could track him down I had to ask four times, redfaced, 'Is Alan there?' She wanted him to come to tea on Saturday. Alan, sounding pleased but surprised, said yes, he'd love to come.

It was not a success. Right from the beginning, wincing when he said 'pleased to meet you,' my mother showed how it was that she'd earned her nickname 'the Duchess of Bratherton'. When Alan, asked to admire Pugin sleekly dozing on her knee, revealed apologetically that he didn't really like cats, she lifted Pugin from her lap and without further comment crossed the room and opened the door; Pugin with great dignity stalked out. From then onwards matters grew steadily worse. As Alan's shyness wore off his nervousness increased; he seemed unable to stop talking. Perched on the edge of the sofa, at intervals drying his clammy hands on his trousers, he talked about his hobbies (hiking, dancing, engine-spotting); about his home life, his four brothers and sisters, his father who was a lay preacher, 'I'm a keen Methodist myself'; and about his job and prospects. 'Anyone would think he'd come to ask for your hand,' said my mother scornfully afterwards. By the time he left, still apologising for Pugin's unnecessary exile, I'd begun against my will to see him through her eyes. It was as if by some alchemy she managed in spite of what I realised to be unpardonable behaviour to keep me on her side always.

I knew this from experience. Several years before, triumphant in my love for the art teacher, Miss Greenwood, I'd invited her to tea one holiday afternoon: certain that her talent and beauty, her aura of suffering (only a few months before her pilot fiancé had been shot down in flames) could not fail to impress. But like Alan's visit, it had gone wrong from the start. My love arrived pink-nosed, apologetic, with a streaming cold; the room was dank and chilly and my mother, who had made the coal shortage an excuse for not lighting the fire till the last possible moment, intimated graciously that because of her asthma she was particularly susceptible to infection. 'Of course, you couldn't possibly have known . . .' Looking cold and uncomfortable, Miss Greenwood sat dabbing at her sore nose; long strands of fine hair escaped from her clumsily rolled bun. Usually it was part of her charm that she looked untidy and wild: in art classes, between rushes around our work, she would lean across the desk—her blouse pulling out of her skirt—writing excited sprawling letters to her fiancé, spattered with exclamation marks and under-linings; by the end of the lesson her hair would have fallen halfway down her back. That afternoon, I'd just sat unhappily, knowing something was wrong but not sure exactly what, while my mother by a series of questions unearthed the fact that Miss Greenwood's father was a railway porter and that her Christian name was Gertie (I had been certain it was Gwendolen).

'Of course I'm sure she's excellent at her subject, and all that,' said my mother afterwards, 'but she *is* a little pathetic, don't you think?'

At the time, I felt only a great sadness: a guiltiness that I hadn't leapt to Miss Greenwood's defence. But back at school next term, all was changed: she seemed to me dull and uninteresting, and a poor teacher—more to be pitied than admired. And although for Alan I felt as yet only easy friendship, gratitude at being rescued that evening, I saw already that it was to be the same old story.

The next day began badly. It was our Sunday for visiting my grandparents, and my mother, who detested the fortnightly ritual, was awkward and belligerent all morning. She often got out of going by some convenient illness; but today she'd obviously decided against this and instead, I well knew, was going to sit the afternoon out, scarcely speaking but wearing a faint smile all the time as if she had some secret. Lunch had been late, and just as we were about to leave Pugin was sick on the front door mat. My father was furious;

47

he disliked all cats and Pugin in particular. Sending me to clear up the mess he went out to crank the Hillman, while my mother ran distractedly into the kitchen to see what was wrong. Nothing much was. Pugin was safely asleep in his Lloyd Loom chair; but she was alarmed nevertheless. Although fat and stiff and old now and very different from the fluffy kitten of 1940 taken in for some evacuees who'd wanted to return home, Pugin was still an object of much love and solicitude: his death something she didn't want to think about.

'For me, you see, Lucy, he's connected with Patmore. You do understand, don't you, darling?'

As I'd known the cat long before I'd heard of the architect, the two were inextricably confused in my mind; but it appeared that Pugin had been responsible for adding a chapel to Patmore in the middle of the last century. ('All that bloody red and purple,' my father said once. 'I don't know what was up with him.') My mother having chosen the name, was delighted: it was short, expletive, a little esoteric, and most important of all, it meant she could be reminded several times a day of Patmore; when Pugin misbehaved, clawing at stockings, scratching the furniture, then she had the added satisfaction of using his full name: 'You *bad* boy, Augustus Welby Pugin!'

We set off for Harrogate at last. My grandparents lived not far from the Valley Gardens, up a little sidestreet—they'd moved there from Leeds in the nineteen thirties, when my grandfather sold up his shop and retired. It was a small house, painted dull brown in and out, its pseudo-leaded windows draped with net curtains which smelt strongly always of Sunlight soap; and except for the kitchen, and the front room on Sundays, it was always freezing.

My grandmother was already at the tiny porch to greet us. 'Father and I'd all but given you up!' she exclaimed. A small, efficient mouse-coloured person, she was dressed as nearly always in a grey jersey suit, her thin hair worn shingled, her actions all quick and nervous, so that she looked considerably less than her seventy-five years.

In the front room, my grandfather was sitting by the Sunday fire; a semi-invalid for some years now, he spent most of his time in the kitchen in a basket chair padded round with cushions, except for occasional short walks seldom stirring out of his brown carpet slippers. I came over now and kissed him: he was big and burly and with so much moustache and beard, some of the auburn still visible amongst the grey, that it was often difficult to find anywhere to kiss. Today I settled for his forehead.

Although I often felt ill at ease with my grandmother, who tended to give me sudden, sharp, critical looks for no apparent reason, with my grandfather I was always relaxed. I had a tough, unanalysed affection for him. And like my affection for Elizabeth, my mother's comments merely bounced off it. 'He seems to have got very grubby with old age,' she had remarked last time (not without truth, for although my grandmother did much mopping and sponging, his dark jacket seemed always stained now with tea or whisky or a mixture of both), but I'd paid her little attention.

When I'd kissed him I sat down in my usual place, on the leather pouf with diamond-shaped patches, close to his chair. My mother was sitting awkwardly on the horsehair sofa, well away from my father. Gazing into the middle distance, she smiled occasionally to herself.

'I heard from Arnold, Friday,' said my grandmother, coming into the room carrying a fat envelope. 'I'm to be a great-grandmother again!'

We heard about Uncle Arnold most visits. He was manager now of a small factory for electrical parts near Glasgow, and rarely came down to Yorkshire. When he did however, my mother kept out of his way. Big, heavy, like my grandfather in physique, he was a practical joker (on his first visit to Leeds after my mother left Patmore, he'd put a farting cushion under her chair). But most important of all, he had never, from the very beginning, thought the marriage had a chance. (That he'd been proved right only made it worse.)

My grandmother began reading the letter aloud, making comments as she went along. He wrote a rather dull letter: laboured, ponderous with detail. There were several sheets to come yet, and bored, I let my eyes wander, following round the photographs which hung all along one wall and ranged the length of the sideboard. Everyone seemed to be there. All the Taylors and Illingworths I knew about; and many that I didn't. The famous Ethel: in Land Army breeches, solemn-faced and surprised-looking, barely recognisable as the girl described so affectionately by my mother;

49

Uncle Norman, weedy and not very tall, unbelievably young-looking in private's uniform. Uncle Arnold himself, head and shoulders only, dressed for football. My father—first as an early boy scout, bullet-headed, frowning, then later, in stiff new Sam Browne, as an officer. There was even Aunt Lucy as a prim, tight-bodiced, moustacheless young girl. And many, many more. It didn't seem that a picture had ever been put away that could be put out.

'Lucy's off dreaming.' said my grandmother, folding the letter and getting up. 'She can give me a hand to get the tea.'

I went through with her to the kitchen. It wasn't a very big room and an enormous range took up most of the space, giving out an almost unbearable heat. My grandfather's basket chair was drawn up to the table, which was crammed with food. Rich dark parkin, moist from the apples it was stored with, fruit loaf, cold fat bacon, apple pie and cheese, Yorkshire curd tart. It had always been like this ever since I could remember, even in the worst days of the War. There was a confident assured air about it all too—a custard for instance, would never had curdled for my grandmother.

My mother ate little during the meal. She had remarked often that this was an uncivilised hour to eat: 'However, it's what they've been brought up to Lucy, and you are *never* to comment,' (I had not been going to.) 'After all, noblesse oblige.'

My grandfather was spreading mustard thickly over his bacon. 'A little bird told me you've a young man now, Lucy,' he said, taking a noisy gulp of his tea and spilling some of it onto the large napkin tied under his chin.

'It wasn't a *little bird* at all,' said my mother sharply. 'You get all your information from Peter. Peter was over here last night.'

My grandmother, pursing her lips together, said, 'Father's only showing interest, Winifred.'

She didn't say any more, but lifting up the teapot carried it over to the stove; my father muttered something which I didn't hear. While her back was turned my grandfather poured a swig of whisky into his cup from a bottle hidden amongst the cushions: he winked at me and I winked back, and I saw my father give him a quick, friendly look.

My grandmother came back to the table. Turning to me she said, 'This White Rose, now, we've not heard much of it, Lucy. We've nothing but what your father's told us.'

I caught sight of my mother's expression. Her superior smile, which she couldn't keep while eating and drinking anyway, had begun to fade, so that she looked to me pathetic, and I began to feel protective immediately. I said carefully:

'Well, we have to work very hard of course.' I described the school a little. 'But it's all very interesting.'

My grandmother was pouring out tea. 'It sounds very fancy to me,' she said. 'And it'll give you *ideas*.' She reached over for my mother's cup, filling it without asking her. 'You're wasting your money, Winifred. Next thing, she'll be courting and wed—and not a penny back.'

This was the first remark, in my hearing, that she'd ever made about the project. I suppose I'd realised that they must have discussed it at some time: the Patmore legacy, the uses to which it was to be put, and so on; at no time had my father ever hinted that he didn't believe my mother's story. But it was a rare thing for my grandmother to comment openly. Although in the circumstances neither of them could have been by now very fond of my mother, very little was said, apart from the odd remark now and then: the 'oh, well, Winifred' which I heard sometimes, when I went there alone with my father. On the whole, I think the situation was accepted like Acts of God and the weather. Not much to do about it.

Today my mother let the remark pass. In the close atmosphere of the kitchen she was beginning to look very flushed and as always when she was too hot, her hair gave the illusion of being too heavy for her head. But I could see that my father was growing more and more annoyed with her; and a few moments later, he showed this by making some reference to the elocution lessons she'd arranged. (I wasn't even sure how he'd heard of them.)

'So you see, that's not all with the legacy. There's money gone on brown cows too.'

I blushed. My mother cast him a look of dignified hate.

'What's that, eh, what's that?' asked my grandfather; then began to laugh before he'd seen any joke. I didn't say anything; and my father didn't repeat the remark. My grandmother who was clearing the table hadn't seemed to hear.

We left soon after. There was a wireless programme my grandparents always listened to on Sunday evenings and my mother found it very convenient to remind them of this: she herself always listened to the Radio Doctor on Friday mornings, so she knew, she said, how it was.

My grandfather, leaning forward in his chair, kissing me goodbye, said, 'Be nice to that young man, Lucy!' His moustache was wet and smelt strongly of whisky. Just as we were leaving, feeling a surge of affection for him because of his warm undemanding approval of me, I ran back to kiss him again.

We were alone in the kitchen. As I was moving away he began to mumble, but as if to himself. 'She'd do best not to come, you know,' he said, twice. 'There's nothing right. Nothing suits. She'd do best not to come.' He reached forward for his cup and took a few big gulps. 'There's no pleasing Winifred, she'd do best not to come. Aye,' he said, 'that'd be best—that's right. Taken all round, that's best.'

Then he noticed I was still there. He winked at me rather sheepishly.

'You haven't to tell her,' he said.

The next Tuesday I began with Miss Lister. My lesson was for five o'clock, but we'd had our first shorthand test that afternoon and hungry after the strain, I made a swift, expensive visit to Fuller's; then I realised that I was going to be late and ran all the way, so that when I eventually arrived at Miss Lister's address in the Cold Bath Road I was not only apprehensive but breathless as well.

I didn't know anything about elocution teachers and the image I'd made for myself was of someone bustling and efficient—a sort of gymnast of the vocal chords; the reality of Miss Lister however, was something quite other. Her first words to me as she stood dramatically on her front door step, were, 'You are Lucy!' spoken in a deep, vibrating voice. Then repeating, 'You are *Lucy*,' with a sweeping gesture, she led me inside.

Tall and horsefaced, dressed in a tight black silk blouse, her brown cobwebby hair piled up high, she struck awe into me at once. As we walked through the hall, the hem of her long velvet skirt trailing along the linoleum, she said in a sad tone, 'Pupils should arrive at least ten minutes before their lesson is due. Where is your breath, Lucy?' Her own as she leant towards me, smelt of violet cachoux.

The room she was to teach me in was large and dark with a lot of heavy drapes of the same plum-coloured velvet as her skirt. While she asked me some questions about myself, I sat on the edge of a knobbly sofa and gazed for reassurance at a stuffed canary in an ornate wicker cage; she herself sat very upright in a high, carved chair, shuddering as I spoke.

'So flat!' she said. 'Such *slovenly* sounds.'

My vowels, she explained to me sadly were the ugly vowels of Yorkshire townsfolk—never, never of course to be confused with the lovely, country dialect. 'I often sit, quite quietly,' she said, 'on my beautiful visits to the Dales, listening, listening to the shepherd, the ploughman, the herdsman, the—' She searched for another example, but not finding it she waved her arm airily. 'Their dialect is sacred,' she declared. 'I would never tamper with it.'

But my vowels, it appeared, weren't ready for improvement yet : I would have to begin with breathing. Breathing was of the greatest importance; and for what seemed an age, I had to sit before a large diagram showing me in red and black the whole complex of larynx, pharynx, lungs, windpipe, while Miss Lister, blowing violet over me, pointed them all out. Then we did some simple exercises which I was to continue faithfully at home, fifteen minutes every evening. In the meantime we would approach the vowels by stealth as it were, forcing them through beautiful poetry. To this end, I read aloud from the *Golden Treasury*; Miss Lister wincing at regular intervals.

In the middle of *The Lotos-Eaters*, she interrupted me.

'Do you ever go up on the moors, Lucy?' she asked.

'Well, yes,' I said, starting. 'Sometimes. In the summer.'

She stood up suddenly.

'Emily Brontë!' she cried. She threw back her arms, straining the buttons of her blouse. Then in her most dramatic voice, she announced, 'Lucy, next time you are up on the moors—I want you to *run*. Run, run, flinging your arms wide like this,' she made another wild gesture, 'run away, away! Call out your vowels, Lucy. Ah, ah, ah!' She sounded in pain. 'Hear the wind catch them—a wonderful, rising, falling, dying-away sound—ah, ah, ah!'

I said that certainly I would see about it, and she sat down again, refreshed. Then with my eye on the grandfather clock, I read her two more poems, watching relievedly as the hand approached the half hour.

The second poem, 'Innisfree', I was to learn by heart for next week. 'Lake water lapping with low sounds by the shore,' declaimed Miss Lister with relish, lingering on the word 'low'. 'I have a great deal of the Celt in me,' she confided as she showed me out. 'I find it a *wonderful* help in my work.'

When I got home my mother thought that I sounded better already: and she was thrilled by the homework.

' "Innisfree", Lucy—Gervase used to read me that!' She told me yet again, 'Gervase read so beautifully then—his voice was so gentle, so controlled. We would have gone to Ireland on our honeymoon, you know, Lucy. The West Coast, Sligo, Galway. A stonyhurst friend had offered us a house.'

Later on, she said:

'I tried once to read some other Yeats poems, more modern ones, Lucy. But they weren't *at all* like "Innisfree". They were about old age, and sex, and some were frankly disgusting. All the *romance* lost. Not what I call poetry at all, Lucy.'

Two evenings later, it was my date with Alan. I met him straight from his work and as it was still quite early, we went into a milk bar before the cinema.

Most of the day I'd been agitated: that morning my mother had hinted that homework and early bed and Miss Lister's exercises were of greater importance, and without actually forbidding me to go had made me feel that I was being ungrateful to her and to Uncle Gervase. Also, since the tea last week I'd been prepared to feel awkward in Alan's company; and now, although ashamed of myself, I saw, as if through her eyes, that his suit was all wrong; so was the way he was cutting up his pork pie into minute pieces.

But perched on a high stool beside me, he chatted animatedly about his work, and after a while I began to relax.

He didn't mention Saturday again, except to say, 'My mother won't have a cat in the house. When she was a kiddie her baby sister was suffocated. It got in and laid on her. Now she can't see one but she thinks of it.'

Talking had brought the sweat out in beads on his forehead and his face was flushed, but close to he smelt inviting. We sat on companionably. There was a loudspeaker in the milk bar playing tunes from *Annie Get Your Gun*; he sang some of the words: 'The girl that I marry', 'Doin' what comes naturally'.

'I'm really enjoying this,' he said.

There was quite a queue for *Brief Encounter* but we were early and got good seats. Throughout the renunciation scene we clasped hands stickily. When we came out, wiping his palms on his handkerchief he apologised profusely for the clamminess. 'I always perspire like this. You should see me on a new call—my hands slipping all over the samples case.' I said I didn't mind, because I didn't; that he should have wanted to spend an evening with me at all filled me with wonder. On the way home, walking from Bratherton bus station, we discussed earnestly the moral issues raised by the film. Celia Johnson had done right to renounce Trevor Howard, Alan said: there were the children to consider, and Bob was a good husband.

'I'm maybe old fashioned. But there were lies told. Once you've got lies—'

'You could see she'd never get over it! The ending was in for the censor,' I said. 'You aren't allowed that sort of happy ending.' I was worried, distressed suddenly; but about what I didn't know.

'It could be a very dangerous film. If you think about it,' went on Alan, telling me how many people shouldn't make marriage vows if they didn't mean them. 'A promise is a promise, like.'

I saw then in a sudden flash a picture of my mother visted by a resurrected Gervase; frail gilded youth of 1913. 'Choose,' someone was saying; and I saw her crash about clumsily happy, rushing out of our lives: the past made right at last. She came before my eyes as I'd always wanted her to look—joyous. 'Tell Peter where I've gone, would you?' she cried; the beige felt hat pulled down hard; not minding or needing me any more, scarcely bothering to say goodbye. 'We'll see you next summer, darling—tea at Gunter's as usual!'

'Penny for them,' said Alan. We were turning the corner of the avenue coming up to the house; our feet squelched in a pile of sodden beech leaves.

'Anyway,' he said, giving my hand a squeeze, 'it seemed the right ending to me! Not that I'd know much about it really. At home—

they're a couple of love birds still.' He opened the gate for us, then as we came up to the porch he leant over suddenly and pulled me to him, kissing me awkwardly at first, then as I didn't resist, tightening his hold; I felt his lips press harder and harder. His skin, not smooth as it looked, had a pleasing roughness, and surprised into enjoyment, I leaned back.

As he released me, he said, 'I wanted to do that all evening!' Then as if suddenly overcome, he clasped my hand quickly and skipping almost, hurried down the path, turning for a moment at the gate to call, 'Cheerybye!'

Inside, there was a light on downstairs but no one about. I supposed my mother had taken a sleeping tablet: when she did this no sound seemed to disturb her. I turned off the light and went upstairs.

In the bathroom, my lips which had been tingling began suddenly to burn and looking in the glass I saw that they were swelling rapidly. At first I was agitated, wondering if they'd be right by morning; then I became all at once very proud of them. Reverently smearing them with vaseline I thought of how, in Elizabeth's eyes at least, I could be said to have begun to arrive; and for that—and for making a pale thing of red-headed Brian's kiss last Christmas—I felt towards Alan a great rush of gratitude.

It was only later, hearing the door bang downstairs, the creaking of the top steps on the staircase, that I realised how much I'd hoped in fact that my father would be at home when I came in. I'd been proud of course that someone had asked me out; but that wasn't what it was all about. I had wanted, I knew now, his anxiety—even his anger. I had wanted him to fling open the sitting-room door, to march out, anxious-faced, full of orthodox righteous indignation: 'Where the hell have you been?' Worried, caring, on his twentieth cigarette of the evening. 'Did that lad bring you straight home—tell me that now. Did he? Did he bring you straight home?'

Chapter 6

We all began, gradually, to get used to the White Rose. I got on well enough with the other girls—to some extent a dislike of Miss Metcalfe united us all. But as I'd suspected, most of them had fairly vivid outside lives, which they discussed in loud confident tones in the cloakroom, and although I chatted occasionally with a lively blonde called Jennifer in the row behind, Marjorie was still my only friend.

I worried for her continually. Her typewriter was a clawed monster, which she approached fearfully each morning, as if the keys were about to strike her, not she the keys. Most of us had got the eccentricities of our old uprights more or less under control—except for Marjorie; her machine had a life of its own. It was Marjorie who'd been the first to tangle a typing ribbon, pulling and twisting unending coils of it with her sore hands—which now that the cold weather had come were stiff and swollen with chilblains. Twice a day she coated her fingers hopefully with wintergreen, and Miss Metcalfe, passing by, would sniff ominously. In every respect, Marjorie's misery seemed to aggravate her in a way that no cheerful incompetence could have done. In shorthand class she would stride suddenly across the room, snatching up Marjorie's nervously chewed notebook, waving it in front of us all and making some withering exclamation, such as, 'Ladies! How *not* to practise grammalogues ...'

It all came to a head one Friday morning. We were practising typing exercises before lunch, a barely suppressed feeling of week-end liberation in the air. Miss Metcalfe had been prowling about the room for some time. She came over our way now, and stopping suddenly by Marjorie's desk, looked at it for a moment. Then leaning forward, she tore the paper angrily from the machine.

'Over *three weeks* of practice,' she shouted, in the ringing tone we'd all come to dread. 'And the paper still in crooked!'

From my seat in the front row I didn't dare look at Marjorie. Miss

Metcalfe went up on to the dais, and after a little while, when she began looking at some papers, I was able to glance across quickly.

Marjorie was sitting motionless, her sore red fingers hanging by her sides, tears coursing silently down her cheeks. I thought of trying to write a comforting note which I might slip across, but before I could do anything, she stood up suddenly. Saying in a loud voice 'bloody hell,' she banged against her desk and ran, jerkily, out of the room.

It was a dramatic gesture—and a final one. In the afternoon Marjorie was nowhere to be seen.

When we returned on Monday we were told, in the course of a short homily, that she had left us.

I didn't pay a lot of attention to Miss Metcalfe's words, because that morning I'd had a letter from Alan which had upset me very much. Since our outing, I'd been half-expecting him to telephone and was surprised that after nearly three weeks I'd still heard nothing. Now this letter had come.

'I have phoned three times now,' he wrote, in a scratchy, sloping hand, 'but on each ocassion your lady mother told me you were not At Home. I have been wondering therefore if my 'Goodnight' after the pictures was out of turn, I must say that you seemed to enjoy it. But perhaps however you do not want to see me again and if that is so I shall quite understand, but Faint Heart never won Fair Lady, so please forgive me writing this . . .'

The morning after I'd been out with him, there had been a scene with my mother. I looked exhausted, she said; did I think really I was being fair to Uncle Gervase, who had invested so much in this White Rose course?

'There's plenty of time, darling. I've told you. When you go to London—' She broke off and looking at me closely, 'Lucy, do try and understand. It's not that I'm snobbish in any way—but just because someone is worthy, doesn't mean they're *suitable*, you know.'

'But I only went out with him. I'm not going to *marry* him—'

'Oh darling!' she exclaimed sadly, shaking her head. 'Darling.' Then suddenly intense, she had hugged me to her closely.

'Lucy, all Mummy wants for you, in the end, is to make the sort of marriage you would have made *if* you'd been brought up at

Patmore! And this isn't the way to go about it.' I was terrified as she released me to see that her eyes were full of tears. 'You do want me to be happy, don't you, darling? You do *see*, Lucy?'

This morning, after opening Alan's letter, I'd mentioned the telephone calls to her, timidly; but she was recovering from a weekend migraine, and rubbing her hand to and fro across her forehead she only said, wearily, that there *might* have been one or two calls. 'However, with the way I feel today, how can I possibly be expected to remember that sort of thing?'

Her behaviour over this had induced in me one of my rare fits of rebellious anger–none the less real for being so rare. I said nothing at the time, but when I came out of the White Rose at four o'clock I didn't feel that I could face going straight home; and turning off at the bottom of the crescent, instead of walking up to the bus I went off towards the Valley Gardens.

My mother disliked the Gardens, and seldom went in them now; but when I was a child she had had to take me there occasionally. The outings then had been peppered with comments, all the way through from the entrance gate, up till Harlow Moor. 'Pathetic! After one has been brought up with *acres* to roam in . . .' 'I find these gardens so artificial. So *public* . . .' Hands in the pockets of her old tweed coat, she would amble along grudgingly, while I ran to and fro just ahead of her, clatter, clatter, up and down the corridors of the sun colonnade.

This afternoon it was already growing dark. It had been a damp day and the few children going off home were all in wellingtons; an old man, head bent in his mackintosh collar, looked up startled, when I heard myself say, out loud: 'I want a home like Alan's.' Walking along to the sun pavilion, my steps echoing, I realised that Alan's face was already hazy in my memory, but that the picture of his home life, which he'd given when he came to tea and embroidered on during our outing, was completely clear to me in every detail—and filled me with inexplicable longing.

I saw the warm, firelit room where they sang in the evenings: Wesleyan hymns, I thought probably; or just-out-of-date dance tunes. 'At weekends we often go hiking,' he had said. 'We do youth hostelling too.' His sisters thought he was wonderful, and he returned the compliment: 'Jean's a swimmer. You should see her—good as Esther Williams she is.' While his mother fussed endlessly over his too-

59

hardworking father, who was always thinking up small, inexpensive surprises for her: ' "You've got to guess first," Dad says always, "then you can have it!" They're a couple of love birds still . . .'

In my fury I walked the length of the Gardens, through on to Harlow Moor; it was almost dark now, the air damp and resinous. After a while I came out by the reservoirs: the filter beds, clean and shallow, lay just visible in the disappearing light and behind them, the reservoirs themselves, black and deep and sinister. My mood of rebellion nearly spent, I shuddered. Years and years ago, walking that way with my father, he'd told me, 'Two boys got drowned there. They'd been fooling around, for a dare. Then there was this accident. Night time it was.' Since then I'd tried never to go by the reservoirs, because for me the boys lay there still. Against all commonsense I fancied their bodies had never been removed; and tonight, unable to look at all, cold and shivery, I began running and running, not stopping till they were right out of sight.

Then, on the bus back to Bratherton, ashamed of my fears I felt foolish, and flat. Everything, really, seemed pointless: the White Rose, torments like Miss Lister, deciding whether or not to make an issue over Alan, going to London; and, above all—this trying to live for ever as a Patmore might-have-been. Why, why, why?

But when I got in my mother didn't remark that I was late, and I said nothing more to her about Alan's letter. I didn't answer it either, and never heard from him again.

Marjorie's machine didn't remain vacant for long. The next day, coming back early from lunch to finish some homework, I saw a strange girl sitting in her place. My first reaction was surprise; not so much at the speed with which Miss Metcalfe had filled the vacancy, but because the replacement was obviously so much older than the rest of us—well into her twenties, I thought. She seemed altogether a far more sophisticated, finished product than was usual for the White Rose. Under cover of my Pitman's manual I took a good look at her.

She was reading a magazine, a cloud of expensive scent wafting round her, and hadn't seemed to notice when I came in. Everything about her was very neat and slightly fragile, not brittle like china but with the small-boned delicacy of a kitten. Fashionable ankle-strapped shoes showed beneath her long skirt and lilac cashmere sweater, and on her bent head the light brown hair was cut very short to fit like a cap; her skin, dry and rather delicate, had the remains of a strong tan.

Sensing my gaze perhaps, she looked up and smiled: a slightly crooked smile which gave the impression of being for herself alone.

'What sort of a penance have you got there, darling?' Her voice was very quiet, and when she spoke she seemed to round the words in her mouth, drawling them almost. 'Let Juliet see.'

I handed her the opened book; she looked at it for a moment idly. 'What is the least price at which Briggs and Baker will deliver their brass paste in glass bottles?' she read out. She made a little shape with her mouth, then shrugging her shoulders, handed the book back. 'Are they tongue twisters, darling, or what?'

'It's to practise initial hooks on straight strokes,' I told her. 'Or that's what it says. We're having a test.'

'But how boring, darling,' she said. She reached over for her handbag and took out a gold cigarette case and long tortoiseshell holder, 'I can see that poor Juliet is going to suffer from the most dreadful ennui.'

She offered me a cigarette and when I refused she lit one herself; then with her free hand she began fingering Marjorie's machine.

'I did some typing of a sort, in the WRNS. But that was all over in forty-six. I shall look at the keys of course.' She pulled at the guard carelessly, 'I have my own fingering anyway; Juliet's system.' Her hands resting on the machine were small, and plumper than I would have thought.

Back looking at her magazine again—I saw that it was the Queen—she asked me a little about the typing lessons: half-listening to the answers with a small, secret smile, saying finally, 'but really?' so that I wasn't sure whether it was the White Rose or I who was being laughed at. Then reaching for her handbag again, she took out a portable ashtray and unfolded it on the desk.

'I really ought to let you get on with your hooks, darling,' she murmured, puffing lightly. 'Naughty Juliet.'

She was still smoking when the other girls came back, (although admittedly Miss Metcalfe was away for the afternoon, her daring in continuing to do so even after Miss Laycock had clapped her hands for order, amazed me). She didn't stay for long afterwards: just went over and discussed one or two points with Miss Laycock, then quietly strolled out.

Realising that she'd probably be beside me for many weeks to come, I wished I'd been less shy and had asked a few questions. Fortunately I ran into Jennifer in the cloakroom at going-home time. She was a mine of information:

'That's Juliet *Hirst* you've got next door! I kept trying to pass a note over to you,' she twitched at the roller towel. '*You* know— Blackett's. The sauce and jelly people. I've often seen bits about her in the paper—she's the only daughter, and terribly rich.'

We were the only two left in the cloakroom now, but as it was my day for Miss Lister I was very keen to stay on talking.

'I think from what someone said, she must be doing the Shortened Course. War Heroines, you know. It used to be in the prospectus when my sister was here. All sorts of blah,' she put on Miss Metcalfe's voice: 'vital years of your lives, sacrifices for King and country, etc. etc. There used to be loads of them doing it, ATS and Land Army and so on. But it's a bit stupid now.' Pulling heavily on the roller towel, she sent it spinning. '*Anyway*, I don't expect she'll stick it for long.'

Unable to put it off any longer, I began dawdling my way to Miss Lister's. I was even more reluctant than usual because I hadn't really been practising my exercises: in our small house, I found it quite impossible to raise my voice to the frantic full-blooded tones she recommended; and this week I hadn't learnt my homework properly either.

'O Death in Life, the days that are no more,' I recited, stumbling from line to line, while Miss Lister prompting me, tapped her fingers impatiently on the wooden arms of her chair.

My breathing was much, much too shallow:

'Direct, drive, *push* the air out!' she urged, blowing at me a cachou of a different scent—rose perhaps? Then she placed her hands firmly round my waist and as my diaphragm tensed to her command, she demonstrated how I was able by my breathing to move her fingers apart.

'You have no catarrh, no adenoids,' she declared. 'Nothing to come between you, and a beautiful, deep, *controlled*, breath.'

'Harrogate is a Spa! Aaaaah . . .' I repeated after her, ad nauseam. My vowels it appeared had not improved at all.

'We've a long way to go,' she said sadly at the end of the lesson, setting me part of *The Lotos-Eaters* for my homework.

'All day the wind breathes low with mellower tone:'

she chanted,

> 'Thro' every hollow cave and alley lone,
> Round and round the spicy downs the yellow Lotos-dust is blown . . .'

'Have you been up on the moors yet, dear?' she asked.

On the Friday of that week, my grandfather died.

I'd come in from the White Rose, later than usual because my mother had sent me shopping, to find my father standing by the telephone in the hall. Still in his macintosh, he looked white and shaken. He told me shortly: 'We've just heard. Your grandpa's dead.' He began at once to move towards the front door.

I'd begun to tremble as soon as he'd said it. I asked urgently to his retreating figure, 'But what happened? He was all right on Sunday—'

Through the open sitting-room door I saw my mother, her legs up on the sofa, a handkerchief pressed to her face.

My father took out a battered cigarette packet and lit up quickly. Then without looking at me: 'Mother'd been round the corner for an evening paper,' he said. 'She'd left him having his tea and when she got in—she thought he'd fallen asleep. A neighbour phoned, just a few minutes back.' He pulled at the cigarette. 'I'm just off over there,' he said, his hand on the front door. 'She'd best not be alone.'

When he'd left, I went straight through to my mother. She hadn't moved from the sofa and seeing me come in, she blew her nose loudly.

'How awful—' I began. My voice was very wobbly.

She got up suddenly. 'Nonsense!' she said, with a false briskness, 'we all have to die, Lucy—it's *quite* unnecessary to dwell on the subject.' She blew her nose again, more vigorously this time. 'I've a cold beginning,' she explained. 'It isn't emotion.'

I wanted to cry but it was as if she had forbidden me. She made me give her a full account of the day's classes, with a blow by blow account of the Friday etiquette lecture.

'At least you'll know *how* to behave,' she commented.

But later, in the kitchen making some toast, while I opened a tin of sardines, Pugin mewing round my ankles, she was unusually silent. She let the toast burn: the acrid grey smoke billowed round the cooker; then, as she threw the charred pieces in the bin, she turned on me suddenly:

'Anyway,' she burst out, 'what *good* was he doing, Lucy? As old as that—and sitting by the fire all day?'

I turned my head away quickly. Under cover of getting some more bread I went into the larder. Bent over, rattling the bin, I felt the tears begin to flow, scalding, uncontrollable.

'Don't say we're out of bread!' called my mother.

'Housekeeping really is a wearying business,' I heard her go on. 'I wasn't brought up to it at all. With all the worthwhile things I could be doing—to be fussing over bread, and rations, meat, butter and so on. And the endless *dust*. Dust everywhere, Lucy. I think often, you know, that that's what's at the back of my asthma. Dust!'

At the weekend my father and I went to visit my grandmother. Still very shaken, she nervously arranged and rearranged jars, pans, plates on and off the dresser. There was a dismal tidiness everywhere.

I wanted very much to say something consoling. Looking at her agitatedly patting the leaves of a trailing plant, I felt confused sentences jostle for order in my mind: there seemed not too few, but too many words. Sadly I said nothing.

She talked a lot of the time, going over and over again her account of how he died. In all she must have told us four or five times at least. Of how she'd just poured him out a cup of tea, with a drop, 'just a teaspoon', of whisky in it.

'Then when I were in again with the paper, there he was fallen asleep. And I was vexed with him, Peter, because he'd let drop the

64

cup.' It had been quite a few moments before she'd realised the truth and even now, grief was still tinged with a little outrage.

'To be smelling of spirits like that at the end. His trousers sodden with it, Peter. It didn't satisfy him the bit I put in, you know. He was putting more and more in his cup every day. On the quiet like.'

During the journey back my father seemed distant and pre-occupied, and I was tense, as always when alone with him in the car. In a way it was simpler when my mother was there too. The sullen build-up of taunts and fury, subtly charging the air, much as I disliked it, made me feel safer, more protected, earthed as it were.

He spoke to me only once. As we approached Bratherton–the beech trees, damp and drooping, stretching over towards the Drop-ping Well, the castle gaunt in the afternoon gloom–he said in a firm rather cold voice, 'This is bloody well an order. We're burying him Tuesday, and you've got to get leave from that finishing school. Understand?'

My mother's cold grew worse, and she wasn't able to come to the funeral. It was early November now, and the weather raw. As we stood in the graveyard of the little moorland church where my grandfather was to be buried, a cutting east wind blew in our faces; around us, their inscriptions worn not so much by time as by the high winds over the moors, stood tombstones with the family name. For a couple of hundred years or more Taylors had farmed this district: now the shopkeeper was going back to his roots.

My grandmother with bent head was standing a little way from me; my father was on one side of her, and Uncle Arnold, his mouth set in the firm line I'd so often seen on my grandmother, was on the other; a handful of friends stood near. With our collars turned up, we formed a bleak little circle round the pit. It seemed to me frighteningly deep. In my ignorance I'd always imagined people buried only just below the earth's surface, and gazing down now, I thought with horror of my brother: faded photographs and hearsay only, but once flesh and blood, never seen or heard or touched by me, and now lying as deep as this.

The words of the burial service rolled on around us; in the background I heard a sheep bleating down in the valley, the sudden cry of a peewit.

And then as if from nowhere, a picture of Miss Lister floated before me. She was standing up on the moor, arms flung wide, head thrown back; her vowels echoing, her bosom rising and falling, she called out to the wind across the faded heather. The image, ludicrous and unwanted, wouldn't go away and a moment later, without warning, I felt a giggle begin: pushing at my ribs, shaking me, forcing tears to my eyes. Slowly, but relentlessly, a sacrilegious grin of mirth spread over my face.

My father saw it almost at once. Stepping forward, he grasped me by the wrist, then half-pushing, half-pulling, led me over to the car. Jerking the door open, he pushed me roughly inside. 'Laugh in there, will you.'

My wrist was sore where he'd pressed it. I huddled in the corner, a handkerchief over my face, till it was time to drive away. On the journey home, we took three of the neighbours while Uncle Arnold drove my grandmother. I sat choked and silent, looking out of the window.

Our route back went through Bratherton, and as we passed our house my father stopped the car:

'You get out now,' he said, coming round and opening the door. He spoke to the people inside: 'Lucy'd do best not to come to the tea,' I heard him say. Then, as I was about to walk shakily away, he appeared behind me.

'The others all think you were overcome with grief,' he said. 'Hysterics. And I've left it at that.' I tried to say something, but no words came. He went on, in a low voice:

'I've had enough. I reckon you wouldn't find a Patmore funeral such a bloody laugh, would you? Would you?'

I turned my head away, pretended to be looking for my gloves.

'Get on in and tell Winifred all about it,' he said. 'Split your sides—the two of you.'

Chapter 7

My father forgave me I suppose, that is he didn't refer to the matter again; but his general mood over the next week was gloomy, and my mother by this time was wheezing with the asthma which inevitably had followed her cold. She sat about a lot—her Roger's inhaler at the ready—so low-spirited that she didn't even bother to quiz me about the White Rose. As yet, I hadn't mentioned Juliet Hirst to her and as I always found it difficult to tell her old news nonchalantly, the respite was welcome.

Juliet had been at the school nearly two weeks now and was still a source of wonder to many of us. As far as we could see she obeyed none of the rules. She had her own car and, expensively and immaculately turned out always, she came and went when she liked. We found it hard to believe that the Shortened Course was in reality so liberal, but Jennifer, who was fascinated, and jealous in a hearty way ('this month's *Vogue*—walking and talking,' she would hiss behind her hand to me), had by the end of the second week come up with a really consoling fantasy.

'I've worked it all out,' she said, from her favourite perch, hanging on to the roller towel—most of our giggling was necessarily done in the cloakroom: 'It's *blackmail*. You see, the Metcalfe's got this sister, and she's not awfully clever and she's worked in Blackett's ever since she was twelve, or whenever it was they used to leave school, and now she taps away all day with one finger just hoping and *longing* for her pension—and Juliet's got this terrific hold over the Metcalfe because of this. I mean, it could be all up with the sister tomorrow. Juliet just has to appear at Blackett's and wink at her father, and say "Off with her head!" '

I didn't want to spoil it for her by pointing out that Miss Metcalfe was probably making more than enough to support both of them through a luxurious old age: fantasies like Jennifer's were cheering, and over the next few days we embroidered it considerably. But I had already guessed the real secret of Juliet's relaxed attitude. It was

67

very prosaic: a state of mind that couldn't be faked even by the most cocky amongst us. She truly didn't give a damn.

One great advantage of the Shortened Course it seemed, was that work was done either alone or at worst with Miss Laycock, so that it was very rarely that she came under Miss Metcalfe (not that the odd sarcastic remark upset her anyway: beyond looking slightly surprised, she would go on exactly as before), but it did mean that I saw very little of her, and apart from that first afternoon we'd scarcely spoken.

Then one Wednesday—it must have been about her third week there—I was alone in the typing room just after four, half-heartedly cleaning my machine after an angry tirade against smudgy work, when she came in, very quietly, and began looking vaguely about her.

'I thought I left a *Tatler* in here. Have you seen it, darling?'

'It's wedged under your machine,' I said. I'd noticed her push it there at lunchtime.

She took it up and yawned. 'That job looks impossibly filthy,' she said: I was picking with a pin at small 'h'— an action which reminded me of Elizabeth and my frantic nail-cleaning before school inspection. 'I think I shall get a man at the works to clean mine.'

Her machine was a shiny new portable: Marjorie's upright had ground to a standstill a few days ago and Juliet had brought one of her own along.

She yawned again, then flicking open the ring-watch on her right hand she said wearily:

'Juliet should be meeting some friends for tea at half-past. But she's not at all in the mood.'

I picked up the old toothbrush and began to work on the typewriter keys. She watched me for a while, then yawning yet again, she said:

'Why don't you come along too, darling?'

The suggestion, taking me completely unawares sent me into a panic. I saw it as a Royal Command.

Yes, of course I'd come, I told her.

Together, we went to the cloakroom to get ready.

When I looked in the mirror my appearance depressed me, increasing my panic. How could I go out like this? The gloom at home had spread to my dressing and the sensible outfit of Gor-ray skirt and ex-gym blouse looked even more dreary now than on the first day. At least I wasn't wearing lisle stockings, but my rayon ones, worn shiny side in, had a long cobbled ladder up the calf.

'There's no hurry, darling,' said Juliet, dawdling in what seemed to me an incredible manner.

The whole cloakroom smelt of Jean Patou 'Colony'—some days it was the only indication that Juliet had been in the building at all. A big bottle of it as eau de toilette stood above the basin now and she was splashing her wrists and neck with it. Then after doing over her face completely she took out a silk scarf and rubbed at her hair till it shone. Glancing at my watch, I saw that it was already twenty to five.

Just as we left she lifted up the skirt of her beige Jaeger dress, showing a small red arrow on her nylons, just above each knee. 'Seam correctors, darling,' she explained. Then picking up her hand-bag, she went over to the mirror for a last, loving look.

Although we were to meet her friends at Fuller's, not many minutes' walk away, we went by car. On the way she told me a little about them. 'Quentin runs an antique or junk shop—whichever you like to call it. Richard's a solicitor. He's quite sweet but *much* too fond. Juliet finds it a little bit boring.'

Climbing the stairs to Fuller's behind her, I felt already the trembling legs, the prickly sweat, which heralded an attack of shyness. I tried hastily to decide what expression to wear—since I didn't think any expression was going to come naturally: then Juliet walked straight over to where two men were sitting at a table in the window and, in a moment, the worst was over.

The fair one was Richard Ingleson; the dark one Quentin Myers. This was as much as I'd taken in—and Richard was already leaning towards Juliet asking her whether she wanted toast or teacakes— when a fresh worry hit me.

It was to do with my accent. As a result of Miss Lister's campaign, which was beginning at last to have some effect, I'd become rather like a boy with a breaking voice—never sure how it would come out; far from lengthening my 'a's' permanently she'd merely made them unpredictable, and after saying 'how do you do' and opting hesitantly for teacakes I decided to stay completely quiet. It didn't look impossible: Quentin had said, 'ah, Lucy Locket' and Richard had said 'oh dear' sympathetically when he heard I was from the White Rose, but after that they began at once to talk amongst themselves.

Juliet made no apology for being late; although Quentin, after the order had been given, remarked:

'Madam, we've been here *twenty* minutes, you know.'

'Don't you two do any work?' she said. 'Sitting around in tea-shops on a weekday—'

Richard said, 'Quentin's been at a sale actually. All afternoon.' He shrugged his shoulders, then added, smiling: 'And I'm playing truant. Just for once.'

'Which I'm all for,' said Quentin. 'That's the sort of fall from grace which makes you *human*, Richard. Don't you agree, Juliet?'

Juliet merely smiled, but didn't answer. Quentin, catching my eye, smiled at me: I smiled back—and would have gone on looking except that I was afraid it might make him talk to me. I liked his face. Full, with a slightly dimpled chin it just missed conventional good looks; faintly olive skin, dark hair worn quite long and curling at the ends; a bright waistcoat, which in those days of drab dressing struck an unusual note. My mother, I guessed instinctively would have distrusted him. He had a foreign look. What exactly this reaction of hers was all about, I was never sure (some chance remark of Robert Tinsdale's, her mother's, even Gervase's which had stuck?) but she'd had this attitude ever since I could remember, making room for it amidst her pre-occupations with the niceties of the English social scene. Foreigners worried her; she was unable to place them. Even their titles were suspect.

The waitress brought tea, toast, teacakes. The handle on the teapot was too hot for Juliet, and Richard lent her a big handker-chief. While she was pouring, Quentin said,

'Richard and I were at the Kenworthys' dance last night, Juliet. Did you enjoy your—theatre, was it? at any rate your *conflicting* engagement?'

Juliet ignored him. She said to Richard, sweetly:

'How was the party?'

'Fancy even asking him!' said Quentin, putting on a shocked expression: 'I quote:

> "How did the party go in Portman Square?
> I cannot tell you; Juliet was not there ..." '

Juliet blushed, the colour flooding her thin skin; as she passed his cup over, Quentin said, 'Extraordinary! You have a lovely colour today, dear Juliet.'

It was Richard who changed the subject. He seemed embarrassed by Quentin's obvious baiting of Juliet, even though, it seemed, it was on his behalf. He began asking me a few polite questions about the White Rose, and I found myself answering easily: their attention after all, wasn't really on me. Juliet, I thought (and it was a comforting notion) had probably brought me along as a sort of buffer.

For a while they chatted on, mostly about people and places I hadn't heard of. Gradually the atmosphere became less edgy, although Richard, I noticed, was hardly able to take his eyes off Juliet. For him, she seemed to be the only person in the crowded teashop.

'I shall release myself at Christmas,' she was saying: Quentin, bringing me back into the conversation, had asked her how she was getting on at Miss Metcalfe's? 'The place is so impossibly boring Juliet can't take it seriously.' She said to Richard: 'Mama nags me about getting something to do—as you know. But there *are* limits.'

Richard said, laughing, but gazing straight at her, 'Well, darling, you know you've only to say the word—'

'But not here, Richard,' said Quentin. 'You haven't a hope.' He passed his cup over to Juliet. 'What girl wants to remember that she said "yes" in Fuller's? Bendicks, Gunter's, the Ritz (*just*), Joe Lyons, an ABC—but *Fuller's*—'

'Oh God that's enough,' said Richard half-laughing, half-serious.

While Quentin was talking, I'd been taking a good look at Richard. With his tall, heavy build, went generous rather rough features—the skin already a little lined, his forehead creasing when he talked; his colouring was the almost traditional, fair-haired Englishman. In a way I didn't find him as interesting to watch as Quentin, but I did recognise him, timidly (my mother would have done so joyfully), as belonging very much to the world from which

71

she insisted I had come, and to which, if I loved her, I would try to return.

I recognised his clothes: the tweed jacket with its leather elbows, telling me of someone who could afford the best but couldn't afford not to take care of it. And his voice—the sort of sound my mother would have liked tumbling about my ears daily. His manner, a mixture of diffidence and clumsy ease, I recognised too—not so much from first-hand experience as from memories of outings with her when, quite without warning, she would suddenly assume her *grande dame* manner.

'Those were Ampleforth boys,' she would say to me later, of some trio we'd seen waiting to go into the cinema: or 'that undergraduate was wearing a Christ Church scarf, Lucy. Gervase's college, you know . . .'

Quentin was saying to Juliet:

'But I thought they were especially kind on this Shortened Course? After all that you went through for your country, too. Sunning yourself in—' He raised his eyebrows, 'Where was it? It's awfully sad really, that we never saw you as a little Wren.'

Juliet, refusing some cherry cake, said with a small pout, 'Juliet was quite *fond* of the uniform. The stockings suited her legs.'

Richard nodding enthusiastically, smiled at her. Quentin looked over at me; he said suddenly:

'You see—Juliet has *travelled*, Lucy. Even before the War, she graced a school in Switzerland—although I believe they did try and contain her at Queen Ethelburga's here, for a term. But since then she really has been places—can't you sniff the Gauloises and garlic? They compete very successfully, you know, with the smell of brown sauce—thick or thin. And fruity jelly, bubbling in cauldrons—'

'Easy does it, Q,' said Richard, angrily almost. 'Easy does it.'

Juliet said nothing, although she had coloured again. It was Richard who changed the subject once more, asking me, with the same polite eagerness, what I thought about Bratherton and the sort of place it became in the summer? He never seemed to go there now—Was it as bad as it looked? Often it was, I said—thinking of Elizabeth and me and our summer afternoons down by the river. I was finding it quite easy to talk now. Although my voice came out quieter than I intended, it was my own—Miss Lister had not, after all, got through the doors of Fuller's.

72

Soon after that, Juliet murmured that she'd have to go. We all broke up, and I accepted a lift from her as far as the bus station.

Quentin said: 'I hope we'll see you again, Lucy Locket.' Juliet, putting on her gloves, started up the engine—Richard still in sight by the car door. A half-hearted rain was coming down in the darkness outside.

As we drove off, she said:

'I hope you weren't too bored, darling? It was really very sweet of you to come along and support poor Juliet.'

When I said politely that I'd enjoyed it, she said in a rather purring voice, 'Quentin wasn't very nice today, was he?' adding, 'he's madly disapproving of me, you know. He imagines I may do Richard some fearful harm.'

We had stopped behind some traffic. Talking more than I'd ever heard her, she told me that both Quentin and Richard had been prisoners of war, in the same Stalag; and that after the War when Quentin had been visiting the Inglesons, he'd decided on Harrogate as an obvious choice for his shop. 'He fell rather heavily too for Richard's sister, Nell. She's up at Cambridge now. *Juliet* doesn't like her terribly, though. She can be very offhand and bitchy—all the good nature at the Inglesons seems to have gone into Richard.' She paused, gloved hands on the wheel. 'I can't think what the spring will be like. The four of us are going to Rome together—Quentin's half-Italian through his mother, and his aunt has this lovely flat there. Nell and Richard were over last year; and this time Juliet's invited along too.' She gave me a half-smile. 'It's really rather tempting, don't you think? I shall certainly go—that is, if I can stand Richard's proposals. One a month, darling, at least, and none of them indecent.' She suppressed a yawn. 'Just endlessly, "will you marry me, Juliet?" It's all those lost years, darling—they've given him a terrible nesting fever.'

We had come up to the bus station. Pushing open the car door for me, she said, 'I feel so restless sometimes. And bored too.' She yawned again, gloved hand over her mouth. 'Juliet does so *hate* to be bored.'

'Whoever were these people?' asked my mother irritably.

She was sitting, as if stranded, in the big armchair; ignoring my father's presence, saying insistently, accusingly, 'but who *is* this Juliet?'

When I told her, 'Oh *trade*, Lucy!', she said scornfully, with a little flash of her eyes; then: 'But the boys—you still haven't told me anything about the boys.'

Richard Ingleson and Quentin Myers; one fair, the other dark:

'Anyway, they weren't boys,' I said—feeling a need to be provocative. 'They were men.'

My mother spat out her frantic interest. But who *were* they, and what did they *do*? And why had I gone out looking such a mess? ('really, Lucy!') And had I actually, while I was there, talked *at all*?

My father came out suddenly from behind the *Yorkshire Evening Post*: 'Give over interrogating!' Gathering his paper in one hand, he slapped it hard against the coal scuttle, ripping the pages. 'You're worse than the ruddy police. Give *over*, Winifred!'

My mother's face quivered, I saw her try to arrange her mouth. A moment later, more mildly, he remarked,

'Myers I wouldn't know, but Ingleson—that'll be the solicitor. I've met the father. The family's RC and I'd have thought by now they'd be on your secret list, Winifred. The son's quite presentable. And Ma Ingleson is on every committee that's going, Catholic Mothers, Legion of Bloody Mary—the lot. If you ever got up off your backside and went around you'd have met her by now, and then who knows?'

He bent over, picked up the torn newspaper. My mother said with angry dignity: 'I've never made any pretence, Peter, of trying to enter Yorkshire Society, *so called*. From this background—I should be wasting my time.'

She flounced out leaving the door wide open.

I trailed after her—although I didn't want to. I couldn't face staying: didn't know what to say, feared what might be said to me.

'He's so vulgar!' she exclaimed, banging the enamel colander full of potatoes into the sink. 'These gibes at Catholicism. He's *never* realised what my religion means to me, Lucy!'

The inquisition, I thought, was over. But standing in the doorway of the larder, her head to one side, she pleaded suddenly:

74

'Lucy, these boys—or if you like, these *men*—couldn't you tell Mummy a little more about them?'

I saw with dread her mind clanking into action, about to make out of this small self-contained dead-end experience, some embarrassing project or plan. Hopeful of ending it all, I said:

'Quentin's pretty well engaged to Richard's sister. And Richard and Juliet—they're going to be married I think.' As a finishing touch I added, 'Quentin isn't really English, he's half-Italian, they said.'

Her eyebrows lifted. 'A *dago*, you mean? Now that I think of it, there must be Jewish blood too, with that name. Still, it was all practice and will help for London.' She handed me a tin of Spam. 'You open this, Lucy, you're better with your hands. When I *think* of the food at Patmore! More at breakfast than we eat in a week here. It never seems worth bothering, really . . .'

By the end of the week it became obvious that my mother wasn't getting over her cold: often when I came home at five, she would already be in bed for the night. Then at the weekend, she told me that Doctor Varley had suggested a complete rest. She was arranging a fortnight with the maiden aunts in Wiltshire. Although these aunts had never been to Patmore (hadn't in fact kept up with my grandmother at all after her second marriage) they liked, I think, to listen to my mother's reminiscences, and it was probably this as much as the rest and change of air and good food, which made her trips there such a success.

During the last visit about three years ago, my father and I, left together, had formed an uneasy truce: with me disappearing to stay with the Horsfalls while he went over to Harrogate—appearing only on the last evening to take Elizabeth and me out to dinner. The dinner had been a great success. We went with one of his work colleagues—I'd seldom if ever met any of his friends, and never his drinking pals. Alec, a big jolly man, expressed surprise at my existence. 'Where does Peter hide you, eh?'

But Elizabeth, who talked almost non-stop, was the real star of the evening: my father reminded her of the first time they'd met— nearly ten years ago now—when Elizabeth, sitting on top of the piano, legs swinging, had sung to his playing:

'She was a *good* girl, and I can never understand . . .
Why did she fall for the leader of the band?'

He'd seemed proud of me too, that evening. It was the first time
I'd drunk wine and he thought I held it well. 'Winifred doesn't
drink,' he explained to Alec. 'She'd a father who couldn't stop.'

This time however, we both stayed at home, theoretically anyway; there were no signs of any outings to come, nor as far as I
could see any particular interest at all in what I did or where I went.
Our few conversations were purely practical; most evenings he went
straight to my grandmother's from work, often staying the night
there, and in the mornings he was often up and gone before I came
down. We both wrote notes for Mrs Pickering.

After a week of this I felt tired and restless. The White Rose term
was in its second half; a dull grind which looked like never ending,
while Miss Lister—against whom I'd borne a grudge since the
funeral—seemed to me more than ever a giant waste of time. Also,
and I wasn't sure why, the tea with Juliet had unsettled me. I'd find
myself reliving it in bed at night or on the bus going home,
sometimes even amending the dialogue so that I came out of it
better. Juliet hadn't mentioned it again; Richard I saw once on my
way to the bus, going into Ogden's the jeweller's, but he didn't see
me. I was afraid to call out and didn't think he would recognise me
anyway.

Most evenings I just sat up in my bedroom; I'd always more than
enough homework to keep me quiet. The night before my mother's
return, there was for some reason less than usual; I'd already done
it, *and* a perfunctory run through of Miss Lister's exercises, by nine
o'clock. Sitting on the bed I flipped now through a pile of old
magazines from Elizabeth's hotel.

Summer numbers, they were mostly full of how to renovate a
dingy winter complexion, what to do, say, wear on the beach, how
to cope with the hot weather. Then seeing a diagram for making a
fitted headscarf out of an old blouse, I remembered that I had a
paisley one I'd always disliked: forgetting that I'd probably dislike it
even more as a headscarf, I got it out and measured it up with my
White Rose ruler. Then I hacked away at it for a while with my nail
scissors; but they weren't very effective.

76

My mother, I knew, had a good pair in her sewing chest in the bedroom. This chest, antique, rosewood, a Patmore relic which she'd rescued through Gervase sometime during the War, was usually—though not always—kept locked. Today I was lucky. I slid the top tray out carefully, then as the scissors weren't there, gently pulled out the blue satin basket underneath. This was in great confusion—she mended as seldom as possible, buying new reels of cotton and cards of wool each time, and never putting away needles. I'd pricked myself twice, and was about to give up, when I came against something very hard right at the bottom. It was a bundle of papers, tightly wadded; I lifted them clear of the tangled wools and cottons, but as I did so they slipped from my hand. Sheets of paper covered in my mother's handwriting lay scattered about the floor, so that I was frightened—even at first glance I could see they were private. I started at once to gather them up. Then, instead of replacing them, on impulse I rushed with them across the landing and back into my bedroom.

There I began to examine them; trying frantically, with a guilty greed, to read them all at once. Isolated phrases leapt out at me: 'Gervase love', 'worship you', 'my beloved heart', 'my darling darling'; and I relaxed. These were simply her Great War letters to Gervase (returned by him when she married my father?). And as if to prove it, a stiff photograph fell from one of the folds. Sepia, creased at the corners, it was one I hadn't seen before—a studio portrait taken in uniform. As he gazed serenely at the camera—his beauty almost shocking—the lips, the angle of the head, the arrested perfection of feature, all breathed a calmness which in the several years of sitting opposite him at Gunter's I'd never so much as glimpsed.

'To my beloved, who *must* have faith,' he'd written above the date: December 1914. 'I have done wrong, I have done wrong, I have done wrong,' my mother had added, in an undated pencilled scrawl.

I picked up the letter it had dropped from.

'All day every day,' I read, 'I've been flooded with gratitude darling—when you said so very quietly, I'll pay Winifred—and Gervase I've already sent off the forms and they'll interview Lucy soon, when you said that I wished Gunter's was empty except for us—because I died to reach out and touch you but I couldn't just *touch* you Gervase I'd have to clutch and cling. I'd be desperate, the flesh that *could have been mine*—Gervase we only throw away, lose deliberately what we really care about and my punishment is many things but its most of all that I can't touch you—That if I touched you it wouldn't be that same you, they say Gervase only *seven* years to make a new body—'

I stopped, my heart thumping, my mouth dry. There was no date on the letter. I could find no dates on any of them at all. The fresh blackness of the ink should have told me these weren't old love letters anyway. I wanted to stop then—not see another word.

'Foul! Foul! Foul!' she wrote, 'when I think he's going to touch me. Peter mustn't touch me—it's the *not being touched* by you Gervase makes it all worse so much worse—*Once* he asked me to—No *I can't write it*, I wish I didn't know anything at all and you could teach me darling darling—Mother said *nothing* to me about it *ever* except once she said *Gervase* will teach you all you need to know. O thank God its not often now and I sometimes wonder if he gets it somewhere else—I would *die* rather than ask I care *not at all*—he's very cruel Gervase he said once—alright alright, but if ever *you* want it Winifred you can whistle for it—he's so vulgar Gervase you wouldn't know you are so *pure* my darling you don't know what its like to live closely to bump into accidentally someone you—I was bewitched Gervase he must have known some tricks that trapped my flesh, how else could I have been taken from you my own parfit gentil knight—do you remember that I used to call you that and you made me write it out and *spell* it right, you laughed anyway—I didn't listen when you used to talk about poetry I was too young. There aren't second chances. I feel so tired and flabby—such rare fits of energy now darling—I think its disgusting to call it the *change, nothing* will change, I know that, Perhaps 1948 will be better—but *how can it be*? if I only held the key to your heart Gervase and you held the key to mine—Love holds the key to set me free, and Love will find a Way from the Maid of the Mountains—oh *you* always held the key to my heart darling, *Why* didn't you use it? . . .'

'The White Rose Gervase, the name is so *pure*—she started there today my love and I want to tell you something about her. She has no push—no push at all, what will she *do* with your gift Gervase? you see shes so quiet and Peter has all this life in him, he could have given her some of that but hes kept it to himself—perhaps he gave it to Michael, he was a great lusty noisy baby wearing me out with his tantrums able to get his way from the beginning. Peter could have given some to Lucy but he's so vengeful. Even in his *seed* you know he's *vengeful* Gervase. What shall I do, it doesn't matter you see what I tell her—shes an exile from Paradise—but she doesn't *know* it . . .'

'This morning darling on the wireless there was a forces request— was it Clarice Mayne used to sing it Gervase? we had that record with the big scratch at the beginning, Let the great big world keep turning never mind if I have you—I sang it inside all day, some of these tunes they *knock* at my heart darling, You have *simply set me yearning*, I wept you see, I couldn't help it—I sang For I only know that I love you so—that there's *no one else* will do . . .'

'I've had that nightmare again darling—*four times* since Christmas now. I never wrote it down for you before—this wood, I'm in this wood looking for you and I call Gervase Gervase everywhere—I *know* I haven't married Peter, But I've lost you in this wood and I'm searching then I start to lose hope—and the pain starts. Then suddenly I hear your *voice* Gervase! Oh darling the *flood* of relief it comes all over me, I shake in my dreams! I can't *move* in my happiness—But then I see you—oh its terrible—I *see* you, You are coming through the trees. A long way away and you come closer and closer, you are a *skeleton* Gervase—oh I cant write it, your face—and then the rags and bits and shreds of khaki theyre clinging to your bones—but its your *face* is the worst. I scream and I scream and want to run But suddenly there's only *Peter* to run to. Oh God its so terrible, I wake up and Im fighting for breath I think Im *suffocating*—'

A door slammed downstairs. With a guilty start, I jumped up-right, then gathering all the bits of paper together I crammed them hastily into my chest of drawers. For a while after that, I sat trembling and listening, but there were no more sounds from below. My legs felt very shaky; the drawer where I'd hidden the letters burned in my vision with the clarity of a cut-out. The room felt like a sprung trap. But I sat on, quite motionless. When I heard my father climbing the stairs to bed, I took hold of my pillow; then clenching it with my teeth, I sat rigidly—terrified, yet hopeful, wondering if he would come in.

But the steps—remarkably quiet for one who'd slammed the door so heavily—passed by, went on up to the attic room. After about half an hour I went through to the lavatory and was violently sick.

Chapter 8

The next day, I had a row with Miss Lister. She attacked me as I stood beside the stuffed canary, trying to remember selected lines from 'The Old Vicarage'.

'Ah God!' she moaned, 'to see the brahnches stir
Across the moon, at Grahnchester!'

Then, 'You don't know it, you haven't learnt it!' she exclaimed, tossing her head like an over-reined horse. I mumbled something. 'And my time,' she asked hotly, 'what about my time?' I said nothing. 'My time is *precious*,' she announced, snapping shut the pages of Rupert Brooke: the *Complete Poems*, 'precious like the bronze, the silver, the gold medals for which my *real* pupils work.' She flung up her head again. 'Your heart is not here, I have felt this for some while. And you scarcely improve. Why should I waste my time?'

Why indeed? I thought.

Surprisingly however, my mother wasn't cross about it at all. Just back that evening, not coughing or wheezing and looking rested and well fed, she was prepared to be most gracious and understanding. It was I who was the unhappy one. After the letters I felt miserable in her presence, feeling—I couldn't think why—that it was not she who was naked, but I; so that to take refuge in something superficial like Miss Lister, was a relief. We should stop the lessons at once, my mother said: she'd never really thought them very good, or even all that practical. 'I was falsely informed,' she said.

Over the next few days, a great deal of her renewed energy went into enthusiastic plan for my going to London in the autumn. As usual, none of these plans were at all practical, but it worried her that I didn't seem interested enough: possibly I hadn't been eating properly while she was away? ('I can't believe Peter bothered in the *slightest.*') I looked tired—did I think perhaps the White Rose was working me just a little *too* hard? When I said that it was, she looked sympathetic; and a shade triumphant at the same time.

But during the next few weeks I realised that I'd spoken truer than I knew, for as the pace accelerated and the end of term came into sight, the sense of hurry which began with the grey early morning run for the bus and was still there when we spilled out into the dark winter afternoon, grew worse; there seemed to be a test of some sort always hanging over us, while Miss Metcalfe, always critical, never satisfied, constantly walked amongst us, urging perfection.

Only Juliet seemed exempt from all this. Occasionally Miss Laycock, stop-watch in hand, could be seen testing her for typing speed, but otherwise she appeared to do no real work at all and continued to be scarcely in the building; I supposed that at any moment she was about to leave.

Then late one afternoon I ran into her, coming along the corridor. After saying 'hello', she added casually, 'By the way, darling, I think you're about to be bidden to a party.'

'Me?'

But she'd already bent over, and was looking at her stocking. 'These Italian nylons aren't a patch on American ones. Poor Juliet! A ladder, and on the *outside* too. I shall have to change the legs around.'

She turned towards the cloakroom. I followed her, asking 'what party? where?' Trying to sound calm.

'At Richard's I think, darling. When Nell comes down.' She reached for her coat: it was new, dark green with a coachman's cape collar and I'd admired it only a few days before in a shop window. 'I expect you'll get a card,' she said. 'It's just that Quentin asked me for your name, darling. "Let's ask your friend of the flaming hair," he said—in his *silly* way.'

I didn't mention it to my mother because I didn't really believe anything would come of it; but two days later an invitation arrived, addressed to me at the White Rose ('We are *not* a Poste Restante here, Miss Taylor,' remarked a disapproving Miss Metcalfe); and in the evening, dreading her excitement, trembling almost, I showed it to her.

'What are you going to wear?' she asked at once.

82

The old problem. And this time, whether it was cocktail or evening length, I was sunk: I'd spent all my coupons and some of my savings on a Jaeger dress, a couple of sweaters and a skirt, in the fervent hope that a sudden invitation to tea wouldn't catch me shabby again. Elizabeth, I knew from past experience wasn't a suitable source, and my father I was too proud to ask for coupons or money. Even my mother couldn't help—she'd surprised me by getting herself a new winter coat and dress in Salisbury last month.

I was saved in the end by Juliet. Sitting, legs crossed, up on Miss Metcalfe's dais one lunch hour, eating a bar of chocolate and turning the pages of *Harper's Bazaar*, she asked: 'Shall you come next week, darling?'

I explained my plight. She said immediately, 'But have one of mine, darling. You're about my build.' When I hesitated, she added, shrugging her shoulders: 'a little *fuller* perhaps? Anyway, *Juliet* will look you one out, darling.'

'Juliet's lending me a dress,' I told my mother, 'I've to go and collect it on Tuesday evening.'

But when I turned up at her home—she lived in the Duchy Road—it was to hear that she'd gone away. Someone obviously her mother, answered the door. Small and birdlike, she was a chirping caricature of Juliet, resembling her only in the tiny bones and neat head.

There was a parcel for me, she was certain. 'It *is* little Lucy, isn't it?' Juliet had left a parcel for me in her bedroom; she remembered this definitely: 'Lucy, with red hair, would call for a dress.'

She went upstairs ahead of me. Where Juliet would have glided, she bustled. Opening the bedroom door, turning on the light:

'It's somewhere in this mess,' she announced helplessly. I looked around. The disorder was terrible: scattered shoes, pants, petticoats, an enormous wardrobe open and crammed with dresses and coats; on the dressing-table lumps of dirty cotton wool beside open and split bottles, broken lipsticks, pancake make-up without a lid; on the roughly made bed more piles of clothes.

Mrs Hirst flitted about attempting a little order here, a little order there. 'You wouldn't think the naughty girl had been in the Services, would you?'

She picked up a nylon nightdress, one of its lace straps broken. I wasn't sure whether to help or not. Looking around, I could see nothing like a parcel anywhere.

'Juliet rushed off up to Town. One of these *sudden* invitations, you know. A first night, Gertrude Lawrence at the Aldwych. She *loves* first nights! It's with some old friends. *Naval*, you know.'

By now she'd stopped tidying; as she stood in the middle of the room she fiddled nervously with her rings—two or three on each hand:

'I'm afraid Juliet's not the teeniest bit serious about this shorthand-typing—you'll have noticed that. Of course, she doesn't *need* to work—she comes into her money when she's twenty-five you know. But her Daddy says she must do something, until. Not that she won't be able to get round him, she always has.' She looked over at some of the clothes: 'She gets all the money she wants *now*.'

I stood awkwardly, while she began tidying up again. I felt a remote sort of envy for someone who could so obviously buy unlimited coupons, as well as filling her wardrobe on her travels.

'It was the War did the damage,' went on Mrs Hirst, 'I blame the War—she'll settle to nothing now. Of course what her Daddy and I would *really* like is to see her married. There *was* someone—in the Navy, in the last year of the War. But it came to nothing.' She leant over, adjusting the bed cover, 'And now there's Richard Ingleson—*most* suitable. She could marry Richard tomorrow. Do you know Richard? He's quite *devoted* to her—'

She lifted a couple of sweaters off the bed, revealing a brown paper parcel: it had my name on; and a scrawled message: 'Please keep—don't want.'

'The naughty girl!' Wouldn't I like to try it on now, at once?

But it was getting late, and I made some excuse. I felt unaccountably trapped in the scented untidy room; I didn't think either that I could stand her chirping comments.

'Well,' she said, showing me out, 'I don't know when Juliet will be back, dear. But if it doesn't fit, just give us a tinkle, and we'll try again. The naughty girl's got *far* too many dresses . . .'

Home again, the carelessly tied bundle unwrapped, I stared in amazement: I'd imagined some quite adequate cast-off, but for this careless luxury I'd been quite unprepared. My mother, fingering the soft folds ecstatically, cried that it was of course *real* silk. The label, from a shop in Rome's Via Veneto, excited her even further.

'She hasn't *given* you this, Lucy—surely?' It didn't fit, I explained. Juliet was thinner than me.

'But it's lovely, darling! Exquisite!' Almost tearful, she kept lifting it up, fingering the lavish tiny pleats at the waist, exclaiming at its expensive simplicity. 'And such a lovely shade of beige. Try it on *now*, darling!'

Amazingly, it seemed to me, it fitted perfectly, and its length gave me all I desired of the New Look. I came downstairs to show it to her—she gave me one surprised glance, then rushing up from her chair she flung her arms round me. She seemed barely to notice my stiff resistance. 'Darling,' she said. '*Darling.*'

Shy and angry and confused as I had felt since the letters I could not bear now to be a witness to her emotion. For a moment I feared that she was going to cry; but then, holding me away from her, gazing at me intently, 'Oh darling this party, if *only*—' she began; then breaking off, putting her head on one side, she said almost coyly, pleadingly:

'You won't spoil it all by being shy, will you? Promise Mummy you won't be mousey, darling?'

Saturday came, and although a clear night it was piercingly cold, so that I wasn't relishing the idea of the journey with its two or three different buses. The Inglesons lived in Harrogate, in the Cornwall Road, and we'd decided I should make my own way there and hope for a lift back: my father, who didn't know about the party, had said earlier he'd be spending the day with my grandmother fixing some things in the house before going on to a 'Messiah' rehearsal in the evening.

But at seven o'clock I was standing ready in the doorway of the sitting-room, my coat over my arm, self-concious in the new dress, when suddenly he walked in. For a moment he stood quite still, looking me up and down.

'What's all this, Winifred?' He banged his cold hands together, stamped his feet. He'd brought the night air in with him so that he looked frosty even to the moustache. 'What's up, then?'

'A party,' my mother said coldly. He paid no attention to her: 'The singing's cancelled,' he said to me briefly, 'I'll run you to wherever it is.'

It was the last thing I wanted: already nervous; that's all I need, I thought. My mother, heavy-faced, made no comment. I realised that at least I would be spared a dramatic send-off: lumpish with irritation now, she'd obviously been planning an evening alone, dreaming of my possible successes.

It was cold in the car and I shivered with chill as well as apprehension. At first my father didn't talk; he whistled most of the time, a tune I didn't recognise; then when we stopped for the level crossing halfway between Bratherton and Harrogate, he said suddenly,

'That's a nice dress.' His tone was friendly. 'Who's the fairy godmother?'

He lit a cigarette. Juliet, I told him.

'You've not one of your own then?'

I shook my head. For one wild moment I thought he was going to make some offer, express regret, say something like 'you've only to *ask*.' But his tone of voice had deceived me.

'Any idea why the Ingleson's asked you?' he said. I didn't answer —nothing I thought of sounded quite right, so I merely shrugged my shoulders; then wished immediately that I hadn't. He said rudely, switching off the ignition and looking straight ahead, 'I hope you'll not forget to talk loudly. Value for your mother's legacy— How now, brown cow. The rain in Spain—all that ruddy crap.'

A goods train, its waggons rattling, was being shunted towards the crossing. In the street light I saw that his hands were clenched white on the steering wheel.

'And don't bloody well answer me either,' he said angrily. 'Just *sit* there!' Lifting his hands off the wheel he brought them down again smartly, then laid his forehead against them. I thought for the hundredth time that perhaps there was some magic formula by which I could speak, or be silent, at the right moment and in the right way. Once, I had known it. Now, I just wanted to get out of the car and walk away: I had my hand on the door, when the train clanked back again and the crossing gates opened. Tight-throated and silent I sat beside him, till just as we passed the White Rose he said casually, but not unkindly,

'How are you making out in the Chamber of Horrors?'

'All right,' I said guardedly.

We turned up past the Valley Gardens. 'It's a racket right enough

—you'd have done better at the North of England.' I thought then, he was going to make another remark about the legacy; but after a pause he added, in an amused voice,

'Ah well—if it tastes so nasty, it must be doing you good. What do you think?'

But after he'd left me at the Inglesons' gate—I hadn't encouraged him to take me up the drive—I realised that I was still upset. All my usual fears about parties had come over me as well, and any confidence I'd felt from the dress had been lost on the journey. The house looked enormous, a light shining from the open front door as I walked up to it; behind me a car flashed its lamps and I pressed myself hurriedly against a hedge. Three men were getting noisily out of a car, and as they went in I joined on behind.

A tall elderly woman, an air of brisk efficiency about her, greeted us in the hall. Her large beaky face reminded me of Richard—I supposed her to be Mrs Ingleson; dressed in plum satin, she gave the impression of having been thrust into it unwillingly at the last moment. The party seemed already well under way: voices, laughter, clinking of glasses. I wondered if Juliet was there? The dress seemed wrong already—Mrs Ingleson was in full length, and so was a girl crossing the hall.

Upstairs I laid my shabby tweed onto a bed already covered with coats, then went over to the glass for reassurance. I thought I'd be flushed, but I was pale, pinched with cold: I slapped my cheeks a few times. The thought of actually going down there was so terrifying that when after a moment or two there was no sound of anyone coming up, I went over and sat down in the basket chair by the gas fire.

It was a comfortable, shabby room, which had obviously been cleared for the party—on the dressing table there was only a bottle of Guerlain 'Mitsouko'; but there were books everywhere, crammed in the shelves, stacked under the table desk, newspapers and magazines in a toppling pile by the window; a small leather-framed snapshot of Quentin stood by the bed. Nell's room, surely? I would have liked to stay, secure in the warmth and casual disorder, but sounds on the stairs sent me hurrying back to the glass, pretending to fiddle with my hair, as two girls, loud-voiced and confident in the way that I dreaded, came crashing into the room. Both were in evening dress.

87

They flung fur coats onto the bed; then one of them came alongside me at the glass. 'God, I look a mess,' she said, peering closely, pulling the skin down under her eyes, '*Awful.*'

'Look Caro—when I *bend*, can you *see* anything?' said the second girl, standing in the middle of the room, 'I mean *honestly?*'

'It's my skin,' said the first one, 'it's ghastly. All sort of muddy. Oh God.'

The second girl was bent right over, her head twisted awkwardly. 'Damn, you know you *can* see, Caro.

'It's no sleep,' said the first girl, 'it's murder. God—I need an early night.'

I slipped out.

Halfway down the stairs I saw a door open and Quentin in dinner jacket and scarlet cummerbund come across the hall. He was carrying a tray of glasses and saw me at once.

'Lucy Locket, how dear.' He put down the tray, 'And what a lovely dress!' I'd reached the bottom of the stairs, and taking my hand—he was frowning slightly now, looking at me closely— 'A *lovely* dress. I just wonder—?'

But he left the sentence unfinished. My face flaming, I felt certain that my being in cocktail length was a matter so terrible that probably the best thing would be for me to run off home. But Quentin had me by the arm now, and was saying, 'let's get you a drink', handing me a glass of something warm and faintly medicinal, taking me straight into the crowded room, and over to a group standing near the door. The noise was deafening, but looking around I saw to my immense relief two, three then four girls in cocktail dresses.

'This is Lucy,' Quentin was saying, 'she's a barmaid at the White Rose. Full time.'

The group who'd been deep in conversation looked mildly annoyed I thought, as Quentin introduced me. Then as he moved away, a plump girl in a frilly yellow off-the-shoulder dress said,

'Honestly don't you think Quentin gets worse and worse? Sort of terribly *unfunny?*'

A bearded man at the edge of the group, shifting his weight from one foot to the other as he spoke, said 'I would hazard a g-guess he's been t-testing the punch.'

Some of them laughed. A fair-haired girl, very thin and intense, said did Quentin mean that I went to that terrible secretarial place, because her sister'd been there two years ago and wasn't it true that the principal was quite out of another age but really the training was awfully good and if you were clever you could get a jolly good job after it, and what sort of job would I like? The bearded man said, didn't all g-girls want c-cushy jobs as c-confidential secretaries with all day to sit around f-filing their nails and telephoning boy-friends?

'It's an absolutely ghastly place to *go* to though,' said the plump girl.

'You might s-say then that the White Rose has thorns?' ventured the bearded man. He laughed at his own joke. Creakingly the conversation got going again—they all seemed to know each other well and although they didn't deliberately exclude me they didn't try to draw me in, so that after a while I began looking around, trying to see if Juliet had come. No sign of her at all. I sipped frequently at my drink—it was soothing, and mysterious passing hands kept filling my glass. The talk moved on to hunting: the thin girl's horse was lame, 'And I hadn't been out *once* . . .' Behind me, a loud conversation was going on about cricket:

'It'll depend you see on what happens in Durban.' Compton, Hutton, Simpson, Washbrook: the names floated across.

'364 not out,' someone said. 'Just before Hitler's do, that was. The Oval, in '38.'

A girl with a very penetrating voice said,

'Personally I think Len is rather ducky.'

'*I* go for Bedser,' said another girl.

'You go for *what?*'

A man said, 'You heard, oaf' and the girl with the penetrating voice replied, 'Oh smart Alec, *well.*' Another man's voice said reproachfully,

'You're laughing at us, girls.'

They moved away. A moment later, Richard, taller and bonier than I remembered, came into the room. He clapped his hands for silence.

'Dancing's begun next door. Cabaret in here,' he announced, as Quentin sat down at the piano. There were a few cheers and mock groans. Quentin began singing in French, in a light assured voice.

'Monsieur Trenet I presume,' said the bearded man. Our group drifted over to the piano. Several people were already leaning

89

against it; someone was holding a glass to Quentin's lips. 'Hutch, now,' he said and broke into 'Smoke gets in your eyes.'

'Can't someone get him up to date?' said a girl. 'Where's *Nell*?'

We stood, pressed up against the piano. I'd just finished my drink when a man tapped me on the shoulder. Would I care to dance?

In the room next door several couples were already moving round to the radiogram. My partner was elderly, with thin grey hair and an abstracted expression; at intervals he would murmur, 'Ah, yes.' I never discovered his name because he tended to swallow his words, and just as he was introducing himself someone turned up the radiogram. We waltzed stiffly around. Still no sign of Juliet. My partner's hand round my waist felt like a steel grasp: I thought that I wasn't doing well, and to make conversation, I asked hesitantly, 'Do you know the Inglesons well?'

'A great many years,' he replied, flatly. Silence again.

We passed the doorway, and at that moment Richard came in. He was partnering a generously built, ash-blonde girl, who resembled him just enough for me to guess it was Nell. They began to dance, and after a moment, bumped into us. Richard turned to apologise.

'Why, hello.' He smiled. Then hesitating, he looked at me curiously for a second, frowning almost. As they moved off again he said something to his sister, and a little later I saw her turn round and glance at me quickly.

'An attractive girl, Nell,' said my partner, into the back of his throat. But I was in confusion. What had I done wrong? Perhaps they'd never meant to ask me and this was all some joke? Miserable, I heard the record come to an end, and a voice call out, 'Gentlemen's excuse me.'

'I trust some young man won't whisk you away,' said my partner —not very feelingly.

A few turns later, I was surprised to see Richard beside us. Bowing slightly, he said the formula. But although his manner was polite as we moved off, his face, slightly averted, was set, and he seemed to be embarrassed. It was a slow foxtrot; we were out of rhythm, our knees knocking every few steps, and without thinking, remembering the hours of thumping round with Elizabeth in her Victor Sylvester craze ('*You* be the man, Lu. I need the practice.') I said out loud, 'Slow slow quick-quick slow.'

'I'm awfully sorry.' He flushed, 'I don't seem to have got this right at all.'

I had coloured too. Tensely, we circled once more; then he said, very suddenly,

'Look. Could I—may I ask you something?'

'Of course.'

He was very flushed now. 'It's rather personal, I'm afraid.' We bumped clumsily into a couple alongside—I felt menaced by the word 'personal', and wondered why I'd ever come to the party at all.

'Your dress—' he began; then after a pause: 'Look, I know this sounds frightfully silly—I'm muddling this terribly—but it's just that I, *we*, wondered—whereabouts you got it?'

Relieved (so that was all!) the words coming out in a rush: 'From Juliet,' I said. 'It's a cast-off of hers. I hadn't anything to wear and she says it doesn't fit and I can keep it.'

I looked at his face, expecting to see on it warm pleasure at his beloved's kindness. But I saw that on the contrary he was upset, his face working: puzzled, I floundered about—only making it worse.

'It's real *silk*,' I was saying desperately, when we were interrupted: a small, plump man, clasping me to him at once, said, 'My excuse me.' And to Richard:

'Your Juliet's here you know, old man. Just arrived.'

Dark with curly hair, snub kind features, and a reassuring Yorkshire accent, he seemed to me a saviour. 'Real conversation stoppers, these excuse me's,' he remarked, as we moved off to an easy rhythm. I saw Richard walk out of the room. 'Bob's the name' he told me, 'Bob Turner. I'm in the antique business.'

The record changed, and to the tune of 'Buttons and Bows,' he began to show off a little, doing neat side steps and patterns. 'Know anyone here?' he asked, tightening his grip.

I explained about Juliet.

' "East is east and west is west and the wrong one I have chose",' he sang. 'She's stinking rich, you know, love. Blackett's. The only child.' He tightened his hold again. ' "Let's vamoose where women keep wearing those silks and satins—" Our host looked pretty browned off, didn't you think?'

I nodded, still smarting from a few moments back.

'He's welcome to her,' said Bob. Nell, leading Quentin by the hand came into the room. 'The lady of the house. No prizes for guessing *that* happy ending.' He side-stepped expertly, ' "and I'm all yours in Buttons and Bows—" Quentin's a good bloke though, I like Quentin. He's in my line, in the junk trade. Know his shop, love?'

Two, three dances later, we were still together. 'I like you, love,' he said, giving me a squeeze.

We sat out the next one, drinking the punch: 'This is my lovely day!' he sang to the record; with surprise I realised that I was beginning to enjoy the evening. He talked without stopping: about his work, his friends, his war. 'The Liberation. Going through Brussels,' he said, 'best thing ever, that.' At intervals, he squeezed me, saying again, 'I like you, love.'

When a little later, supper was announced he took it for granted we should stay together. 'Don't dally, love. Eats look good,' he said, as I went off to the lavatory; and when I got back he was already waiting with two plates of chicken and salad: '*There* you are, love! I thought you'd gone down the what'sit—' He'd bagged us an easy chair and he sat on the arm of it, chatting. We drank some more punch; it was very hot in the room and my head a little wuzzy. Bob seemed to know everybody—a succession of strange faces stopped, spoke, laughed, passed on.

Juliet, in long strapless, caramel-coloured velvet, floated by, Richard in tow. It was the first time I'd seen her that evening. She didn't see me; smiling her satisfied cat smile, she looked very contented. Richard, less so.

'Whew,' exclaimed Bob under his breath; then draining his glass, he added confidentially, 'too much money, that's her trouble—and don't you wish it was yours, love?'

Soon after that, we went back to dance. The lighting was low, the air full of cigarette smoke, wine. Quentin and Nell, cheek to cheek, arms round each other's waists, waltzed by. I was relaxed: if I'd nothing to tell my mother—so what? Her concerns seemed very far away.

With renewed energy Bob turned Latin American: 'Take back your tango ay, your rumba ay, your samba ay ay ay . . .' he sang above the voice of Edmundo Ros; hips swaying, feet like quicksilver: 'South America, take it away!'

At the end, 'That's good, love. You're good,' he said. He collapsed into a chair, mopping his brow. Then getting up again: 'I'm dried out, love. Let's go see if they've laid on any beer.'

Out in the hall, we blinked at the bright lights. Saying, 'Follow me, love,' he crossed over to a green baize door by the staircase. Just as he was opening it I felt my arm gripped suddenly.

'Ah! Lucy Locket,' said Quentin from behind me. *'My* excuse me. I think.'

He was swaying slightly; but still holding me firmly he pulled me along into what appeared to be a small study. It was cold, and musty-smelling; leaving the door ajar, he switched on the desk lamp, then from behind the pool of light he looked at me angrily:

'Did Juliet put you up to this?'

Down the corridor, the radiogram was playing 'Buttons and Bows': for the fifth time. Gusts of sound, thumping of feet came to us.

'Up to what?' I asked, in a shaky voice.

Very slowly and deliberately, as if he were talking to a fool: 'Your *dress,*' he said. 'Or rather I should say, *Juliet's* dress—the one you so charmingly described as a "cast off".'

'I don't understand—' I said. My legs felt weak and I sat down on a chair stacked with journals: it made me feel awkward, un-naturally raised. I'd begun to shiver too.

'*Richard* bought it for her,' he explained, in a very precise tone: I realised that it was probably because he was tight. 'Last spring. Unaided. Quite a feat—if you know that sort of Englishman. A real labour of love. Now *you* walk in with it.'

I was shivering uncontrollably now; in the shadowed light, his face looked menacing. Someone turned up the radiogram: 'I love you in buckskin, and the clothes that you've homespun . . .'

'She's never worn it.' he said, 'of course. No doubt you're in it together—one of her little *games?* Cock-teasers of the world, unite. You have nothing to lose but your—' He shrugged his shoulders, 'I'm sorry.' Then hiccuping: *'Idle* little b,' he said angrily, 'nothing to do but play the coquette. I thought her sort went out with anti-macassars and flutterings in the conservatory.' He hiccuped again. 'I shall *sell* her,' he announced, 'marked down of course. For people interested in shoddy Victoriana—'

'I'm sorry—' I said; my voice was thick with tears.

Nell appeared in the doorway. She too was swaying slightly.

'I heard you, Q,' she said. 'You're mischief-making. Don't be so *bloody.*' Pushing the door to, she leant back against it. 'Poor love—you're *Lucy,* aren't you? I've heard all about it, Quentin's being absolutely bloody. Forget it, poppet—it doesn't *matter—*'

'It suits her,' Quentin said, rather sadly. 'The dress *suits* her.' Nell came round and took his hand. 'You're being bloody,' she said, 'I'm very angry with you. You're absolutely bloody, but I love you.' She pressed her head against his shoulder. 'I do love you, don't I?'

'You do,' he said heavily, 'you do. All over Europe.' She kissed him. 'Paris, Milan—'

'Fool,' she said.

'Rome. Leeds. In and out the Appian Way. Up and down the Headrow—'

'*Fool,*' she said again, nuzzling up against him.

It was as if I weren't there. Out in the hall there was no one about, and I ran straight upstairs, searching blunderingly for Nell's room and wondering if I was going to cry. I rummaged among the pile of furs and long coats for my old tweed, dragging it on and buttoning it up to hide the now hateful dress.

Bob, looking very concerned, was waiting for me at the foot of the stairs.

'Where ever did you get to this time, love?'

There'd been a misunderstanding, I explained feebly: I'd been talking to someone. My voice was still shaky. 'I want to—have to go home, please.'

'I'll take you, love.' He disappeared, coming back a moment later wrapped in an enormous teddy bear coat.

On the way back, he drove carefully, with the heavy breathing of concentration. He didn't notice that I wasn't talking. 'Cigareets and whusky and wild wild women,' he sang, as we came over the bridge into Bratherton. 'That was a good evening,' he said. 'You *made* that evening, love.' Before opening the car door, he kissed me beerily. It was comforting, and for a moment I buried my face in his furry coat. Then he wrote my telephone number in a little notebook, held upside down:

'You'll be hearing from me—no, I *mean* it, love.'

In the house there was no sign of life. I got straight into bed, and lay there washed by waves of enormous fatigue, but sleep wouldn't come. My throbbing head was full of insistent rhythms—tango into foxtrot into samba; my legs, aching, seemed still to be dancing.

After a while I got up out of bed. The curtains weren't drawn and in the moonlight I could see the dress where I'd thrown it on the floor. I picked it up, and crushing the silk into a heap, stuffed it angrily to the back of my wardrobe.

Chapter 9

On the Monday morning Juliet came into the typing room just as we were leaving for lunch. She was wearing a pencil skirt so tight she could barely walk; hobbling, she crossed over to her desk and began tidying it out.

'I shall leave today. Poor Juliet is *not* being given the magic diploma,' she said, smiling.

But I had had a miserable weekend. Surprising myself with my courage, I accused her directly of making mischief.

'But darling—' she began. I noticed with satisfaction the rush of blood to her delicate skin. 'It was only to give Juliet a little *amusement*. And I was hardly there, you know; I only stayed an hour or so—I had the curse and felt fearfully fragile. Juliet knew *nothing* about Quentin's dramatics.'

Lifting two lipsticks out of her drawer, she tried them on her wrist, then dropped them together with an empty scent bottle into the wastepaper basket. I felt frantic. I would never see her again; wasn't at all sure that I wanted to, but my anger, which had been smouldering all weekend, flared up.

'You can just take the dress back,' I said sharply. 'I don't want anything to do with it.'

She looked surprised. 'What a storm in a teacup, darling. Quentin's to blame of course, and I'm sure he gave you a horrid time, but why don't you just forget it, darling?' She smiled—a small, secret smile. '*Richard* has.'

I didn't say anything. A little later, looking at her watch—a wrist one today—she said, 'Juliet really must go.' She opened the drawer: 'Some *Queens* and *Tatlers* for you there, darling.'

At the door, she said, 'We must meet sometime, Juliet would like that. I'll be in touch, darling.'

I expected to hear from her about as much as I expected to hear from Bob. In fact, I hoped to hear from neither, and only wanted to wipe from my mind the whole unhappy occasion. Even the moments I'd enjoyed were sicklied over. Luckily, my father hadn't asked me about it at all, but my mother's questions were incessant, and the more she asked the less I told her: I must have seemed to her more than usually vague and exasperating.

'I hope you didn't *drink*, Lucy,' she said at one point: harking back to one of her greatest fears. An odd worry, in a way, since Robert Tinsdale had kept a good cellar—she still spoke of it with pride. I could only suppose that it was her mother's influence (helped on perhaps by half-buried memories of her father) which had prevailed.

But whether I'd been drinking or not, it was obvious, she said, that I'd wasted my time there. Had I really nothing to tell her, about anybody? What about this boy, this man, who'd brought me home —who exactly was *he*? And so on; on and on in this vein. Looking hurt rather than angry, she implied that Cinderella had come back with both slippers firmly on: worse—had not even danced with the prince.

'I suspect of course,' she said, 'that you didn't even try. How *ever* will you manage in London?'

Christmas came: never a great success in our household. The forced togetherness only increased the tensions; present-giving invariably went wrong; and by nightfall there was sure to have been a scene of some sort.

Ten days or so before, a wave of nostalgia for Patmore would overwhelm my mother, and she'd devote an entire afternoon to buying Mrs Pickering's present: coming back with something totally unsuitable and unnecessarily expensive for which Mrs Pickering had never expressed any desire, and which she would receive with polite surprise. (When I suggested once that she might prefer the money, my mother was indignant, hurt, uncomprehending: 'One of our *greatest* pleasures in December, Lucy, was the outing to buy Christmas presents for the staff . . .')

This year, while she was over in Harrogate making her annual search, I received a present myself. An enormous scarlet azalea was delivered to the door; with it a note, which read: 'Love, from a repentant Nell and Quentin.'

I looked at it with mixed feelings, as I did also a small parcel from Juliet two days later. It was a handbag size of Houbigant's 'Quelques Fleurs'. 'In memory of the White Rose,' she'd written, 'and *do* forgive Juliet.'

'So suitable for a young girl,' said my mother, sniffing at it. 'Papa, you know, always bought me *Floris*. 'Gardenia'. Every Christmas from 1911.'

The meal, not usually a success, was even less of one this year. My grandmother came over: still very upset, she sat withdrawn, hands restless on her lap, while my father salvaged slices of drying turkey (last year it had oozed pale red juice), and spooned out portions of underboiled austerity plum pudding—its centre still cold and clammy.

After the meal, my mother as usual blamed all her culinary disasters onto the post-war world. Running the two wars together, and moving straight from food to bigger issues she remarked of the world today that it was 'fit only for spivs and squatters.'

'Nothing makes sense since 1914—who can blame the squatters? Where *are* the homes fit for heroes? In 1917, and in 1918—'

'Keep those years to yourself!' interrupted my father, suddenly and angrily.

'Winifred's only giving a political opinion, Peter,' said my grandmother mildly; but with some of her old spirit—surprisingly taking my mother's side.

My father leant over and snapped on the wireless for the King's speech.

'You and your memories—I'll give you 1918, Winifred. You weren't even sewing shirts for soldiers then.' He gave the fire a kick. 'Just ironing them for officers.'

Christmas over, I sank into the usual holiday torpor. With my mother I felt ill at ease, although her mood was equable enough and she'd stopped nagging. The discovery of the letters, which I thought I'd put out of mind, disturbed me still. Beneath my present feelings of emptiness, it lay festering: joined now by memories of the Inglesons' dance, and all to do with it. I didn't water the azalea—I'd just plonked it down in the sitting-room—but it flourished obstinately: cared for, I suspect, by my father.

Then, just after the New Year, Elizabeth had a few days off. Not wanting to stay at home—Mrs Horsfall was evidently worse than ever—she spent most of them with me. She was very cheerful: Andrew, who was still mad about her, had been on leave. But her real life, I sensed, was in the hotel now. She talked a lot about a regular, George Turnbull, who was in several times a week and who often talked to her in reception.

'He's quite old, Lu—in his forties, and he's got a moustache; I've never been kissed by a moustache, Lu; and I can't help thinking—he's that *fresh* you know, sometimes. He's good-looking, too, Lu. Not as good-looking as your Dad, but not bad at all, and smart like. And ever so well off, Lu.'

Her ways of passing the time however, hadn't changed at all: there seemed to me a greater air of unreality than ever now about her attempts to get notice taken of us—in the cinema, in buses, in cafés and even, one snowy dark afternoon, in Harrogate reference library. 'You see some smashing-looking boys going in there, Lu. Undergrads, and that sort.' But although she chose both the seats and the reading matter most carefully, we had no success. It appeared that the few boys in there, had actually come in to work.

Two days before term began I caught 'flu.

My mother, provided she wasn't feeling ill herself, rather enjoyed playing nurse. Bringing me up some home-made lemonade, ('at Patmore, we always had a jug of this by our bedside—for the *slightest* indisposition') she sat on the end of my bed, and reminisced about the Spanish 'flu epidemic.

'Ethel went so quickly! It was a terrible shock to us all. Just a few days in bed, Lucy, and *seeming* to recover—then all hope gone. An awful colour, struggling for breath (I should know about struggling for breath, Lucy). It was unbelievable. And she looked so *healthy* too—all that work on the land. One would never have thought. But of course the food wasn't good then—we had no resistance. And it's the same story now, Lucy, thanks to Cripps and all this austerity . . .'

Her third day as a nurse however, she became a little restless and after lunch announced that she was going to the cinema. '*The*

Guinea Pig—about white-coated scientists I should imagine. I feel rather in the mood for something like that.'

Thinking that I felt a bit better, and tired of lying in bed, as soon as she'd gone I got up and began to wander shakily around the house. Passing her bedroom, I had a sudden, very strong temptation to go and look if the workbox was unlocked—and to see if any more letters had been added. Although I knew passionately that I didn't want to read them I stood, my hand on the doorknob, for several minutes. Then turning away suddenly, on impulse, I wobbled instead up the narrow stairs that led to the top of the house: to the attic and boxroom.

I didn't go up there often; couldn't remember in fact when I'd last been—nor was there any real reason for going now. The boxroom was crammed with rubbish most of which could well have gone for salvage, while the attic was just a dumping place for any overflow—although it did have in it as well a bed, a small electric fire and a gramophone, dating from the first days of the War when it had been cleared out and converted for an evacuee. Now my father used the room as a refuge, sleeping in it when he came in late or when he'd had open warfare with my mother. He was probably there more often than I realised because it didn't smell musty or damp and there was a lingering scent of eau de cologne.

I turned on the electric fire and sat on the end of the bed waiting for the room to warm up. Outside, it was already growing dark and through the small high window the sky was leaden, full of icy rain. The room with its sloping ceiling felt oppressive: junk everywhere, piles of newspapers in one corner; in another the wind-up gramophone and a cardboard box of old records. I never bothered with these. Once, years ago, Elizabeth and I had played through them all, but we hadn't thought much of them; collected by my father as a boy—and some of them must have been secondhand even then—they were mostly scratched hissing ballads, muffled Caruso, worn Gerald Kirby or G. H. Elliot. We much preferred the old 'twenties ones at Elizabeth's home: with titles like 'Something in my disposish', 'Diga diga doo' and 'My canary has circles under its eyes', they'd all belonged, unbelievably, to a young Mrs Horsfall. There was a radiogram there too, so that when later Elizabeth and I bought records jointly—Joe Loss, Glenn Miller, Geraldo, Ambrose—it was always at her house we kept them.

But now, for want of anything better to do I looked through the ones in the cardboard box; then played a few of them. I wasn't enchanted. Age and wear had given them a false rhythm and tone—John McCormack, in the garden where the praties grow, had become arch, almost hysterical. Then, after 'The Mountains of Mourne' I forgot to rewind, and 'A Perfect Day' died down with a baritone moan. The room was warming up, and turning the gramophone handle vigorously I began to feel lightheaded. Heavy rain was beating now against the window and the skylight.

Back at the box, I came across—sandwiched between Gertie Millar and 'The Rosary'—a thick one-sided record of Handel's 'Where e'er you walk'; its label was blurred so that I couldn't make out the singer's name; the quality of the record was poor also, and at first I listened only half-heartedly, irritated even as he sang of cool glades and shades. Then, arrested by some quality in the voice—the sound, now faint now scratched now oddly pitched—I tensed.

It was nearing the end. 'Trees where you sit—' The singer's voice rose—'shall crowd into a shade': lovingly, he played on the words. 'Shall crowd into a shade,' he sang. Final, rounded, triumphant.

Surprised that I'd liked it, I played it over again; sitting back on my heels beside the gramophone, trying to ignore my throbbing head. Outside, the rain turned to hail drummed against the skylight. The room seemed very warm; confused images, most of them meaningless, jostled for a place in my mind. Then I shut my eyes and, suddenly and clearly, saw Richard.

He was exactly as I'd seen him at the party; exactly as when, dancing with him ('may I ask you something?' he'd said) I'd given my happy reply: 'A cast-off of Juliet's ... never fitted ... doesn't want it ...' In my confusion I'd barely noticed his hurt; later I'd been too upset and too angry. Now—long after the event—I saw it quite clearly. The flushed forehead, the struggle behind the eyes, the lines about the nostrils. the mouth working. He might have been in the room.

The gramophone needle, record finished, grated to and fro; I did nothing about it; pierced by pity—useless now—I sat quite still, hands clenched, nails dug into palms, fighting his image.

And then, just as suddenly as it had come, it was gone again and I was aware only of the throbbing in my head. For a while I didn't move; then getting up dazedly I cleared away the records, turned off the fire, tidied up the bed and crept back, shivering, to my room.

I must have fallen asleep almost at once. When I woke up, my mother was in the room.

'Such weather!' she exclaimed, drawing the curtains to hide it, 'I should never have gone out.' She sat on the end of the bed, after placing a cup of watery Bovril beside me. 'And it was *so* disappointing! Such a silly film, Lucy. All about a public school which has to give a place to a working-class boy—the result of some Government report or other. Anyway, of *course* he doesn't fit in. *The Guinea Pig*, it's from a play, I believe. I *had* hoped it would be something like Madame Curie—'

She looked tired, pinched. Later, she brought her supper up and ate it with me. 'Peter never even said he wouldn't be in,' she grumbled. I felt uneasy with her, as if I had some secret.

That evening my temperature went up to a hundred and three, and all that night I lay: half awake, half asleep, my mind full of ghoulish, terrifying images. Outside in the darkness, the lorries that had killed my brother crashed their gears and came rushing towards me— the room shaking; shadows on the wall, downstairs a door banging; hot and cold by turns, I was haunted too by anxiety: a question hung, half-formed—as if something once known had been forgotten; all the next day, tossing and turning, I searched and searched.

On the second morning, I woke late, weak but cool, my head clear. I'd had a dream, I knew that, but I could remember nothing of it. Through the half-open curtains the sky was a sharp blue, a light winter breeze rattling the window frame; as I lay there, a sudden intense joy swept over me; a memory of such sweetness, that it lent radiance to everything around me—chipped shiny chest of drawers, faded curtains, heavy dark wardrobe, threadbare carpet. And then I remembered. Greeting what I'd been searching for in my delirium : I love him, I thought; I love him. I love Richard.

It was the most joyful knowledge. Masked by fever, revealed to me now on a crisp January morning, it needed no action, no thought. It was just a wonderful discovery, a secret source of

strength which all that day grew and gew—precious, because delicate, yet tough : a beginning of such simplicity and satisfaction that
I couldn't imagine it otherwise.

And it made me well again; so that when later that afternoon my
mother, clutching her forehead, said that she'd caught my complaint
('so *dizzy*, Lucy!') I was able to nurse her, strong enough to run up
and downstairs time without number, finding nothing too much
trouble.

My father was away : 'Thank God Peter isn't around— Not of
course that he would catch it. He's *never* ill.'

'You must rest,' she said feebly, the second day. 'You should be
resting, Lucy.'

But rest, like thought, I didn't need. Sitting up in the attic, I
played the Handel record: three four five times, over and over.
Mostly I didn't need even that—knowing that any time, at any
moment of the day, I'd only to halt in my tracks for the wonderful,
inexplicable sweetness to suffuse me again.

It was still with me when, three days later—my mother well
enough to be left—I climbed the stairs of the White Rose once more.
Blissful, confident, banging away at my upright, my fingers weak,
my head like cottonwool in the fuggy heat, I was unassailable.

And it was the same in the afternoon, sitting in the shorthand
room, while smoke from the paraffin stove rose and made our eyes
smart. Miss Laycock, looking exhausted already, dictated :

'Queen Victoria had a necklace of pink pearls which was worth
$80,000, but the ladies of the Rothschild family possess pearls of far
greater value—Baroness Rothschild has a pearl necklace valued at
£50,000 . . .'

Miss Metcalfe, coming up behind me suddenly, looked over my
shoulder and snorted.

'Where is our mind today, Miss Taylor?' she asked loudly. 'Where
is our *mind*?'

Depression struck towards the end of my second day back. It was alarming in its sudden onslaught as if, deceitfully, it had only been lying in wait: one moment, calmly rolling a new sheet of paper in my machine, I was happy; the next—all was gone; I was without hope or purpose, where the sweetness had been, a dull ache.

Unable to face going straight home after the White Rose, I walked instead, like an automaton, in the direction of the Valley Gardens. It had been one of those January days, never fully light—now it was darkening fast and an icy wind starting up. The Gardens were nearly deserted: in the sun colonnade there was only a woman in a pixie hood hurrying a small child home. Hunched and shivery, I sat on a bench a little above the stream and rockery. The seat felt icily damp, even through my coat; as I gazed out at the tall grey houses tiered behind, I wondered, common sense flooding in, what ever could I have been about these last few days? In what Never Never Land had I been living? What *could* I have been thinking?

It was then that I remembered Juliet. Mysteriously, miraculously, I'd forgotten her existence until today. Yet, adored by Richard, she might well by the year's end have married him; and in the meantime, unless my mother changed her mind suddenly, I'd be leaving Yorkshire anyway. When should I ever—*why* should I ever, see him again? Even if finally Juliet didn't want him for herself, what was the most I could hope for? the odd glimpse, the stray report, and if I was persistent and haunted the right places, perhaps the casual encounter. All very small coin—even if through longing and desire I turned them into treasure trove.

In the wake of my quiet happiness—my rich feelings of only a few hours ago—had come something sharp, demanding: above all, hungry. But it couldn't live on nothing. That I wanted it to stay, I was certain: an emotional vacuum which I'd barely noticed, nature had abhorred—to return to that state now was a far, far worse prospect. Sitting there, self-indulgently hopeless, miserable: I'll settle for the hunger, I thought.

My mother was up again; weak and querulous, breathing with difficulty, she didn't suppose that she would feel better now until at least the spring. Princess Elizabeth had measles, she said, as if this royal irrelevance somehow dignified her own ill health.

My own quietness and general low state weren't much noticed, fortunately; they were anyway easily explained by post-'flu depression and overwork at the White Rose. She did comment however, on my lack of appetite, remarking also that I was very pale.

'We must ask Dr Varley for an iron tonic. *Gervase's* mother was very anaemic as a young girl,' she said; leaving me to wonder how ever this tendency could have been passed on to me.

My father, to irritate her I think, suggested a bottle of Wincarnis.

He was snubbed. 'Tonic wine,' she replied haughtily, 'is just an excuse for people of your background to take alcohol.'

But after a while, probably because she was still feeling low herself, she stopped her comments. I settled into a mechanical, conscientious routine : White Rose all day, homework checked and double checked all evening. Between times, I was lost. Weekends were the worst, and I tried several times to get in touch with Elizabeth : feeling her cheerful self-absorption might be just what I needed, or ought to need. But she was never there. The fairy tales, which half-ashamed I tried to return to now, had gone dead on me: I wondered what beauty I'd ever found in them. Only the Handel record still held its magic, and rationing myself strictly, afraid always it wouldn't last, I'd creep upstairs and play it, over and over again—almost as if it could give me some answer.

During the week, instead of spending my lunch hour sensibly in Jennifer's company I'd make various excuses to wander off on my own. It was the same when we came out at four o'clock. Not wanting to go home, I'd go up to Smith's bookshop and browse idly, never remembering what I'd seen; or haunt the cosmetic counter at Marshall and Snelgrove's—the warm air, the heady blend of scents, the creams, powders, soaps, the suggestion of potential extravagance were all for some reason comforting.

More often though, I would go to the Valley Gardens. The weather was still icy; guiltily aware that I could well be visiting my grandmother, I'd sit on the bench above the stream till I was stiff with cold, then wander up and down the sun colonnade or in and out the paths; sometimes even through on to Harlow Moor. Once, though I'd promised myself I wouldn't, I walked up to Cornwall Road: strolling, nonchalantly I hoped, twice past the Inglesons' house—pretending, finally, to put something in the pillar box on the corner.

One afternoon, I was sitting on the usual bench; we'd been turned out of the White Rose half an hour early, so that it was still quite light. Three children, hooded, muffled, woolly-legged, came running along the path below, then stopped by the water to throw bread to the ducks. A uniformed nanny was with them and while they jostled each other for the creased paper bag she stamped to and fro in her sensible shoes, impatiently, rubbing her brown woollen fingers.

The paper bag burst. '*Now* look what you've done!'

At the water's edge the children were all fighting over the pieces of biscuit and bun. As I watched them, a man came by; his head was bent, the collar of his British warm turned up.

Between sight and recognition there was a second only of shock; I couldn't speak, and he was almost past, before, weak-legged and with beating heart, I called out, 'Hallo—hallo, Richard!'

He turned at once; his hawklike features sharpened by the cold, looked at the same time familiar, and yet hardly known at all. 'But hallo!' he said, smiling. I felt sure that he was asking himself who I could possibly be, was hastily trying to remember where on earth he'd seen me before. But no: 'It's Lucy, isn't it? How *awfully* nice to see you—' I'd got up from the bench and was standing awkwardly beside him, 'I had to take some papers over to a client. Conveyancing. Then I thought I'd walk back—some damn silly notion about the need for healthy exercise. Only it's always further than you think—and cold with it.' He hesitated:

'Were you just leaving the Gardens?'

'I'm going for my bus,' I said; my voice coming out with a squeak, hitting the cold air. 'The Bratherton one.'

'Then look, I'll walk up with you—if I may? Our office is in Victoria Avenue, so I go most of the way.'

I nodded, incredulously.

'This really is an awfully pleasant surprise,' he said, as we walked along. Then, 'Are you still at that frightful place? Juliet's awfully pleased to be out—I know. Not that she took it very seriously—'

The duck-feeding children came running up behind us; one of

them, a boy, darted across our path, and the nanny called out angrily, '*Mind* how you go, Lionel!'

'Poor little b's,' said Richard, as she stalked out of view. '*We* had someone frightful like that when we were children. Not brown though—a sort of *grey* witch. Awfully superior. She ruled over our insides. A real reign of terror. Nell thinks probably she was costive herself, and her mood every morning depended on her success or not after breakfast. Anyway—we found prep school a riot of freedom afterwards.'

'Who's we?' I asked: this time my voice came out breathy and small.

'My brother Philip. He was killed at Alamein.'

We were just coming up to the gateway; on the stone shelf at the side a solitary glove, stiffened in the cold, waited to be claimed. 'My brother was run over—' I began hesitantly. But it sounded odd, an unfair bid for sympathy and I added, 'a long time ago though. Five or six years before I was born—'

'All the same, how terrible. What a terrible thing to happen!'

As we walked on out I glanced at him, stealthily. Our pace, although it was probably on the slow side, seemed to me unnaturally accelerated: as if to fit the racing by of time; and it *was* racing by; even in thinking, he is really here, I have only now—even in thinking this, I was wasting the moment. Already we'd reached the White Rose. In its projecting upstairs windows a few lights were still shining; below in the chocolate shop the dragees, the truffles, the violets, the gingers were laid out temptingly. I rarely looked at them now as I hurried in and out, but Richard, stopping in front of the window, said:

'These look awfully good.' He hesitated, his hand in his pocket: 'I seem to be much too well off for coupons—hardly a sweet tooth in the house . . .' Then rummaging: 'Look—would you—may I get you some?'

I stood trembling by the counter while the girl made a selection. My mother liked crystallised violets, I told him. For myself, I hurriedly chose dragees. Richard pulled out a ten-shilling note and some dog-eared coupons; I watched him: his face creased, eager, a little uncertain; and suddenly I was reminded of Uncle Gervase.

It was a fleeting resemblance only; of manner not of physique: something in the impulsive, almost extravagant gesture; Uncle

Gervase on the pavement outside Gunter's, wanting us on the spur of the moment to stay up, to go to a theatre, to let him give us this, that, the other. I could see him as in a faulty photograph when one exposure over another a second and ghostly figure stands behind. And for a moment I felt as if the world of my mother had invaded this other, intensely private one. Then, in seconds, it was over. Richard was handing me the carton; opening the shop door.

Outside again, the cold hit us forcefully.

'What time *is* your bus?' We turned into the narrow Ginnel leading up into Parliament Street: I wished it a mountain and he helping me up it, 'Couldn't I get you a cup of tea or anything? Are you *sure*? The Kiosk's just here. Or—or we could brave Fuller's, or Betty's?'

But I was unable to accept. Frightened at the prospect of such riches, I assured him that it ought to be, had to be, the next bus. And then—because I knew I must sooner or later, and desperately didn't want to—I asked, 'How's Juliet?'

'Oh, she's *very* well.' His face had lit up; I sensed an excitement in him to be speaking of her at all. 'She's leading the idle life at the moment. Sort of getting her bearings. Recovering from the White Rose and all that.'

We came up out of the Ginnel, straight into the freezing wind; the icy air whipped our faces. (Shall you marry Juliet? When will you marry Juliet?) I glanced over: he was looking straight ahead and where the wind had lifted his hair, the tips of his ears were red with cold, the skin of his face drawn with it.

'We go to Rome you know in the spring. A foursome, with Nell and Quentin. Q's aunt has this flat in the Corso Vittorio Emmanuele —then a villa on the coast. We're looking forward to it tremendously. Nell and I were over last year, but it'll be Juliet's first visit—'

We were crossing the road, into the evening traffic, up the other side of Parliament Street. The greater part of the walk was over, my time was nearly up, and remembering my thin, pointed hunger I began, almost without realising, a fierce catechism.

But he answered easily; didn't seem surprised at all. It was awfully nice of me to be interested— Yes, he had been up at Cambridge— John's, before the War. 'Only a couple of years though—then the Army of course.' No, he hadn't gone back. He'd done the rest of the work in Germany. 'Thanks to the Red Cross, I could bash the books out there. God knows there was time enough . . .'

Yes, he had tried to escape. Once. But it had been a miserable failure. 'I wasn't the type. And by that time, Q had turned up. He didn't even try—much too lazy, he said. We just settled down really to making the best of a rotten show. He read an awful lot, did some quite remarkable drawings—and I had the exams of course. But it was a pretty frustrating War . . .'

We were nearly at the top of the hill. 'I'm afraid I've rambled on terribly about myself—'

We stopped just by Jaeger's window, opposite the War Memorial where four or five roads meet and it's always windy, whatever the time of year.

'This is where we part, I think.' We stood there; he made no move. There was a rush of people coming by; on the road a car trying to cut across another braked suddenly, and two sets of horns fought each other.

I said: 'I used to be afraid of the police horse here—'

'*Did* you? I wish sometimes I'd been . . .' He pointed over to the Imperial café, 'I must have spent pounds of pocket money over there, buying it enormous Bath buns—'

A bitterly cold rain was blowing across now, icily hitting our faces. I said, clutching the carton to me, 'Thank you very much for these.'

'Not at all. It's been—awfully pleasant.'

We stood there shivering. He seemed about to say something. Then:

'I'm sorry, it's terrible of me keeping you standing in this incredible cold. It's just that—' He hesitated. I saw in the street light that he had coloured. It's just that—look—I should have apologised before. That business at Christmas—you should never have been involved. Quentin exaggerated everything rather but we *all* behaved badly. Really, I'm fearfully sorry. I hope—we're forgiven?'

'Yes, yes. I mean, it wasn't *anything*,' I said. 'I'd forgotten all about it.'

I heard my words die away. A moment later, his hand raised in a farewell gesture, he'd gone. For a long time, I just stood on the corner; at first I was frightened he might glance round and notice me still there, so that I had to pretend to look in Jaeger's window. Forgetting to shelter from the wind, ready at any moment to fix my gaze on a belted camel coat, price eight pounds, I watched him, till he was right out of sight.

Chapter 11

Over the last few weeks my mother's health had been improving gradually; her breathing easier, her cough less. She was all set in fact for one of those sudden attacks on life, fits of enthusiasm I knew so well. Now, as Lent began, she launched herself, zealous and fervent, into six weeks of piety.

For once I was glad to see her like this, feeling that totally absorbed as she was she wasn't likely to stumble on any of my secrets. I had in any case been feeling easier with her—I seemed to have grown a skin now over the affair of her letters. But I trembled still that I might give myself away about Richard.

Every evening now she went off to church, usually to the Stations of the Cross; she'd have been pleased if I'd gone with her, but I made homework a convenient excuse.

She had decided to observe a full fast in Lent. She explained to me carefully exactly how much and how little she was allowed:

'At Patmore there were always these little gold scales standing on the table. Cheese, or biscuits, or toast—they could all be weighed. One was able to be *quite* sure that one was keeping the rules . . .'

My father, watching her one evening pick ostentatiously at half a potato, remarked:

'I'd thought anyway your Pope had let you off all that nonsense—'

'*Thank* you,' she replied coldly. 'I prefer to keep the spirit of the law *and* the letter.'

Exasperated: 'What about that RC cat Pugin, then?' he flung at her—at us both. 'What of him? Shouldn't *he* be bloody well fasting?'

Scarcely able to believe the meeting with Richard had ever really happened, during the next few weeks I lived it over and over again: wastefully, prodigally, telling myself I was impressing it on my memory: knowing I was using it up, sucking it dry.

February turned into March; and at the White Rose term dragged on: still nine typing specimens to go; and tests, tests, tests. Tuesday and Thursday afternoons now we typed to Victor Sylvester ('rhythm and relaxation, Ladies! I want to see *both*'). Miss Laycock worked the gramophone, an antiquated machine which seemed to vibrate to the pounding of the typewriters while, mistakes piling up, we listened to the records—often surprisingly modern: 'Shrimp Boats', 'Buttons and Bows', 'Slow Boat to China'.

'I'd like to get you, on a slow bus to Bradford,' sang Jennifer in the desk behind: in her element, fingers flying.

A few more weeks, and it was spring. It came suddenly, arriving as it were overnight. Warmth everywhere, sudden sharp colours, fresh scents, piercing greens; a blackbird was nesting in the bush by the front gate.

I was in the Valley Gardens as often as ever; but whereas in winter there had seemed to be hordes of children, running, sliding, stamping through the cold, now there seemed to be only couples. Strolling hand in hand—not talking, or striding out together, arms swinging: then the sudden burst of laughter, a sleeve clutched, the joke shared. Sometimes an impulsive kiss, the girl's head pulled roughly against the man's collar; once, sitting on the bench beside me, a long-drawn-out bee's kiss.

Stupidly, I sat always in the same place: reasoning that if only I sat there long enough, often enough, Richard would come by again. One lunch hour, seeing a sports-jacketed figure in the distance, I rushed forward with crazy conviction; but panting and puffing, hunting frantically for memorable words, I knew before I arrived that I was mistaken; and looking with near-hate at the body which by some trick, set of shoulders, shape of head, had deceived me, I mumbled an apology.

At last, term ended. We were released at noon and coming out, I went straight to Marshall and Snelgrove's, to buy my mother an Easter present; something frivolous and unlikely—the religious bout I reckoned, must be nearly over and disaffection would set in soon. I was standing among the talcum powders and boxes of soap, looking, when a voice behind me said: 'Darling, *hello.*'

At the next counter. finger poised over an open jar of cream, was Juliet. Seeing my surprise, she gave me one of her little smiles; she had, as ever, her air of contented kitten.

'Mm—and well, how has it been, darling?'

In spite of the mild day, she was wrapped round in stone-coloured tweed; I noticed beige gaiters too, and a long thin umbrella propped against the counter. Staring at her, I was struck by sudden panic: certain that by looking at me she could see, could guess, that I loved and pined for Richard—as if her own position gave her immediate insight.

Putting aside the cream, she gazed at me for a moment. ' "Darling you look tired he said" ' she murmured, quoting a skin food advert that once we'd joked about together at the White Rose.

' "And a tired look is an old look," ' I said, finishing the slogan, feeling it described exactly my present dusty, lukewarm condition of mind and body.

'I can see it's been a *terrible* term, darling,' she said, pouting slightly. 'That woman shouldn't be allowed.' She turned away a moment, took up another pot of cream. The assistant—smart, a little anxious—asked: 'For day or night use, Madam?'

Juliet ignored her. 'I must have something really *rich*, darling,' she said to me, 'or the Roman sun will frizzle me completely.' She shrugged her shoulders: 'Silly Juliet should wear a sun hat of course. But she never does.'

She picked up a tester lipstick and tried it out; it was a pale rose colour. She looked at it critically.

Hearing, unwanted, an urgent note in my voice: 'When do you go?' I asked.

'A few days after Easter.' She gave a little yawn. 'I don't know. Richard has the arrangements.' She tried on another, brighter lipstick, 'It's this currency allowance business which is so boring, darling—he's supposed to be doing something about it. Or Quentin is.' She gazed around her; the assistant was still hovering. 'But *pas discuter ici*. We may need to go abroad again, you see—if Juliet should weaken, for instance.' She smiled, 'I couldn't really imagine a honeymoon spent in the British Isles, darling, could you?'

Her scent wafted about her, rising above even the mingled shop scents; looking at the paper-thin texture of her skin, I realised, trembling inwardly, that this was the flesh Richard touched. As she stood there, I could sense it, could trace where his bony hands had stroked.

'*Not* Lizzie Arden,' she was saying. 'Her jars are too heavy—for my wrists, you know. What about Guerlain? or Dottie Gray?' The assistant's smile was fixed in patience. 'Nellie Rubenstein possibly— although I rather like Lancôme. Yes, now I think about it, *Lancôme*. Do you have their Crème du Jour?'

I tried to sneak away. I thought she wouldn't notice, but even as I made a move, she turned:

'Don't wait for Juliet, darling—I shall be an age. I find it so *boring*—choosing.' She gave another yawn. I muttered something like, 'Have a lovely time, and lots of sun.'

'But yes.' She turned back. 'Goodbye, darling. I shall send you a card.'

As I left, she was smiling to herself, one of her secret, satisfied smiles.

Her card came about two weeks later, a blue and golden picture of the coast near Rome. In her careless rounded hand she'd written: 'Lots of sun and good food, darling, we're all lizards. Richard peeling horribly . . .' I carried it about in my shoulder bag for several days, grateful for any news at all; was even tempted to show it to Jennifer—half hoping perhaps to be asked 'who's he?', even to be lured, so late in the day, into talking about him.

I'd seen a lot of Jennifer this holidays. Her home, with its relaxed jollity, its liveliness, woke in me the same envy I'd had for Alan's imagined family.

Elizabeth I hadn't seen since the New Year, and with the emotional muddle I was in now, I wasn't really keen to. Then in the last week of the holidays she rang me up, very early one sunny morning.

She was in a bad mood.

'Lu, it's my day off—and she says I've to spend it all in the fresh air. You hear that? But I said I wouldn't, only you came too.' She gave a breathy groan, 'Fountains Abbey—that's her idea. On bikes. Heck, it's *miles*, Lu—'

She was in the kitchen looking sulky when I arrived. Mrs Horsfall was packing lunch for us: beetroot sandwiches and some unattractive squares of cheese. She told Elizabeth several times over, 'Your system's clogged up, you know. Her pipes are all furred,' she said to me; she sounded always as if she'd culled her vocabulary from laxative advertisements, 'Furred with stale air, Lucy. It's not good, isn't that job.'

We'd only been cycling about ten minutes when Elizabeth said the meal looked so foul she'd have to have something for it to sink into. 'We'll find a café, first thing.' As we pedalled along on a flat stretch, she sang: 'I want some red roses for a blue lady' through her nose, over and over again. In between times, she kept up a stream of questions and comments:

'You see *Up in Central Park* Lu—Deena Durbin at the Odeon? *Bonnie Prince Charlie*, you ought to go to that, Lu!—there's this scene, ever so sad, Flora Macdonald, with the colour all lovely, and the boat going away. "Speed bonny boat, like a bird on the wing ..." I cried like anything, Lu.'

After three or four miles we found a café. So far she hadn't talked about boys at all; but now, over lukewarm Bev and a choc-ice, she hinted at revelations to come. Pulling a face at two boys she would have ogled only a few months ago, she said scornfully, 'Look at them. They ought to be in short pants, they ought.' Then, scrumpling up her choc-ice paper:

'Still, heck—if *they* were all I'd got on my mind!'

But it wasn't until well in the afternoon that she told me anything. We'd made Fountains in good time, and after we'd eaten, exhausted by the long and hilly ride, we lay sprawled on the grass. It was quiet, too early in the season for many tourists, the weather balmy and gentle; an early afternoon sun cast shadows across the river Skell, while by our faces the grass smelt sweet and fresh. But I'd reached that stage of unrequited love where all natural beauty is painful, and guiltily, I was wishing Elizabeth away.

Lying on her back, her feet in her old plimsolls pointing outwards, she seemed to be asleep. Opening my bag, I took out Juliet's card. Beneath an impossibly blue sky, pine trees fringed the edge of the beach; I began a set of fresh useless imaginings. Perhaps, standing together at the kiosk, Richard had helped her choose it? But Juliet's voice purred in my mind, '... And I nearly forgot—a card for that pathetic little thing, the one I brought to tea that day—remember, darling?' Her bent head intruded, as bare arm touched bare arm; I lost his face—felt the chill goose pimples rise on my own untouched flesh.

'What's that, Lu?' asked Elizabeth, sitting up suddenly.

I rammed the card back into my bag hastily—too hastily. 'Go on, give us a dekko,' she said, shaking her head vigorously, bits of grass sticking to her frizzy hair. 'I bet it's a boy. You're a deceitful beggar.'

I had flushed. It was just a White Rose girl, I explained.

She pulled a face:

'I wish I didn't have to believe you—' She lay back again, hands behind her head; she asked: 'Ever go with that Alan now?'

I shook my head.

'Oh well,' she said, 'he wouldn't have set me on either.' She picked up a blade of grass and began chewing it at the juicy end. 'Lu,' she said, 'remember that George Turnbull? The one I said about the moustache and the kissing? Christmas time.'

I tried to think what she'd told me—I didn't think there could have been very much; but it seemed an age ago, another life.

'It's just—I don't know what to do. I'm in a right pickle. It's daft —but—' She spat out the chewed grass. 'Lu, this George—well, he'd like me, you know, as his—well, sort of fancy lady. Mistress like.'

She propped herself up on one elbow and looked at me; she was giggling, but she'd gone very red. I tried to remember something— anything—about George, but all I could recall was her saying, 'he's good-looking; but not so good-looking as your dad—'

'What's he like?'

'In business,' she said. 'He's in business.'

She took up another blade of grass. 'You know, Lu, it's all going a bit fast like. Even for yours truly.' She shrugged her shoulders, 'I mean, when it all began, he just used to come over to reception to have a chat like. That was all. He's in three nights a week, you see—been coming for years. And his wife too sometimes. *And* his son—a great big boy, Lu, and older than us! Only, after Xmas we weren't that busy and he was in a lot—alone, Lu—and he'd ask me, you know, for a drive afterwards. Well, he's got this great big Rover—he's in business like I said. "Let's go for a quick spin, love," he'd say, then I'd give him a look. "Don't fret yourself," he'd say, "I can get petrol! All I want, love." ' She pulled a face, half-laughing: 'Heck, what *we* do, Lu—it doesn't use much petrol—'

She was quiet a few moments, thoughtful. Then she said suddenly:

'I'm not *daft*, you know, Lu. I didn't think like I was in that bally Rover to admire the moonlight. But this, it's jinks, real high jinks, Lu.' She had gone very red again. 'I mean, you know *me*. I'd used to think like a boy was that daring if he had you feeling his cock. But now—'

She sat up and, leaning forward, clasped her hands round her knees. 'Heck, I dunno!' She paused; bits of grass were still sticking to her hair. 'There's another thing, Lu. You know, him having a son like that—it gives me a right funny feeling.' She screwed up her face, 'You know, he'll stop his fumbling suddenly and look at me—really odd like. Then he'll say, "Don't you wish now it was that son of mine doing this, *don't* you, eh?" And I'll say how I don't. Because I mean what'd I want with him? but that only sets him on more, and then he goes all rough and he's saying all the while, "It wouldn't be like this with *Douglas* would it now, would it eh?" Then in a bit, he's after me to go the whole way—only I won't. Then he sulks, Lu.' She gave a great sigh : 'Heck—it's dodgy.'

She reached into the haversack for the fizzy lemonade we'd bought at the café, then drained the bottle, laying it on the grass beside her. For a while, neither of us spoke. Then 'He wants to buy me some clothes,' she said. 'I mean, he would, *if* ... But I'm not bothered.' She began rolling the empty bottle to and fro. 'Only, jewellery now—I could fancy that, Lu. A bit of something good, you could look at it and say "I *earned* that".'

'What about his wife though?'

'*Her*? She just sits around on her fanny all day, playing bridge. I've no time for her. And she's dead scared of George—I know that for a fact. I'm not worried, Lu—'

A moment later she asked, matter of factly:

'What shall I do, then?'

It was so unlike her to ask for advice: I was taken by surprise. But I needn't have worried. Before I could answer her, indeed say anything at all, she suddenly changed the subject.

'You got a boy?' she asked. Then when I shook my head, she began talking about the hotel instead.

'Smashing dinner dances they have there, Lu,' she said. 'I wouldn't mind getting asked. Real do's they are.'

On the way back she kept singing, 'We're a couple of swells, we stay at the best hotels'. She didn't seem too worried. Just once, as we were freewheeling down a slope, she called over:

'You'll not tell, Lu—will you? You know *her*. She'd crown me, she would, if she ever got wind of this little lot!'

We were back in the Horsfall home for tea by seven. I was exhausted, with the familiar drained feeling I got always from a lot of Elizabeth's company. Over the meal, I yawned continually.

Mrs Horsfall was very pleased. The ride must really have done us good.

'There's nothing like a bit of God's own fresh air,' she said to Elizabeth. 'It'll blow away anything.'

Chapter 12

My mother's religious bout (after a short period of exhaustion and three days in bed) had given way to a frenzy of spring cleaning. The April sun showed up thick layers of dust, and Mrs Pickering was away, ill. No she didn't want any help from me, she would do it all herself.

My father, appalled at the mess and discomfort went over to stay in Harrogate; and a disturbed and moulting Pugin for whom she had no time now, was turned out of his Lloyd Loom chair, the wicker scrubbed, the cushion beaten. While I waited anxiously for the moment when her energy would suddenly give out—and Mrs Pickering and I would be left to clear up the confusion—she emptied drawers, took down curtains, rubbed, sponged, scrubbed.

One morning, I came through from clearing the breakfast and found her kneeling by the big cupboard in the sitting-room. It was the last Saturday of the holidays, and she'd been cleaning for nearly a week.

'How can anyone tolerate such a mess!' she exclaimed, opening the doors. The contents hurtled out: piles of yellowing newspaper, a couple of gas masks, two chipped china dogs, some souvenir booklets and theatre programmes, a broken Mickey Mouse clock.

'Perhaps we could make a pile for a jumble sale, Lucy?' she said hopefully. She rifled through the rubbish, making the disorder worse, stopping all the time to comment.

'Frightening things,' she said of the gasmasks, pushing them, black rubber flapping, to the back. The newspapers she lifted into a pile, then sitting back on her heels began idly glancing through them. 'So trivial,' she commented, 'these provincial goings on.'

Then something caught her eye.

'Look!' She sat up again, very erect, her face taking on that expression of surprised light I knew so well. 'Look here, Lucy!'

The paper was dated sometime in the 'thirties. She pointed to a small paragraph low down the page:

'. . . the exhibition, which deals with monastic life up to the time of the Dissolution, was opened by Mrs Alice Ingleson, wife of the Harrogate solicitor. Mrs Ingleson, who before her marriage in 1919 was a Miss Foxton-Tuke, is a direct descendant of Blessed Piers Foxton-Tuke, martyred at Lancaster in 1584. In her speech, Mrs Ingleson said . . .'

'But Lucy!' my mother cried, 'that family—the Foxton-Tukes. They lived near *Patmore*. Fifteen, twenty miles away only!' She was trembling with excitement, 'I didn't know them *well*, but Gervase was at Stonyhurst with the boys: and I certainly met some of them—many times. They were a huge family, Lucy. Then *I remember*, Father Ainslie—before he came to be our chaplain—he spent a summer there!'

She sat back again, the newspaper slipping from her knees; a stray tendril of hair lay flattened against her damp forehead. 'But what a *discovery*, Lucy! It's like some *voice*, darling, back from the dead!'

There was no more tidying that morning. The pile of rubbish was pushed in again, the catch on the door forced shut. She walked round the room, talking all the time, excited, animated.

I sat very quiet. I was stunned by the news: treasure so enormous I wanted only to go off and sit by myself and think about it. She pressed me:

'See if you can remember anything about Alice Ingleson, Lucy. That party, before Christmas. You *must* have met her?' But my mind was a blank: I remembered only plum-coloured satin, a bony face.

'You're not very observant,' she said. Then, still in high spirits, she announced suddenly: 'I shall call on her, Lucy. This very afternoon.' She glanced at the clock. 'Peter comes for you at two. He can give me a lift over.'

She was beside herself with excitement. Straight after lunch she went upstairs and changed into her Gunter's suit. Talking all the time, she took down and rewound her heavy hair, pulled on the velours hat.

'I wish you could come along too, darling,' she said twice. But I had already promised a long-overdue visit to my grandmother; Richard was anyway still in Italy, and I doubted that I could have borne sitting in his house in my mother's presence. Surely I would weep or blush or stutter, disgrace myself, give everything away?

Frank from next door was being given a lift into Harrogate too; my mother insisted that he sit in the front. 'Lucy and I have a *lot* to talk about,' she said mysteriously : hoping, I think, to be asked what the excitement was so that she could refuse to answer. But my father carefully avoided speaking to her.

My grandmother had improved very little: her house, although spotlessly clean, had still the same unloved look I'd noticed earlier. And just as before, she moved restlessly about the kitchen, arranging and rearranging plates, mugs, knick-knacks. She remarked several times that for the spring to come round without my grandfather didn't seem right.

'He'd wait always, would Alfred, for those daffodils round at back.' Then she said to my father, 'They're no good, Peter, what we've planted on the grave. It's too cold up there, too cold and all on that moor.'

Towards the end of the visit my father said he wouldn't be driving back. He'd stay on with her for five or six days. 'You girls can get a bus,' he said when my mother reappeared. She ignored him, barely concealing her impatience to be alone with me. As soon as we'd left the house, she began talking excitedly:

'Lucy—she *remembers* me! She came over to Patmore once at least, maybe twice. I would have been about seven, she thinks. I can't get any picture of *her* though—even when I saw her. But of course she's several years older than me. And she was abroad in 1911. Then during the Great War she was in Malta, nursing.' She was walking so fast that I had to run almost to keep up with her. 'And then, my drama, Lucy—she thinks she remembers *that*! Only vaguely, but she recalls that she was very surprised there was so much upset.' We were standing on the kerb by Queen Victoria's statue, waiting for the traffic to clear: 'I did *not* tell her,' she said, in a sudden fierce tone, 'what a terrible mistake it's all been.'

The thought seemed to sober her, for a while; but then just as we were climbing onto the bus, she clutched my arm:

'Would you believe it, Lucy? She hadn't realised Gervase was still alive. But of course she hasn't kept in touch—their own home was sold up you know. I hadn't realised. All *five* of the boys were killed, Lucy—'

She chatted on. I was afraid to ask questions, longing for and

121

dreading the moment when she would mention Richard. But she said nothing till we were almost into Bratherton, and then it was only: 'I saw photographs of the son and daughter, Lucy. *Very* fine-looking. And both, I gathered, more or less engaged—'

She looked thoughtful for a moment. We were crossing the bridge now; the evening sun illumined the dark green of the trees massed on the cliffside; up on the viaduct a train was rushing by.

'Do you know,' she said suddenly, 'her telephone rang *six* times while I was there? So *busy!*'

On the way back, she seemed exhausted, flat. But later when we'd both gone up to bed, she came into my room suddenly, carrying the Memory Box.

'Lucy—but how silly of us!' Sitting on the end of the bed, she scattered photographs about the eiderdown: 'Look me out any that are a group will you, darling? *Stonyhurst* are the most likely:'

One by one she held them up to the light. Then her face drooped:

'You know—there was one remark of Alice's which *really* shocked me. About her early life. "I scarcely give it a thought," she told me. "We're here to do good in the present—not mourn the past." '

She peered closely at a blurred group in fancy dress: 'I don't think really,' she said, 'that I shall call on her again. Other than this childhood link—I can't see that we have anything in common. Can you, darling?'

We went back to the White Rose. It was for a few weeks only, a token term, with all the frills removed and nothing but shorthand and typing. There were daily tests. Next month Miss Metcalfe would go abroad, not returning till September, but meantime the room echoed to her shrill commands, 'Wrists up, Ladies, wrists *up!*' or her shocked discoveries: 'Miss Taylor—*eraser* dust in your machine!'

Obsessed with the thought of Richard, counting the days till he might be back, I inhabited a kind of no man's land: bouts of intense concentration alternated with heavy-limbed dreaminess. My mother meanwhile, had calmed down over her Foxton-Tuke discovery. She'd written to tell Gervase about it but his reply—being mainly enthusiasm—had told her very little. Her only other reference to it all was to say one day, out of the blue, and almost coyly: 'What a might-have-been! If this Richard had been free, and nearer your age—and if everything else had been favourable. Then—who knows, darling?'

What she did talk about a lot though, now that the White Rose was nearly over, were her plans for my move to London, next winter. She wasn't very realistic. Not only was I to emerge, as from some chrysalis, poised and successful, there'd also be a highly-paid, impressive job (Password: the White Rose). The same sort of magic was going to take care of all the practical arrangements; she would say airily: 'Of course, I could spend the first few weeks up there with you,' or 'Gervase will be able to see about somewhere for you to live'—and other unlikelihoods. Once she said hopefully, 'I've read somewhere that there's a very pleasant social club for Catholics starting up, or started, in Knightsbridge—That might be useful!'

I listened to it all: but they could as well have been plans for someone else; I supposed that, since she said so, I would go to London, but once arrived what happened to me would be a matter of indifference: time there, was just something to be passed between journeys back up north, when standing on the windy corner near the War Memorial, I would happen—quite by chance—to run into Richard, who surprised, would take me into Fuller's, or Betty's for coffee. We'd talk, and then I'd say, casually, 'I think you know, years and years ago, your mother knew my mother's family ...' Polite enthusiasm. 'But that's jolly interesting!' A few reminiscences; checking of names, places, then back to Juliet—and the dream would go soggy. 'Well yes, next month actually. You hadn't heard? Yes, it's tremendous—everyone's terribly pleased. The South of France, we think ...'

From the beginning of term, it had been lovely weather, almost unbroken. Evening after evening I would get off the bus early and walk from the riverside. Outside one of the Georgian houses, there was some purple lilac; once, after it had rained earlier in the day I plunged my face into the still wet flowers, drinking in the sweet smell with a sort of passion, walking along home afterwards headily.

Then one evening, I came in earlier than usual. I heard my mother

123

talking in the sitting-room: her voice animated, laughing. A moment later, excited, she put her head round the door:

'Hurry up, darling—a surprise for you in here!'

It was Richard come to see me. I stood quite still, flushed, heart drumming. No time to do anything about my appearance—in the hall glass my face looked back, pouched, startled.

I went into the room; a wave of 'Colony' hit me.

'Here's Lucy!' exclaimed my mother, turning towards Juliet: sitting legs crossed on the faded cretonne of my father's chair. She was very tanned, and her hair cut shorter than ever clung closely to her head. She murmured, 'Hallo, darling,' lifting her arm slightly—the bracelets on her arm jangling.

'Juliet's brought you a present.' said my mother. Over on the sofa was a bulky package, roughly wrapped in pink paper. I walked over awkwardly and sat down beside it, Pugin asleep on the other side of me. The trolley was standing in the middle of the room. There was an atmosphere of interrupted, satisfactory conversation.

'More tea?' my mother asked.

Juliet, passing her cup, said to me:

'I came over, darling, to take some of Papa's foreign business friends round the Castle—but it proved impossibly wearing. I sent them all back in a taxi. Coming to see you, darling, was a delightful excuse . . .' Then as she took back her cup,

'What lovely china!' she remarked.

My mother, wearing her expression of contented grande dame, acknowledged the praise, graciously. She didn't mention that, although she wasn't above using it when she wished to impress, it was in fact my father's china, collected over a period of ten or twelve years. (Alan, needless to say hadn't drunk from it.)

'When I was a Wren,' said Juliet, 'I thought of making a little vow not to drink tea, until I could have it from bone china again. And patterned at that. This is *very* beautiful—'

Although dry-mouthed, I hadn't felt able to pour myself any of the tea yet: imagining already the cups rattling nervously against each other. I hoped just to sit there and not be noticed.

'Utility—the very *name*,' my mother was saying. 'Thick, white. So insensitive.' She looked over towards the sofa. 'Pugin is very appreciative of fine china though. Aren't you, Pugin? With age, however, he's become rather an untidy drinker.'

Hearing his name, Pugin stirred; then stretching slowly, yawning, showing his old yellow teeth, he climbed down and padding over to Juliet, rubbed his head against her leg.

She fondled his ears. 'I do *adore* cats.' Pugin, purring throatily, climbed onto her knee.

'He returns the compliment,' said my mother, smiling. Juliet—the black cat hairs already shedding on her cream dress—smiled back. Then looking over in my direction, my mother said, a little sharply:

'Aren't you going to open your present, Lucy?'

I unwrapped the crumpled paper slowly. Pugin, interested, climbed down stiffly to nose at it as I revealed a handbag: pale, stiff, ornately tooled leather. Touching it sensuously, smelling the rich gamey scent of the calfskin—I began thanking Juliet at once: profusely, repeating the words over and over again, hoping to disguise that I felt no gratitude whatever.

'We stopped over in Florence—just for a few days.'

My feelings frightened me: I felt unable to look at her, sitting there so smugly, satisfied, careless of her precious possession.

'Such lovely things. Juliet thought of you at once, darling.' She added, 'Quentin went a little mad, buying the place up—'

'Quentin?' queried my mother.

Juliet explained.

'But, of course. How silly of me. I was a little confused as to who was related to whom.' She put her head on one side, 'And confused as to who was doing the chaperoning?—but then I come from a *very* different generation. I was brought up—'

The back door bell rang sharply, twice.

'How tedious! Lucy—would you answer it?'

A man had called with a complicated message about some tickets that had, or had not, been paid for. I came back to fetch her.

Alone with Juliet, I sat down again on the sofa, stiffly, the bag beside me.

'Do you mind if I smoke, darling?' She reached for her cigarette holder; it was amber, and very long. She lit up and then leaning back, puffed luxuriously,

'Well, darling,' she said, with a quiet smile, 'Juliet has come to her senses at last. She's *finished* with Richard.'

'Yes?' I said, in a foolish voice. I was sitting tense on the edge of the sofa.

'I can't think now, how I put up with it for so long.' She watched the smoke circles spiralling. 'Nearly eighteen months, darling, of being worshipped and drooled over. Silly Juliet. She should have said no at once, and meant it—instead of letting him *hope*.' She yawned. 'But then he's rather sweet, in a boring way. Like a faithful dog.'

Letting my breath out with a rush I realised I'd been holding it all the time she was talking. I felt a mounting sense of urgency; she was looking now for an ash tray, reaching unhurriedly for one from above the fireplace. Desperate, used always to Elizabeth who needed no encouragement—tell me, tell me, I willed her fiercely. Outside, I could hear my mother's voice: raised, argumentative.

Tapping the ash, she pushed the cigarette more firmly into the holder. 'Richard promised, you know, darling. He *promised* no proposals—and then what happens? A little moonlight on the Arno, and it's the ninth—or nineteenth. I lose count, darling.'

There was a door banging, the sound of my mother stalking past through to the kitchen. I held my breath again.

'Then we were over at Fregene, just for the day—scorching. Quentin and Nell were fooling in the water and Richard and I were lying on the sand. He was leaning on one arm and looking at me in the most tiresome manner—and then I thought, "Juliet, darling, you're going to pass out with sheer boredom"; so I turned to him and I said, "Darling, I'm very sorry, but I think this will just have to end!" ' She paused, 'Only he didn't understand at all—just went on stroking me in the same tiresome way. So that I had to say it again, very clearly. "Darling, Juliet's bored with you. *Bored*, darling." ' She paused again. 'And then it all became rather messy. He cried. And I—'

'Really!' exclaimed my mother, flouncing back into the room. 'He says that *I* said—and other such nonsense. Thank God I so rarely get involved in anything of this sort.' She said to Juliet: 'Is your mother a committee woman?'

Juliet murmured something. My mother took up the remark. Their voices seemed to be coming from a great distance—to belong to strangers even; inside my head words rose clearly, a wail almost. Poor Richard! I thought that if I didn't sit tight, fists clenched, they'd escape my lips. Poor, poor Richard.

'. . . but at that time, electricity had only *just* been installed. And of course in a place the size and age of Patmore . . .' My mother's voice flowed on. Juliet, sympathetic, courteous, slightly in charge (after all, she was free to change the topic; my mother wasn't) asking questions, expressing surprise:

'But what bliss. Unlike this French château I stayed at—in my Swiss school days . . .'

The topic seemed to be baths— How had they arrived there?

'Rather a *tin* one,' my mother said, 'in the warmth of one's bedroom, than all these modern advances. The poky bathrooms of today! Though of course,' she was saying as my father walked in, 'the servants had to work very hard—the bedrooms at Patmore were enormous. Just to keep them supplied with hot water—'

For a moment, my father stood in the doorway. Then, eyebrows raised, he looked over questioningly at Juliet; I was surprised to see that she had coloured, very slightly. My mother introduced her at once, defensively, haughtily.

My father not shaking hands, said merely:

'Hirst—of Blackett's I take it?'

Juliet nodded; half smiled.

'I wouldn't mind a little business like that,' he said easily. He crossed to the trolley: he was wearing his blue blazer and suede shoes, an outfit particularly deplored by my mother. 'I see you're honoured,' he said, looking at the china; then lifting the teapot lid: 'What's in it? Maiden's water?' He pulled a face: 'Worse, it's gnat's piss.

'Have a drink,' he said, turning to Juliet. 'You'll let me get you a drink?'

'Whisky,' she said in a little voice. 'Small. With no water.'

'Winifred and Lucy?' Without waiting for an answer, 'My wife has alcohol in her blood, you know,' he said ambiguously. Juliet gave a little shrug of her shoulders; she was still flushed, I noticed. My mother, ignoring the remark, remained seated very upright, her expression one of remote disapproval. Then, when he'd poured the drinks: 'What's this?' he asked, picking up the handbag.

I explained. He felt the leather appreciatively, rubbing it between his fingers. 'Did you say thank you?' he asked aggressively.

'She's not a child, Peter,' said my mother coldly. She turned to me: 'Wheel the trolley through, would you please, darling?'

'What do you think of the Eyeties then?' my father was asking Juliet as I went out. She was sitting, legs tucked neatly, sipping the tumbler of whisky. When I came back, a few minutes later, the subject was London pubs.

They were talking easily. My mother, plainly, wasn't joining in. She gave me a distant smile as I sat down again on the sofa.

'I lead such a West End life,' Juliet was saying. 'Men talk to me about the City—but they never take me there.'

My father was sitting, legs outstretched, relaxed, his back turned very slightly towards me. Their conversation drifted on. Agitated, my mind in confusion, I only half listened. They had moved on to music-halls now; my mother was visibly impatient; but Juliet, leaning back, sipping occasionally, smoking—my father's cigarettes now—showed no signs of going. She accepted another drink and my mother, excusing herself, went out; a moment or two later, I followed her.

She was in the kitchen.

'Nothing's been done about supper!' she said angrily, banging about. Pugin had retreated onto his Lloyd Loom chair. She turned out into a casserole two tins of dubious-looking meat, and lit the oven.

'I think your friend is rather overstaying her welcome, Lucy.' She looked at the clock. 'Over two and a half hours—for a social call—'

She went into the larder and came out with another tin; opening it, she said, 'You'd better go in again, darling. I'll see to the meal.'

They were both laughing when I came into the room. 'And really,' Juliet was saying, 'if you can *imagine* being teased about it in that way. Schoolgirls can be so revolting.'

My father downed his drink. 'Let me fill you up,' he said.

'They sang it whenever poor Juliet did anything the tiniest bit unpopular. So boring, and it's not as if the firms are serious rivals either—Yorkshire Relish tastes a *lot* better than Blackett's. Sauce after all, isn't our thing.'

She handed him her glass. 'You could sing it,' she said, almost as if daring him.

He poured the drink, then crossing to the piano, sat down and sang, in his strong, slightly croaky voice:

'. . . She's only a factory lass,
And wears no fancy clothes,
But I've a bit of a Yorkshire relish
For my little Yorkshire rose . . .'

'But how dreadfully that brings it back,' said Juliet. 'So *boring*,' and she smiled contentedly.

Twenty minutes, and three songs later, she left.

'Naughty Juliet,' she said, when she saw the time, 'I must have bored everybody horribly.'

My mother was back in the room by now:

'Nonsense,' she said, blinking rapidly, 'the whole encounter has been *delightful*.'

But later, as we were sitting over unappetising fibrous meat, she said to me—in that tone of voice which showed it was meant for my father:

'I suppose it's a good thing, when trade mixes with the professions—*something* must rub off after all— But I'm suprprised all the same Alice Ingleson didn't seem more distressed about this, very probable, match—'

'Juliet?' said my father, his mouth full. 'She's not wedding that do-gooder's son, is she?'

At first my mother pretended he hadn't spoken. Then:

'Probably,' she said, coldly. 'In fact—almost *certainly*.'

The mould of my daydreams had cracked and inside, dazzling and bewildering, ideas could be glimpsed, arranging, rearranging themselves. But the full effect of Juliet's revelations was a delayed one and when it came it wasn't hope or ambition I felt at all, but worry: simple, nagging, unceasing worry about Richard. I worried about his feelings; about how he was managing; about the fact that I could be no consolation.

The last few intense weeks at the White Rose were a helpful distraction. A never-satisfied Miss Metcalfe, her face set in lines of disapproval, her manner icily reproachful, was making the most of her remaining days of tyranny. But the end of the ordeal, when it came, was brisk, One day we were victims; the next, rightful claimants of a diploma. Jennifer and I had both been successful, and weak with relief we giggled our way in and out of a farewell interview: Miss Metcalfe like many larger than life figures seeming to shrink visibly as she lost the power to withhold or bestow favours.

We'd been asked, for every night of our lives if possible, to read a short passage in shorthand.

'I'll be reading it on my *wedding* night, of course,' said Jennifer, her mouth full of coffee cake, as we celebrated in Fuller's afterwards.

The diploma itself was a rather scruffy piece of paper, but it was greeted with delight by my mother. That evening, she insisted on taking me out for a celebration supper.

'Of course the White Rose hasn't turned out to be, socially speaking, quite the place I'd imagined. And I do despair of your accent, Lucy—but you've got a *magnificent* training.' Forking up chicken curry, she said, 'I shall write to tell Gervase first thing tomorrow.' Thinking of the other letters—never to be posted—I coloured, ashamed still.

My father was over in Bradford: 'A good thing,' said my mother. 'He would have been so damping.' Perhaps I might have got some congratulations from him, but my mother, still ebullient the next day, overdid the praising.

'Investing your legacy like that, Winifred,' he said, 'no doubt you'll be hoping to see dividends now?'

Blinking rapidly, she didn't answer. He busied himself opening a packet of Gold Flake.

'Well done, then,' he said quickly, without looking at me.

I was to have a week's rest before I began to look for a job. On the third morning, I came down early to the kitchen to find Pugin dead in his Lloyd Loom chair; he was already quite stiff.

My mother, hurrying down in her old dressing-gown, was overcome. While she repeated, 'He can't have suffered, Lucy, he can't have suffered!' I had to deal with the corpse and later, to remove from the house any reminders of him: throwing in the dustbin a seldom-used catnip mouse, and asking Mrs Pickering if she would like the Lloyd Loom chair. The rest of the day she spent in bed. When I took her up some lunch, she said, 'This is the *second* death —in only seven months. And I'd seen 1949 as a year of such *hope*, Lucy!'

In the evening she came downstairs, but when my father, back from spending the weekend in Harrogate, said surprisingly kindly, 'Sorry about old Pugin, Winifred,' she only snapped back at him: 'Perhaps you could have shown him a little love while he was with us, Peter.'

Three days later, I began the hunt for a job. Jennifer and I had both turned down Miss Metcalfe's offer to obtain one for us: suspecting (probably quite rightly) that it would be mainly prestige, with a lot of hard work and little money; Jennifer was in any case already fixed up to work at a brewery where her uncle was a director. But after a series of fruitless interviews I began to regret my hastiness. The hard truth dawned on me gradually that what most employers wanted was experience; and my ability, on paper at least, to organise a banquet, arrange my employer's flowers, keep his books (and his secrets), fix a trip to Brussels at a few hours' notice—was as nothing compared with the reality, that I had never done a day's work in an office.

Nor did the actual diploma seem very magical; often it wasn't even looked at. Worse still—some people hadn't even heard of it:

'Whatever *is* this White Rose?' asked one man. 'You having me on?' And another said, 'The White Rose? I used to see Sonia Dresdel there, love, when you were in short socks—it's a *rep* company you know.'

In the end I was taken on by a firm of Harrogate solicitors, to work for the managing clerk, a Mr Jowett. Desperate for a job by this time, and filled with romantic excitement at the thought of doing work connected, however vaguely, with Richard, I must have presented a picture both of keenness and a humble willingness to please:

'You'll do—I suppose,' said Mr Jowett. My mother, her face puffy with hay-fever, commented only that she was glad it was a job with a profession, and not in trade.

Working for Mr Jowett however turned out to be a very high price to pay, even for imaginative involvement with Richard. He had indeed heard of the White Rose : 'And I can tell you—I think nothing to it.' Plump and usually short of breath, he had a very red face and shiny pate; his pipe was rarely out of his mouth and his small office, cluttered with overflowing papers was dense always with tobacco smoke. From the beginning he devoted himself to catching me out: delighted when I spelt a word wrong or better still, misunderstood some legal term. My best work he described as 'too fancy'; coughing and spluttering, he'd say, 'We don't need any of your la-di-dah touches here.'

The other girls in the office looked understandably wary when they heard where I'd been trained, and for the first few days passed remarks behind cupped mouths whenever I came in and out. But once they saw that Mr Jowett was giving me a terrible time, their attitude changed completely. Stella, who was fat, engaged to be married, and a few years older than the rest, took me under her wing. 'It's a *shame*,' she would say, every time I came out of Mr Jowett's den.

For the first couple of weeks I was kept buoyed up by the sheer novelty of having a job, and even more important, by the hope—certainty almost—that one day, Richard would walk into the office. But the days passed and there was no sign of him. Mr Jowett became more and more trying, cantankerous and demanding by turns. I began to worry that perhaps, since being jilted by Juliet, Richard had gone into a decline.

June came; the purple lilac outside the Georgian house had turned brown, its scent frowsty. I meant each day to get in touch with Jennifer, but did nothing about it. Each evening I spent sitting with my mother, listening to the wireless and knitting a long shapeless cardigan in blue baby wool. In the meantime, my father went up to London for a three-day business trip: 'It seems pathetic,' she said, 'that he's not even particularly good at his job. I think he just roisters in City pubs.'

The evening he was to return, she went up to bed early. When he came in, seeing me alone, knitting, he said sharply, 'Why don't you find yourself a boy friend, eh?' Then he added, 'Get something that'll make you stay up north?'

Surprised and touched by this near admission that he cared whether I stayed or went, I muttered something, my head bent over the knitting.

He stood in the doorway. 'Please yourself,' he said, shortly. He lit up a cigarette then going over to the piano struck a few random chords. 'Your friend Juliet's in the Big Smoke now,' he said casually, 'did you know that? She's got a job, a receptionist somewhere, dealing with foreigners.'

'Who told you?' I asked breathlessly. My ball of wool fell down; too tightly wound, it rolled across the floor, unravelling as it went.

'She did.' He played a few bars of 'Kitten on the Keys'. 'I met her on the train; she'd been up north for the weekend.' He added: 'If you're wondering what she was doing, passing through third class— she got on late. Only just made it in fact.'

He got up and came over, crushing out his cigarette half-smoked in a souvenir ashtray; then he ran his finger along one of the Wemyss cats, bringing it away dusty. 'Ugh.'

Seeing that he was about to go out I tried to stop him; although Juliet had rejected Richard, to talk of her was still almost to talk of him. Chasing my ball of wool across the floor, I asked, 'Is she going to stay there long?'

133

'*I* don't know,' he replied abruptly, gathering up some papers and going straight out of the room.

But my fallow period was nearly over. A week later, hurrying out of the office at lunchtime—so unimportant as to be invisible—I squeezed past two of the partners in the corridor. They were talking, and I overheard the fragment, '... doubtless you'll be notified. I think Oldenshaw's arranged for young Ingleson to be in court ...'

It wasn't very much. But I ran with it straight to the Valley Gardens: sitting on the same bench, saying over and over again, 'Oldenshaw's arranged for young Ingleson to be in court,' delighting in the new image to add to my now jaded collection; but most of all rejoicing in the knowledge that if he was working, then however inconsolable he hadn't broken down, hadn't pined away completely for love of Juliet.

Back at the office, uplifted by such a trifle I felt the afternoon speed by. My mood must even have communicated itself to Mr Jowett, since he went so far as to admit of some conveyancing typed as a rush job, 'Not bad—not bad at all, lass.'

From that day the weary flatness began to lift. During the next week my lightness of mood surprised me; walking home dreamily in the early evenings, the June warmth ceased to mock me. It was all for no reason that I could see but I was too pleased, too grateful to question it.

Then one Friday evening, as I stood eyes screwed up in the sun, waiting in the thickening traffic at the top of James Street, someone shouted, 'Locket!' I looked up, and a car coming across drew up by the pavement facing the wrong way.

'That hair shouldn't be allowed,' said Quentin, leaning out. 'It stops the traffic.'

I was speechless; I saw that Richard was beside him, smiling at me.

'Come on a picnic tomorrow,' said Quentin. 'I've just thought of it this moment. My Nell comes back this evening.' He turned, 'Okay with you, Richard?' Behind them a car tooted impatiently as Richard, leaning across, said, 'Yes—*do* come, Lucy—'

'Your address, Locket?' asked Quentin. There was another angry blast behind, finger on the horn, and a moment later, shouting 'tomorrow at your house when the pubs shut,' he shot the car dangerously back into the traffic.

My mother, surrounded by photographs and cuttings was having an evening with the Memory Box; my father had gone to London again, and wasn't due back till tomorrow.

'This summer I really *am* going to make an album, darling. We'll get it all done before you go to London. And I was thinking—rather than arrange everything by *people*, we could arrange it by years.'

I'd just met Quentin, I told her casually, and he'd invited me on a picnic tomorrow.

'Isn't he the one who's marrying the Ingleson girl?' she asked, holding up for comparison two faded pictures of the Patmore stables; then, looking only mildly interested, she added, 'who else is going—Richard, Juliet?'

Certain that my father wouldn't have bothered to tell her about the meeting with Juliet, nevertheless I'd been dreading that from some source or other she would find out that Richard was now free; but when I mumbled some answer, it seemed, as I'd suspected, that all her hopes and ambitions were focussed on the wonderful things that were to befall me in London, for she merely said, 'Well, if Richard *is* there, you might ask about Father Ainslie, Lucy. I never got round to mentioning it that day.' Then she turned back to the Box:

'Just look at this, Lucy. 1911. That was a *very* special year! That was the year, Lucy—I first noticed Gervase noticing me. And it was a *wonderful* summer, darling . . .'

At the office next morning, my abstracted state was too much for Mr Jowett.

'It's Saturday is it?' he queried belligerently. 'You're all the same nowadays—summat for nowt.' Puffing smoke in my face, he told me, 'When I got started, in nineteen-o-five, *we* knew what work was.'

When I'd left in the morning my mother hadn't been awake; now as I returned her curtains were still drawn, and when thoughtlessly I turned on the light, she gave a little moan, then half sitting up, clutched her hand to her forehead. Her face was puffy, criss-crossed with pain.

'And yesterday evening I felt so *well*, Lucy.' She lay down again: 'Your picnic, Lucy?' she said anxiously. 'You'll go on your picnic, won't you?'

'If you're sure—'

'But you *must*, darling! After all, they may have asked other friends. And one never knows . . . It's all *practice*, Lucy.'

Could I get her anything, I asked. 'Tea, toast?'

'Just some tea, darling, *very* weak.' Shamed gratitude overwhelming me (I would have gone whatever she said), I ran down to put on the kettle.

There wasn't time for any lunch. It had been a rush back, and I hurried now over my face and hair: putting off the decision about what to wear. Rare luxury for me, I had two dresses to choose from. One I'd bought in the January sales with Elizabeth's help: a conventional print of stripes and dots which nipped me tightly at the waist. 'Pushes you right out on top,' said Elizabeth in the fitting room 'It's grand.' But since then it had shrunk sadly; and when I'd tried it on last night I'd realised the bodice was now a binder. The other one I'd bought at Easter. Simple in style, of russet slubbed cotton, it reminded me of Juliet both in taste and expense (I had only just finished paying for it), and since her visit I'd somehow not wanted to wear it. But today it seemed the obvious choice. I was hurriedly stepping into it—when a car horn sounded outside. Without going in to my mother, I rushed downstairs.

Richard was already walking up the garden path. I tried to look casual; but I was breathless from hurry. The car, a Morris Eight Tourer, stood outside, its roof rolled back. Nell was sitting in the front with Quentin.

Fiery red, I couldn't look at Richard's face. As we walked down, he said, 'I really must apologise. It was a scatty invitation—I'd meant to ring up and confirm it.' Then he added, 'You'll find Quentin a bit over-exuberant. I must apologise for him, too.'

Nell said as we came up, 'Hallo, love.' Her voice, warm, rather fruity, didn't seem so very different from the drinkful one at Christmas. Quentin had his arm round her: 'She didn't get a First, Lucy. She's my paid-up, finished-off, second-class mate—'

'Oh *you*!' said Nell, pushing up the back of his hair roughly, pressing hard against the neckbone; he ducked, then freeing his arm, kissed her; a moment later starting the car, flinging me suddenly against the warmth of Richard sitting cramped with me in the back. Hooted at furiously by a gravel lorry we shot out into the main road.

Tremblingly happy, I sat very quiet. The sun beating down on us was unbelievably hot and the speed of the car lifted my hair up and back. Although I looked out of the window, I didn't notice much of the scenery: the twisting of a lane, dappled light becoming green shade as we drove between overhanging willows; splashing through a ford, and jerking after as we tested the brakes; some rocks, a stretch of dark water, the change to drystone walls.

I wanted to ask about the Italian holiday, but couldn't. Richard, full of sympathy about Mr Jowett, told me, 'He used to be called the Gnome of Princes Square, when your office was there—before the War. His bad temper's proverbial.'

After a while they began to talk among themselves; things, people, I didn't know about. And it was then that I suddenly remembered the kettle. In my haste I'd never gone down to make the tea, and by now boiled dry, it would be a charred mess—or worse still a lump of red hot metal; I might even have started a fire.

'Oh heavens!' I exclaimed, my hand to my mouth.

'What is it?' they asked instantly, all sympathy. But wasn't it electric? wouldn't it cut out?'

'She's sure to smell it,' Nell said; and Richard, concerned, asked, 'Would it help at all if we looked for a phone?'

But frightened that I'd been boring, I assured them that no, no it didn't matter at all. We had been climbing for some time anyway and were now in open moorland, far from a telephone.

We jogged for a mile or two more over unmade road, before rattling to a halt just beyond a gateway. Except for a grey farmhouse in the distance, there was no building in sight. All around us was heather, pale still, and beyond that an expanse of green bracken. On one side of the path some black-faced sheep were grazing.

We all got out, and Richard went to shut the gate; for a moment we stood looking at the view; in the heat, the hills in the distance formed a blue-green haze.

Nell said, 'God, this is glorious.' She poked the ground idly with her foot, revealing a disintegrating condom: 'Hell,' she said. 'The boy scouts have been here.'

'Oh, be prepared,' sang Quentin, and trod it into the ground.

We moved on, all carrying something from the car. 'Shall we keep the champers on ice?' Quentin asked, 'or look for a stream?' Nell and I had the rugs; he and Richard opulent-looking hampers of the sort I'd seen only in jewellers' windows and glossy magazines. When we'd settled on a place we sprawled on the rugs, faces upturned to the sky. For a while no one talked; I wished I could forget the kettle, but it buzzed in my mind—a fat persistent fly.

As if half reading my thoughts Nell said, turning over, 'No insects yet, thank God.'

Quentin put his arm round her: 'Those damned Italian mozzies last summer,' he murmured. 'Drunk on your delicious blood. Lucky, *lucky* zanzare.'

'That *foul*-smelling ointment,' said Nell, her voice muffled on the rug. 'And then, the catchword . . .'

'Seventy zooming zanzare snapping a zany on the zanzariera. Six times right—and you won't get bitten.'

Nell, with her forefinger, idly traced a pattern on his lips. In the unaccustomed sensuous heat this small action aroused in me a sudden delight. Richard, who had said nothing at this memory of last summer, was lying only a few inches away; I felt myself tremble, the skin on my bare arms tautening.

Resting on one elbow, I sat up and looked around: just near were a few bilberry plants, waxy, unripe; higher up would be many more.

I remembered my father—it must have been after some Home Guard exercise, about the third or fourth year of the War. He'd brought back two bursting, stained paper-bags full of the fruit: 'Something for a pie, Winifred,' he'd said. My mother, receiving them (or him) with distaste, had said coldly, 'I never make pastry.' My father, colouring, had replied, 'I should know better than to ask for *anything*.' Then he'd muttered something I didn't catch, adding: 'That is, of course, if it'd be worth *having* now.' My mother, her mouth trembling, had rammed the berries into a bowl still in their paper bags, where I'd found them two weeks later: grey fur growing over the crushed purple. The exchange had hung in my memory like an unsolved puzzle. That it had been sexual I'd not realised till much later.

But my father's was not the only ghost abroad. A few moments later Quentin, leaping up, announced that he was hungry and above all thirsty. He and Richard went to the car to fetch the champagne and Nell, turning to me suddenly, said:

'This outing. I hope it isn't too *ghastly* for you. Richard's been so shot up since the Juliet affair. But we wanted him along for the celebrating, and we were sure he'd have said no to bringing along any friends we suggested. Then Quentin saw you, like that, by chance. And it was all right.' Opening one of the hampers, she took out four silver tumblers. 'That little *b*! Q and I couldn't stand her, and God, she treated Richard badly—we were terrified she'd marry him. Terrified—'

The men returned. Moments later, the first cork shot upwards and fizz rushed, dazzling, down the side of the bottle. We drank to Nell's and Quentin's happiness. Thirstily, I finished almost at once; my tumbler was refilled. Richard, only half joining in the conversation seemed a little removed, and I wondered how, unhappy as he must be, he could bear to celebrate.

We opened another bottle. Their voices around me seemed first to boom then to grow faint. I talked a little myself and once—incredibly—made them laugh. I remembered distantly about the kettle and thought: But it's not important at all.

The food was laid out; it looked lavish, unreal: pâté, several sorts of bread, Camembert, chicken, salad. The heat, as we sat about, seemed to grow. Strawberries, cream, amaretti—I scarcely tasted what I ate. Biting into a biscuit I felt my head, fuzzy, float about me and my hand, enlarged and numb at the fingertips, reach out for my drink, and miss it.

'Have I drunk too much?' I asked: my voice sounded distant as from another person; but Richard, passing me the tumbler shook his head and smiled.

Quentin, lying luxuriously, his head cradled in Nell's arms, said, 'Fancy feeling so bloody good at four in the afternoon—'

'Five, love,' said Nell. 'Five. Five-thirty.'

My feet, like a badly focussed photo ballooned into view. I heard Richard say, 'I don't know why you two bother to bring anyone else along . . .'

Heavy and sleepy, we lay on the rugs; Nell said something about making coffee; then for a while there was silence. I noticed only vaguely the dry click of a grasshopper nearby before, blurred with drowsiness, I slipped into a numbing doze.

I came round, to hear Quentin laughing, protesting, saying, 'I can't, love', Nell pulling him up limb by limb, caressing him as she did so. 'But *love*,' he said, 'you can't want to take exercise!'

Richard sat up. 'Lucy and I'll go for a walk. How's that?'

Nell said from the rug, 'You're a dear, Richard.'

'And you'll be rewarded,' said Quentin. 'We'll have tea for you.'

Richard pulled me up lightly; as we moved off I stumbled almost at once and he took my arm, steering me clear of where the heather, spongy, concealed water. Choosing my words with care I said, 'I'm not really used to drink.' I'd eaten no lunch, I explained, and not much breakfast either.

'Are you sure that you've eaten enough now?' he asked anxiously. 'I could go back—'

It had been an enormous feast, I protested; more than I ever normally ate and really I would be all right. My drink-encouraged heart was thumping: that I should be here with him at all felt curiously unreal and it seemed suddenly very important to make some sort of conversation. The pearl I held was the Foxton-Tukes. 'I think my mother knew your mother . . .'

To get started, I said politely, 'When are Nell and Quentin going to marry?'

'September, October. Q's been waiting, very noisily I may say, for the last three years—Nell refused categorically to be ensnared minus her degree.'

'And your family?' I asked. trying at the same time to remember the name of the Patmore chaplain, chasing it through the fog. 'Are they pleased?'

He was looking ahead as he spoke.

'Yes—awfully pleased really. There are a few complications—Religious mainly. Quentin's an agnostic, and Mother who's rather a keen Catholic is somewhat agitated. We were all brought up as Catholics, you see—Phil and I went to Ampleforth and Nell was at Mayfield. But she's reacted against, rather strongly. Lapsed and come back and lapsed again. I'm not sure what the set-up is now, but

Mother keeps creating about it. Fortunately Father's pretty tolerant. Not, in fact, awfully interested.'

I'd been brought up as a Catholic too, I explained. Of a sort. I didn't feel, I said, that I was the real thing—

'To be honest, mine disappeared during the War. While I was a prisoner. The life there, it seemed to produce either lots more devotion—one chap I know went in for the priesthood straight after—or a sort of drifting away. I don't know—'

We'd been climbing as we talked; now we'd reached the spreading bracken I'd glimpsed earlier. Below us, the rugs and the picnic were out of sight.

I said in a rush, 'I think your mother knew my mother. A place called Patmore, when she was a girl, near the Foxton-Tukes—'

Just as I had dreamt it would, his face lit up. 'But how tremendously interesting— And what a small world!' He had heard of Patmore, he told me; but only as a convent: 'I don't know that side of the family awfully well at all—and Mother hardly ever speaks of her childhood. Phil was the one who was interested in the past. There was a martyr, Blessed Piers—a very grisly affair which we were frightfully proud of at school. But the only Foxton-Tukes living now are a couple of elderly maiden aunts in Sussex. They belong to a third order, I think. Anyway there's a great jangling of rosaries and saying of Office— But I'm ashamed to say I haven't seen either of them since before the War. Another aunt, Frances, I was rather fond of—but she died in the nineteen thirties.'

As I'd suspected, Alice Ingleson couldn't have mentioned my mother's visit. It had been of interest possibly, for the rest of that day; but no longer.

'You didn't go to Patmore yourself, to school?'

He was asking, plainly, out of courtesy; but as if given permission, or better still prompted, I began to talk; I was very calm and felt that I must surely be sober. The words flowing easily; I spoke of my mother, and Patmore, family history, the Tinsdales; then the sad little tale (edited), of Gervase and the kingdom lost. Sometimes as I talked I would glimpse as from far away, that there might be another version, another tale altogether; then straightaway I would go back to continue the gospel according to my mother.

'This Gervase chap—' Richard commented, 'God, what a tragic business.' Later, he asked, 'Do you still go up to Gunter's? Phil and I used to be taken there after expeditions to Daniel Neal's. But even Gunter's ices—and they were *jolly* good—couldn't make up to us for all that measuring and fitting. There was even the indignity I think, of some shoes called "Phat Feet".'

By now, we were quite high up; a light breeze was flattening the surface of the bracken. We'd been following a sheep track, and treading now through a marshy patch we came to a bank with, running below it, a ghyll. We scrambled down.

Richard, looking at his watch, said, 'Let's sit a while.' We lay back where the ground levelled out a little. The water was surprisingly clear, reflecting the clumps of grass hanging at its edge; it moved only slightly, a few sticks floating along its surface.

As I'd done all afternoon, I feasted on Richard's presence. Propped up on one elbow, he was pulling, twisting the long grass; his hands were large, square-tipped, the veins standing out in the heat; as he moved his arm, the surprising white of the underskin filled me with tenderness.

I blurted out: 'Juliet—' Then hearing myself, broke off.

He looked up. Surprised, questioning.

'It was just to say,' I went on; horrified. 'I just wanted to say—' My voice was thick, as if through flannel. 'I wanted to say—that I'd thought about you ...'

As my voice trailed away, he turned; and head bent, his hand still tearing at the knotted grass, he said, 'I *should* talk about it, of course. But I don't. I—'

He was very flushed. 'The subject's more or less taboo at home,' he said. 'Which is probably just as well.'

There was a pause. I thought perhaps he was going to ask me how I knew (yet Nell had supposed it to be public knowledge). My heart ached with saying: *I* would never let you down.

'The worst was over a few weeks ago. I've been damn stupid anyway. Blind, really.'

I waited for him to say more. He was sitting up now, hands round his knees, his head still bent; at the nape the hair was very soft and fair, and reaching out, I began to stroke it gently.

He turned suddenly. I thought I saw tears in his eyes. Impulsively, I knelt upright, and leaning forward, cupped his face in my hands.

For a few seconds, we were still, then freeing his head with a rough gesture he gripped my arm and feeling for my mouth pressed it to his, so that our tastes mingled warm and winey; then his hand plunged warm and hard between my breasts, and intoxicated by the scent of him, the warmth through the cotton shirt, I cried inside: here is what you want. But the smell grew suddenly into the smell of fear; and in a frantic attempt to save my gentle dreams, I pulled away and jerking, fell awkwardly; my body twisted, one foot slipping on the damp grass.

Richard had his arm over his face, like a small boy. Neither of us spoke. Down in the valley a collie was barking, persistent, searching; I stared at some small pink flowers growing by the water and tried to remember their name.

After a while, Richard moved his arm, and looking up, said in a stiff voice, 'I'm sorry. I must apologise. I—'

The conventional words jarred. Turning away, I said, 'I'm sorry—it's me to be sorry.' I had begun to shiver uncontrollably.

We sat a few moments in embarrassed silence; Richard looked at his watch again. 'I think we ought to go,' he said, his voice awkward, polite. 'It took quite a long time to climb up here.' As he helped me up, his hand was trembling.

We walked back slowly. The air had begun already to smell of evening; a rabbit, startled, ran across our path, bouncing, twisting out of sight through the green bracken.

Within sight of the rugs, Nell and Quentin came walking towards us, holding hands.

'You look healthy,' Quentin said. 'She's got the primus going,' he added proudly, 'China tea, *and* she managed to get a lemon—'

At the sight of the little silver kettle I was sickeningly back with the nonsense of what I'd done at home; the worry of it settled now like a dull ache.

We sat about drinking the tea; Richard said, 'God, we needed this.' I was shaky, parched. About the whole outing there seemed to be a flat feeling now. Nell and Quentin had settled into a steady bantering tone towards each other, which I recognised as an extension of their love-making, and envied.

We packed up; the remains looked sordid. *'Fête champêtre,'* said Quentin sadly.

On the way back he insisted on driving again. 'You look fagged out,' he said to Richard; Nell said, 'He always gets flat tired in the heat.'

No one spoke much on the journey; I sat at the back with Richard and worried consistently about the kettle. After a while Quentin began to sing; then Nell joined him and they sang 'Là haut sur la montagne'. 'Our own scabrous version,' said Quentin. We all did a half-hearted Whiffanpoof Song, but no one really knew the words; then Nell yawned and said she must sleep, doing so almost at once, her head lolling over onto Quentin.

In Bratherton they dropped me at the house.

'You've been a quiet couple,' said Quentin. 'Sleepy, Locket?'

I had thought to jump out and run in, but Richard had got out too. At the door, he said goodbye; I thought in a hopeless way that he might be going to say something else—anything else—but pressing my hand quickly, he turned away.

Nell from the car called out something I couldn't hear, and a moment later they were gone.

My mother was sitting on the sofa, wearing a creased flowery dressing-gown; beside her a tray of half-eaten salad.

Her face was flabby, tired.

'Darling, it's nearly nine o'clock—whatever happened? And the *kettle*!' she exclaimed reproachfully. 'How could you be so thoughtless, Lucy? It was absolutely *red hot*. Fortunately, I had to go downstairs—Peter rang to say he's staying on in London over the weekend—'

Overwhelmingly tired, I hoped she wouldn't ask for details of the outing: but after remarking, 'I can't imagine what Peter will do with himself in London on a Sunday—drink the day away, I expect,' she began to question me intensely. In my anxiety to hide anything of consequence, I babbled on irrelevantly; looking pleased she lay back, her fingers stroking her cheek. I was sure that if I listed enough trivia I would escape catechism on more important matters, but too late, I realised that by a chance remark I'd revealed more than I'd intended.

She leant forward, eagerly. 'Do you mean Richard Ingleson has *broken* with Juliet? But *when*, Lucy darling?'

I didn't know I protested; it must be recently, I couldn't be sure.

Panic-stricken: I saw growing in her mind, flowering in her eyes, the beginning of a Plan.

'It can't be *coincidence* he asked you,' she said.

'It was Quentin's idea. Richard didn't—'

'But if he's free—in that way, Lucy!' As often when she was excited, spittle gathered at the corners of her mouth, 'If he's free, everything's different. *Quite* different!' She put her head on one side. 'You do see that, don't you, darling?'

'I'm awfully tired,' I said flatly; I saw that the front of my brown dress was torn, very slightly, and wondered who else might have noticed it.

'We can hear all about it, bit by bit then,' she remarked soothingly. 'There's going to be lots to talk about.' And then, concealing her excitement in a flood of reminiscence, she exclaimed:

'It sounds, you know, in a way rather like the sort of picnics *I* remember, Lucy! There was one in particular. It's as vivid to me as yesterday—*more* vivid, in fact. I had this hat, Lucy, a straw one with streamers. Gervase kept borrowing it to shoo the flies away; it worked better than his boater, he said. And Tom and Bertie were there too, Lucy, and some girl cousins—Tinsdales. Then after we'd eaten, we all sat about and sang, and Tom acted the clown, as always. He nearly fell into the brook doing a Lew Hearn impression, falsetto. Singing "Hitchy Koo"—' She paused: 'That's a tune I couldn't hear now, Lucy, without thinking at once, of that hot, hot summer afternoon . . .'

She sat up suddenly—fixing me with her gaze. 'Oh, darling,' she cried, 'it could have been all right! It's all been such a mess—but it *could* have been all right!'

The telephone woke me. Leaping out of bed I rushed downstairs, in the absurd certainty and dread that it was Richard; standing for a moment trembling before I lifted the receiver.

But it was Elizabeth: 'Lu—something awful's happened. Really awful. I can't say, not on the phone.' In the background I heard Mrs Horsfall's voice. She said hurriedly: 'Can you meet me down the river for an ice, half ten?'

I saw with surprise that it was already nine o'clock. I'd slept badly. Dry-mouthed, my head aching, I went into the kitchen to make my mother some breakfast.

'Who telephoned?' she asked as I came in with the tray. She began to cough almost at once; then like an echo, even a parody of my thoughts, she said: 'I had rather hoped, Lucy, it might be Richard?'

A little later—as so often in the wake of Patmore reminiscences— she asked anxiously, 'You are going to Mass, aren't you, Lucy?'

She sat up, flipping over the pages of the *Sunday Mail*: 'I had a terrible night. Otherwise, of course, *I* would go too.'

Half an hour later, I hurried guiltily past the church. Everyone was just going in—missals clutched, hats balanced, dragging or pushing children.

The weather was close and dull and down by the river a dry wind blew dust and waste paper round the café tables. Elizabeth was already waiting, and without asking me what I wanted, she went up and bought two fizzy oranges and two enormous sundaes. Digging into hers at once, savagely breaking up the elaborate mound of chocolate and synthetic cream:

'Heck, Lu,' she said. 'Oh *heck*.'

Her face was creased and she looked as if she'd been crying—her hair was uncombed.

'I've done a daft thing, Lu. Right *daft*—' she broke off, then glancing quickly around at the other tables:

'Lu,' she said quietly, 'I think I've caught on—'

There was silence for a moment. She gulped down a lot of her orange; then sitting hunched, she twirled her spoon round the softening mound of chocolate. I felt around woodenly for the right words but all I could think of was:

'Are you *sure*?'

She nodded. 'Oh, heck,' she said again; then she began to cry noisily, taking out a grubby handkerchief, sniffing, gulping, blowing.

'Couldn't it—just be held up? Like it said in that book—'

'Two weeks last night, Lu. And don't be daft,' she said despairingly, 'you know me and my monthlies. You could set the *town clock* by them, Lu.' She chased up the last traces of ice cream : 'I've felt sick too, Lu. Friday, that started—sort of poorly all the time I'm not eating. You know what? Real daft this. Last night I'd to go into the hotel kitchens. and just as I was coming out, I saw this piece of pig pie—ever such a size. And I ate it all, Lu—I couldn't help it—*all* of it. Then I thought afterwards—ever such a daft joke, Lu—I thought, "Elizabeth, that *proves* it. You're in pig all right..." '

She gave a half-hearted giggle. We looked at each other; after a moment I pushed my ice cream towards her and she began spooning it in absentmindedly. Strangely for her, she wasn't looking around the café at all. Out on the riverside path, beyond the striped awning, the crowds were milling about. Just near us some girls were dodging a pair of boys, chasing round between the chairs, knocking against the rickety tables.

'Is it George?' I asked.

She was sitting quite still staring in front of her. 'It was a dance,' she said flatly. 'After a dance at the hotel.' She picked up her glass, swishing round the remains of orange. '—They're smashing dances, you know, Lu. I always used to wish like, I wasn't staff.'

I passed my orange over to her; she drank it thirstily:

'George was there,' she said. 'He hadn't his son with him—just his wife and daughter—but he kept giving me that sort of you know—"I can't notice you now, *but*" look. Then, while Pansy and her mam were getting their coats he came over to reception and I said I was off duty half one—and he said, "I'll drive them home first"—*meaning* ... Anyway he said he'd tell his wife some story about a business drink. He thought that was ever so funny, a right good laugh—and I saw then he was a bit tiddly. Only, you know—' she frowned, 'then we turned off the road and it was just the usual carry on—only I couldn't help feeling sort of *proud* like, Lu, him coming back like that—just for me. It made me excited like, you know—and he was breathing in this funny way. Ever so heavy and grunting. "Don't fret yourself," he kept saying. Then, suddenly, "*Damn*," he says, "I've nothing. Have you?" '

She hiccuped loudly. 'Honest, Lu, only he was right on top of me, I'd have laughed out loud. I mean—I ask you. As though I'd be carrying French letters around—' She paused. 'I know,' she said, 'I know I'd only to say stop, Lu. But he'd not have heard. He'd got hold of me that tight. And then, a minute later—he'd done. Just like that, Lu, nothing to it, Just like that.' She paused again. 'Heck, I did feel bad. Awful.' Then, with a touch of the old Elizabeth, she said: 'And that *cramped*. A Rover's not a Baby Austin—but it's no double bed, Lu.' She hiccuped again. 'He looked quite poorly afterwards, mopping his face and not talking at all—it was awful, Lu. And I'd thought, you know, he'd be sorry he'd been rough like—that he'd say something. But he was all sulky. Heck, I was mad. Then, Lu, he didn't come in all that week and I was real scared, and daft beggar that I am I go and ring him at work—he wasn't pleased at all. He'd been ever so busy, he said—he sounded right vexed—and he was just off to Brussels. But that was *three* weeks ago, Lu, and of course the worry came the next week. And last night it was that bad, I got on the phone to his home. It was his wife answered, Lu. "Ho, ho," she says, "George isn't available at present. Can I take a *message*?" I nearly gave her one, Lu. "Tell him Elizabeth Horsfall's caught on and what's he going to do about it?" He'd have looked a right monkey, getting that one—'

She tossed her head. Then jumping up, she went over to the counter and without asking me, bought two big sugary buns and some more fizzy orange.

'If I wasn't so bally frightened, I'd give it a shake. I would, Lu. Only—you can die like that, you know. I'd an auntie went that way—Cousin Elsie told me about it, last year. Before I was born it was.' She bit into her bun: 'Trust *her*—*she* didn't tell me. Burst appendix, she said it was. "Your poor Auntie that had perity-something" . . .

'Want your bun?' she asked, but as soon as she'd finished it, she

148

began biting her handkerchief again, then pulling at the skin of her forefinger. She said suddenly, frantically:

'If *she* finds out—when *she* finds out, Lu.'

I sat quite helpless; I'd never, I realised, been in any situation where Elizabeth really needed me.

Couldn't she go to a doctor? Not the family one, of course—not anyone known to Mrs Horsfall; but if she could talk perhaps. And shouldn't she really try to see George? At least, tell him?

She shook her head feebly. 'I'll not do it. I'll not go near him, Lu.' She began to cry again: sitting limply, with dangling arms, her awkwardly bushy hair and her high colour, she looked like a rag doll. I felt desperate for her:

'If I could *think* of something,' I said. But she just shrugged her shoulders, and for a while we sat without talking. The café was very crowded now; I saw a few people glancing over at us, and to keep our place I took slow sips at the orange.

Eventually, as if coming back to life, she said—with a flash of her old self:

'Fancy lady, *heck*, Lu!' she said indignantly: 'Eh, but it's been a poor do. It has, really. I mean, when I think, how I thought I'd be the real thing. You know—a rented place, Lu; and me in one of those flimsy see-throughs, lying about on the settee eating soft centres, and Mantovani on the radiogram. But know what, Lu? Know all I got out of it?' She drummed angrily on the table: 'A ruddy great brooch I'm scared to put on. And a tartan two-piece he's bought at cost—I'd not be seen *dead* in it, it's that awful.'

Then catching sight of the café clock, she jumped up guiltily: 'I said I'd be back twelve. Heck.' She pushed out ahead of me:

'You coming up, Lu?'

No, I said : I was going to stay by the river for a while; sit around a bit. But I'd do the ride with her if she'd rather?

She shook her head. At the bottom of the hill, leaning on our bikes, we parted.

'Give us a ring sometime, Lu!'

I turned my head away; I was nearly in tears and didn't want her to see it.

When she'd been gone a few moments, I wheeled my bike over to the river bank on the opposite side of the bridge, and parking it, sat down on the grassy slope leading to the water. It was much quieter here: the wide path, flanked by river and meadow on one side and grassy hillocks on the other, led right through into the country. Elizabeth never wanted to come here: without cafés or souvenir shops, it hadn't enough life and bustle. Nor did my mother bother with it (not, of course, that she liked the other side either. 'Vulgar in the summer, Lucy. And *dead* in the winter!'). But when I was a small child, my father had often brought me here on Sunday mornings. I'd been allowed to climb, and then roll down the hillocks—not once or twice, but again and again, eyes tight shut, rolling and rolling; carefree, trusting, 'Promise to catch me!', the grass smelling sometimes damply fresh, or at summer's height, baked and powdery. 'Promise to catch me!' And at the end of the chute, he was always there. Laughing, giving me a little upwards push. 'Again, lovey? Again?'

Then one Sunday, buying me an ice cream, he'd said: 'I'm just off, to see a man about a dog. Wait here and don't move.'

But the ice was soon finished; and when I'd waited what seemed an age, I grew bored. I began rolling down the grass by myself. At first it was fun, then the third or fourth time I picked by chance on a nettle-covered chute: standing up at the end, frightened, I could already feel the blisters forming, all over my face, arms, legs, thighs; by the time my father came back I was crying helplessly, an elderly woman comforting me. He smelt of beer and peppermint: fetching wads of dock leaves, pressing them onto the weals, he said angrily, 'Didn't I tell you to stay put?'

I had never seen him cross with me before, and on the way home I cried again; when he asked what was up, I said it was on account of the puppy—I had thought I was going to get a puppy.

'Have I to make it up to you?' he'd said then, laughing again; and everything had been all right.

But that was many, many years ago.

Across on the other bank the cows stood in groups, chewing, staring, chewing; a punt came by, the pole splashing clumsily. The sun had come out now, but it was very close still—little clusters of insects hung above the water. I sat, hands hugging my knees, and thought about Elizabeth; worrying, wondering, trying to think of some practical way to help. A best friend, I felt, should be more than just confidante. But what, really, to do? For a moment, with a nonsense flight of fancy, I thought of confiding in Nell and Quentin:

as if somehow, nonchalant, amused, assured as they always seemed, they would, against all reason, be able to deal with the problem.

But this sudden wild thought only added to my own confusion. I didn't want to think about the Inglesons. The world of Elizabeth had invaded another world already in turmoil; my own half-stirred, half-terrified flesh was living in yesterday still; when she'd told her story, different as it was I had not been able to disentangle it from mine. All was obstinately merged, flailing limbs, panting bodies, a moorland stream, the back seat of a Rover—what follies, real or imagined, had we not both committed?

In the distance a clock struck twelve. Pushing my bike up the hill to home, a rush of longing came over me: I longed, perversely, for the old simplicity back. For the two of us. Giggling about French kisses, giving the eye to boys on the bus:

'You're *hopeless*, Lu. I've told you till I'm sick—you have to *practise*. Look at Hedy Lamarr like. Even *she'd* to start somewhere—didn't she?'

Chapter 15

That night my mother had a very bad attack of asthma.

'No one can possibly blame poor Pugin and his moulting for this,' she murmured, propped up on pillows, fighting for breath. Before leaving for work I arranged for Dr Varley to visit her.

In the evening when I got home, his car was parked outside; and as I walked in I saw him coming down the stairs, my father just behind him.

On the hall light shade was a cobweb of enormous complexity, but Dr Varley, standing directly underneath, didn't notice it. He said, almost reprovingly, 'You'll have to be some help, Lucy. I'm sending your mother away for a little rest. She's been overdoing it again.'

My father said nothing. He looked edgy and embarrassed.

'A really good rest,' said my mother upstairs plucking agitatedly at the eiderdown. She began to cough; her lips had a queer bluish tinge. 'It appears that Peter has some insurance that covers a nursing home—I don't think the General would have been at all restful.'

She was to go in the morning: as I packed for her, looking around for another bedjacket—the one she was wearing was shrunken and matted—my eyes travelled towards the sewing box; I wondered if I would be able to resist looking while she was gone. What might she not have said to Gervase now?

Downstairs, my father and I avoided each other's gaze with an ease born of years of practice.

'Varley seems to fancy she'll pick up soon enough with some nursing care,' he said. 'It's the change complicating matters. He wants to keep her under observation.'

We were sitting over supper. I made the mistake of asking him whether he'd enjoyed the extra day in London.

Pushing his paper aside, he said angrily, 'Why the hell should *you* care? You're not bothered here. Why the sudden interest about there?'

'I only asked,' I said, retreating behind *Woman's Own*.

He said nothing then, till towards the end of the meal, when flapping the pages of the paper loudly, he remarked, 'I see Princess Elizabeth's to visit Harrogate. What about it—hadn't you and Winifred best start booking front seats?'

Silent, sullen almost, I was reminded at the same time of my Elizabeth, ashamed that I'd forgotten her all day. But when, straight after the meal, I telephoned her, it was Mrs Horsfall who answered. Elizabeth was on duty she told me.

Fearing one of her little talks—she sounded as worried as always —I excused myself hurriedly.

The next morning Richard telephoned, during the tea break. Stella, her mouth full of chocolate biscuit called over, surprised, 'For you, Lucy!'

Never thinking for a moment that it might be Elizabeth, knowing at once that it was him, I lifted the receiver; Stella winked at one of the younger girls, Maureen, who mouthed back at her, 'Boy?'

'Hallo,' I said, nervously.

Richard sounding nervous too, said, 'I tried to—I should have rung you on Sunday—' There was a lot of giggling in the room and I could hardly hear him, 'Then I was away in Doncaster till late yesterday. But I wondered'—there was another loud burst of giggling—'could you—would you like to come for a drink this evening?'

By covering up one ear I could just make out the arrangements. We were to meet outside at six. But as soon as I put the phone down, Maureen said to me, '*Was* it a boy then?' And Stella, cutting in, said, 'Eh, can't you tell the difference?'

'Not with their clothes on, I can't,' said Maureen, stacking up the tea cups, 'ta very much.' They bent over, giggling.

Mr Jowett, coming into the room just then, said disgustedly, 'I've not heard myself think this half hour. Lunch! Playtime in the Infants more like.' He blew his nose very hard. 'If you must giggle—do it in your stockinged feet can't you?' Then he glared at me: 'And I'll have you in, lass. Now.'

Late in the afternoon, he sent for me again, keeping me in till the last minute. As if sensing my tense anticipation he went over every sentence with painful deliberateness. 'And I'll have a semi-colon there. No. A comma, a *comma*—'

In the end I was nearly late. Richard was already waiting outside, and Maureen and another girl running down just ahead of me, cast curious backward glances, before giving their heels that little flick that meant running for the bus.

I said at once, 'I've kept you waiting.' I was surprised that any words came out at all.

'But no,' he looked awkward and hot. 'It's awfully nice of you to come.'

We crossed the road to where the car was parked, under the lime trees; the roofs of the cars which had been standing all day were stickily spattered with yellow blossom. As we drove off, we made stiff formal conversation. I told him about my mother; concerned, he asked, 'Is it serious?'

I explained about the asthma. 'She's had it for years. Ever since I can remember.'

'Phil had it,' Richard said. 'But only as a boy—he'd grown out of it by nine or ten.' In the heat, the sweat was running down his forehead.

'It's very hot,' I said.

'Yes. It's going to be a wonderful summer.'

We had run out of topics. I tucked my feet in their worn sandals under the seat, and wondered in the silence if I wasn't being taken out from a sense of duty: a peace offering perhaps to cancel out Saturday? The picnic was with us in the car; I couldn't look at his hands on the wheel without wanting to touch them.

We sat with our drinks on a window-seat looking out on to a stretch of garden. The hotel was one I'd often passed but never been into; I remember now that there was a great show of roses and that the lawn needed cutting.

'I shouldn't drink,' I said impulsively, 'I'm not accustomed to it. On Saturday—' I took a big gulp of unwisely chosen gin, choking on the smell: 'My grandfather, my mother's father, you see, *died* of drink.'

When I'd said it, I was afraid he might laugh. But he only said, very seriously, 'How tragic, Lucy.' So I explained that my mother wasn't really sure *what* she thought; and it was all complicated, I said, by her feeling that teetotallers were somehow not quite gentlemen.

He laughed at that. We finished our drinks, and then he said:

'I've just thought—if it's all right without any notice, if you're not expected at home that is—may I give you dinner here? It's not the heights gastronomically, but I believe the salmon's not bad.'

We sat once again by a window, the evening sky yellow now. There was some white wine with the meal and I drank freely of this.

'Tell me more about Patmore,' he said, filling my glass, adding : 'I did in fact mention it at home, and apparently your uncle was much swooned over at one stage—not by Mother, who's frightfully unromantic—but one girl they knew was always angling hopefully to meet him. She'd bought a copy of his poems, I think it was?'

I told him about the Memory Box; and the privately published poems. I felt very relaxed, and peaceful.

'Shall you stay with old Jowett?' he asked, later in the meal. 'I can't imagine, you know, that he's awfully good for you.'

I wasn't sure whether to tell him about London: wondering hypersensitively if mention of it might remind him of Juliet. I thought rarely of her now, and when I did so it was to see her that last time, sitting in our house—Richard comfortably jilted—smiling to herself, while my father strummed on the piano and sang and my mother looked annoyed. 'When *I* try to sing,' Juliet was saying, 'just a horrid, *thin* little sound comes out. Poor Juliet!'

'Miss Metcalfe's piece of paper hasn't exactly been a wow,' I said. 'And Mr Jowett did at least take me on. So—' I pulled a face. Then, deciding to tell him all, I described my mother's London plans.

'Do you want to go?' he asked, looking suddenly concerned.

'I don't know. I hadn't thought—I haven't thought,' I said. I finished off my wine, then cutting up some Wensleydale into little pieces I piled them onto a biscuit; when they toppled off, this seemed to me very amusing.

'Couldn't you—' Richard began; he hesitated, his forehead wrinkled, 'I mean, as you say your mother's plans aren't awfully realistic—but that's easily enough remedied. It's just that—the thing is, there's no actual hurry, is there?'

'No, no there's no hurry,' I said with a leap of my heart.

The waiter came over. We arranged to have coffee in the lounge,

F

and in a haze of alcoholic contentment I floated to the Ladies. It was all done in pink and looked like I felt, powdery, cloudy. A woman was bending over one of the washbasins, her rings laid out on the sill in front of her; when she turned, I saw it was Juliet's mother.

I hoped she'd forgotten me, but she said at once, 'Don't I know you, dear?' Screwing up her eyes a little, 'It's *Lucy*, isn't it?'

She reached for the towel, and dried each finger carefully. 'Are you in the bar, dear? We didn't see you there? Ronald and I just dropped in for a quickie—we're on our way back from a party.'

I thought I ought to ask about Juliet. But before I could do so: 'Juliet's doing *very well* in London,' she said, pushing on her rings, 'but naughty, you know—*never* writes to us, unless it's to ask her Daddy for more money.' She gathered up her handbag and gloves: all her movements quick, birdlike. 'I wish Mr Right would come along,' she told me, frowning, at the door.

'Mrs Hirst was in the Ladies,' I said to Richard; I feared very much that he'd seen, or been seen. 'I think they've gone now.'

'Good God,' he said, 'I *have* been lucky—' He was smiling, but he'd coloured too.

I poured out the coffee: 'She's rather incredible, you know,' he said, 'she has this fixation almost, about Juliet and the money. Juliet comes into a jolly big inheritance at twenty-five and Doris is convinced every man must be after it. We're very old acquaintances, and comfortably off and so on, and we're excused—but there was some naval chap during the War— She remains convinced he was on the make. The money's due in August—so God help any worthy but poor suitor after me.'

He'd spoken about her quite easily. The evening wasn't spoilt. The curious feeling of rightness which in the last few hours had been growing, settled. Later, as we came back into Bratherton, he said how much he'd enjoyed it all. He couldn't remember for a long time, he said, anything so pleasant. Please, could we do it again?

Yes, yes of course.

Well then, there was this concert tomorrow evening. The organisers were something to do with one of his mother's committees, he could get tickets very easily. Would I like that? Did I enjoy music?

Before we got out of the car, he kissed me goodnight, very gently. The scent of the lime tree on the corner as we walked up the path together was honeysuckle sweet, overwhelming, heady in the warm June dark.

'That was too bad of Peter,' said my mother, putting to one side a letter I'd brought her from Gervase, 'you *should* know whether he's going to be in or not. Any excuse of course to sleep over at Harrogate. If that's where he was—'

I was frightened that she might ask something about Richard. I imagined that written all over my face was my quiet unquestioning joy: fragile and not to be examined. I had sat with it over an hour in the empty house last night.

Fortunately she noticed nothing. 'I would hardly call this a rest,' she was saying. 'I feel more agitated than at home, just *being* here makes one feel like an invalid.' She sipped some orange squash from the bedside table. 'If you can get in tomorrow, Lucy, would you bring the Memory Box, darling? And that reminds me,' she added, pulling the taggy bedjacket together, 'I wish now, you know, that I'd taken up that friendship with Alice Ingleson, really done something about it. I thought that, perhaps, when I'm better, we could have a small party? A theatre perhaps—then a small supper. Just Alice—and Bernard. And Richard, of course.'

I'd like to be able to remember more about the concert that evening; Saint-Saëns' second piano concerto was the main item, I think: I have a memory of strong rhythms, of tumbling sound and excitement, of audience appreciation; but the crescendos, the diminuendos were for me backgrounds only to my deep joy, as taut but happy I sat beside Richard, so near that I could by moving my head catch the scent of his skin.

In the interval, drinking in the bar, we met two friends of his. We talked about Nell and Quentin. They'd gone away, Richard said, to escape the formal announcement: 'Or rather, the consequences of . . .'

His friends were newly married; they looked closely at me, the girl especially, and at one point she said, 'I hear Juliet's in *London*, Richard?' But Richard merely said, quietly: 'Oh, but that's all off you know.'

157

After the concert we had some supper. Halfway through the meal, during a lull in the conversation, I was struck by a fatigue so complete, such a lightheaded exhaustion that I could hardly hold my head up. I suppose really that for several nights I'd been short of sleep, but this frightening blanket of weariness, my limbs as heavy as my head was airy, seemed to come from nowhere.

I left the rest of the meal untouched. 'All right?' asked Richard. 'Are you sure you're all right?'

Looking at him, his face creased with polite concern, I saw a stranger: the eye of fatigue sharpening the outlines. 'Yes, really,' I said. 'I really did enjoy it.'

And what, I asked inside, is going to come of all this? Seeing that moment, myself in the autumn (perhaps even sooner?) back on the same bench in the Valley Gardens.

On the journey home I was too tired to speak. Richard said apologetically, 'I've kept you out awfully late again. Two nights running.' Tomorrow, he said, he had to see a client; he wouldn't be clear much before nine. 'Could I ring you Friday, or Saturday?'

I wanted to say, 'You don't have to see me each evening;' but I said, instead 'Oh yes.'

Back home again, conscience-stricken suddenly, I rang Elizabeth's hotel. But she was off duty. Leaving a message, I stumbled up to bed.

There was a smell of bacon when I woke in the morning. I came down to find my father already eating, his 1911 Coronation mug beside him full of tea.

I said awkwardly, 'I'd have got that for you.'

He looked up, giving me a quick appraising glance, then said coldly, 'If we each look after ourselves, we'll do well enough.' He drank some tea. 'I write to Mrs Pickering,' he said, 'and you write to Mrs Pickering. It works all right.' Then, looking over the edge of the mug he added casually, 'Who was that took you out last night? Someone from the office?'

'I didn't know you were in—'

'That's not an answer,' he said, staring at me. I was easily discomfited, so rarely did we look at each other, and picking up the newspaper, I hid behind it. The dock strike had worsened, troops had been called out—

'I thought maybe Jowett had taken a fancy to you? It's a nice notion—'

He was wearing a very bright blue shirt which, intensifying the colour of his eyes, made them more piercing. I remembered it as one that more than any other, grated on my mother. 'Such a peculiarly *loud* shade, Lucy!'

'But I don't want to know—as it happens,' he said dismissively. 'If you're starting to lead a normal life, I'm not stopping you. I don't want to know.'

Then abruptly changing the subject, he spoke of my mother. He found visiting her impossible, he said, although he'd been in for the sake of appearances. 'You'll have to see to all that,' he said.

Shaking off my depression, during the lunch hour I bought her a new bedjacket, planning to take it to her straight after work. I was pleased with it: white, elaborate with big drooping sleeves; but because it was of nylon, I worried a little, imagining that she might be disappointed: making her usual remarks about shoddy, man-made fabrics, fingering the material (behind her, more solid business stock than she'd ever care to admit) asking, 'Is this *real*, Lucy?'

But in the late afternoon, when I was taking letters from Mr Jowett, Richard telephoned. His appointment had been cancelled. Could I, would I meet him tonight? Without thinking, I said yes at once: remembering my mother immediately after.

The arrangement had been brisk but as soon as I put the phone down, Mr Jowett who'd grumbled when he handed me the receiver, said resentfully, 'Private calls . . .' Surprising myself, victim of a bad conscience anyway because I wasn't going to see my mother, I replied tartly: 'That was Mr Ingleson. Ingleson and Barraclough. He'd *arranged* to call me.' But I'd already begun to blush and although Mr Jowett, put out, glanced at me with grudging respect, my triumph was shortlived; eleven mistakes in the next two letters completed my routing. By six o'clock I was exhausted.

Richard seemed tired, tense too as if preoccupied. The hotel, a different one this time, was very crowded; we stood with our drinks, the conversation creaking—I wondered whether perhaps two evenings weren't the limit? After that I became boring.

Making an excuse, I went out and telephoned Elizabeth, but the

Horsfall home didn't answer, and she wasn't at the hotel. I could feel, tightening, the knot of worry about her.

'This place is fearfully crowded,' Richard said when I came back, 'and hot too.' Unless I was particularly hungry—what about a walk? The Valley Gardens, if I'd like that—perhaps through on to Harlow Moor?

A child's sock, grass-stained, grubby, lay on the stone shelf at the entrance to the Gardens; I remembered the stiff, frosted glove I'd seen that winter day with Richard, when squirrel-like I had hoarded his every word. This evening as I walked beside him, there seemed few of them to hoard. Once, he said apologetically, 'I'm afraid I'm not awfully good company tonight.' But he offered no explanation. He was very flushed: with the heat, I thought.

I had a feeling of doom. Then as we passed the empty bandstand and came up near the children's pond, he said suddenly:

'Look, there's something I wanted to say. I—' he stopped. He had gone even more red.

'Yes?'

Flustered, he said quickly, 'Sorry, no—forget it, please,' then a moment later, asked me some of the same questions about my mother he'd asked earlier: how was she? would she soon be out? was the nursing home all right?

'And by the way, I forgot,' he said, 'Father Ainslie. I did mention him at home—though I'm afraid as I'd thought, there isn't much.' Brightening now a little, 'Mother's obviously filed it all away mentally and had quite a job resurrecting anything at all. The only item she came up with, was that evidently he'd never eat game. She's no idea whether the embargo was morals or gastronomy or what—but he could smell it out under any guise; devilled, pâté, pie, soup, the lot. Although I gather when things got difficult—later 1917-ish, he ate rabbit and liked it. Anyway,' he said hopefully, 'perhaps it'll turn out to be an idiosyncrasy your mother'd noticed?'

'I'll ask,' I said awkwardly; thinking already with dread of tomorrow.

For a while after that, we talked more easily and as we came out on to Harlow Moor—tame but evocative version of the real thing—we were joking about Mr Jowett. (How had we arrived there, from Patmore?)

Few people were about. It was cooler up here too: the pines

smelling aromatic, resinous, the evening sun showing yellow behind the dark green. We came to a bench in the clearing:

'Shall we—sit down for a while?'

I saw that he'd gone furiously red again.

'Look—' he said, urgently, almost at once after we'd sat down. 'What I've been wanting to say is—' he was frowning now. He leant forward, hands in pockets, head turned away. 'I mean—hell, I'm making an awful mess of this. But the thing is—I'd wondered . . .' He paused, swallowed.

There was a moment's silence; when I looked up, he was staring straight at the ground—pushing with his foot at the scattered pine-needles.

'Lucy, would you—marry me?'

Silence again. He turned and looked at me.

'Yes, please,' I said; tears pricked at once.

'Oh God,' he said, laughing, pulling me towards him, my head against his jacket. 'Oh God.'

Then he saw that I was crying. Trembling, tension releasing itself in great shivers:

'What is it, darling? Lucy, love—what is it?'

It was nothing: just shock, just happiness, 'You see, I thought—' (What was it I had thought?) 'I love you,' I said, 'terribly. I love you terribly.'

'But that's *good*,' he was stroking my hair as he spoke, my mouth still against the material of his jacket, 'God, I haven't done this at all well. I'd meant—I wanted to say, I love you, too—very much. I should have—'

'I thought—you were bored with me.'

'Heavens. Oh God, I *have* done it badly. Darling—I hadn't meant to do it like this at all. It's just that I thought *you* might think—oh God. I didn't know where to begin, you see. The first thing that anyone's going to think, that you're going to think—that it's all on the rebound, only it isn't. God, I *am* muddling this—'

I'd sat up again now. He was still stroking my hair as he spoke; I'd stopped crying, felt calmer, was rejoicing at his fingers, sliding from my hair, pressing my forehead, cheek.

'After that picnic, on the Sunday, I could only think of phoning you—but I couldn't think of a damned thing to say—how to say it even. I just felt . . . Then, well the Tuesday, it went so awfully well,

161

and the Wednesday too. And I thought,' he stopped. 'God,' he said,
'I'm getting this all wrong. Only—you see, it's as if I'd known. It
was one of those—you must think me . . . God, *three days*. Only, I
thought, if I asked you now—as it were *shocked* you, began that
way round—it would be the best—we could go on from that.
Heavens, I'm putting this awfully badly—'

Behind us in the bushes was a persistent scratching, scuffling
sound. A loud voice some distance away, called: 'Mischief,
Mischief—'

'It's like being eighteen, nineteen again. This great age—and I
seem no better at saying anything. Bloody inarticulate—'

An elderly woman, stout, in tweeds, strode into the clearing. She
looked hot and cross. 'Mischief. Where's my Mischief?' Swinging a
dog chain, she glanced over at us incuriously, then called again
'Mischief!', sharp, peremptory. There was some more scuffling and a
tiny Yorkshire terrier came out of the bushes, silken fringe
disturbed, tartan coat dusty, twigs clinging. 'Naughty Mischief,' she
exclaimed, bending down awkwardly, clipping on the lead. 'Wicked
boy.'

'A coat, in this weather,' said Richard as, Mischief under her arm,
she walked off; we laughed relievedly.

And that scene by a freak of memory, is what remains most
vividly of the evening, so that shutting my eyes, I see, I hear the
absurd exchange as if it were yesterday. For the rest: I chase
through a blur. What, really, did he say? He *did* fumble for words,
he *did* find it difficult to say how it could all have been; it *wasn't* a
dream.

But it was a dream come true, and I hadn't—never had—made
provision for that.

Later, over cold chicken and salad, we discussed practicalities.
There were enough of them.

'I feel rather bad—I haven't met your parents at all, and—and
permission, and so on. You're awfully young—I mean, I keep
forgetting.'

About his family: there would be no worry, he was sure of that.
'It's just the suddenness that's going to surprise—and there'll be
frightful cracks about fast work, and rebound—' But then, it wasn't
as if we were necessarily going to marry in such haste. Only, on the
other hand, *not* a long engagement—What did I think?

Unbelieving, excited, I joined in the exciting, unbelieving exchange: the 'I thought that you thought', 'how silly', 'how wonderful', 'but when did you?', 'if only I'd *known* . . .'

(Where was Juliet's ghost that night? Not abroad I think).

'Love first,' he was saying, 'love *first*, and—and get to know afterwards . . .'

Chapter 16

In the morning, I found a note on the kitchen dresser which I must have missed the night before. In Mrs Pickering's handwriting, it read: 'Ring Mrs Horsefall urgent.'

Still in a floating dream—I hadn't for sheer happiness slept all night—I picked up the telephone. Mrs Horsfall answered at once.

'Lucy? Is that you, Lucy?' Her voice was loud, angry: 'Lucy, there's been things kept back. And I'll not have it—'

'What?' I tried to ask carefully, 'not have what?'

Her voice boomed back down the ear piece: I could almost feel her body quivering:

'Things I'd not mention on the exchange, Lucy! Something not very *nice* at all ...' Then, in the voice she usually kept for Elizabeth: 'We're going to get to the bottom of this. You're to come round and see me *this evening.*'

A bit shaken, I promised hurriedly that of course I'd do my best.

I had only just put the receiver down when the telephone went again. Richard. Instantly, everything to do with the Horsfalls went out of my head.

'Are you sure you're all right, darling? Did you sleep *at all?* You're not worrying about anything? Promise? Your father—did you see him? Shall *I* ring him?' Then: 'Everyone here's *tremendously* pleased. Awfully bucked. No worries there at all.' He was arranging for me to meet his parents tomorrow evening. 'And your mother—you'll see your mother today?' Twice I pinched myself; thought: this isn't real.

All morning in the office I was full of suppressed excitement, bubbling inside me so that I felt someone would surely guess: even my footsteps were springy, but except for Mr Jowett looking at me oddly once or twice, no one noticed anything at all.

At twelve o'clock I set off for the nursing home carrying the bedjacket and the Memory Box, which I'd stuffed into a holdall. My mother was half-sitting, half-lying when I came in; her hair, limp-looking today, dusty, was carelessly bundled up. She was gazing aimlessly out of the window, the lines of her face heavy.

'Darling,' she said reproachfully, 'you didn't come yesterday!' Her fingers tapped the sheet. 'No one did. Not even *Peter*. And that letter from Gervase. It's too bad. He wants us early this year,' her mouth twitched. 'But the date he suggests—it's quite impossible.' She sounded near to tears. 'There's not a *hope* I shall be released from this purgatory in time.' A pin fell from her hair and she left it lying on the sheet. 'Is that the Memory Box in there?' she asked, dully. But when I took it out she wasn't interested. 'Push it into the cupboard,' she told me.

At that moment a nurse came in with her lunch. Pale, mutilated cabbage, a slice of corned beef, some waxy potatoes. Steam rose from the oval dish of milk pudding alongside.

As the nurse left, 'Tapioca', exclaimed my mother disgustedly, keeping up the myth that food at home was invariably delicious. 'And in this weather, Lucy!' She toyed with a few mouthfuls of potato.

I took the carrier bag with the bedjacket, and passed it over:

'For *me*?' she asked, half-heartedly curious. She looked doubtful. Then lifting the jacket from its tissue folds, shaking it out, her face lit up:

'But it's lovely, darling!' Trying it on at once: 'But it's lovely,' she repeated, 'so glamorous. So—' she patted it, adjusting the ribbons, searching for words.

Suddenly fearful that I was going to cry: 'And that's not all,' I said, 'there's something else. I mean—something I have to tell you.'

She looked up then, alarmed. 'What's happened, Lucy?' She repeated it, urgently: 'What has *happened*?'

'Richard,' I said in a squeaky voice. 'You know—Richard.'

'Tell me,' she said sharply.

'Well, he asked me to marry him, and I said yes—'

'*What*?' She stared incredulously, I said it again, slowly, spelt it out. But she still went on staring: until quite suddenly, throwing open her arms, her face quite radiant, she called out:

'Darling, come here, darling!' Then hugging me, so violently that I was afraid for her, 'Darling!' she said, breathlessly; I could feel her heart thudding. Something faintly medicinal blended with the characteristic smell of her skin. As she sat back again, holding my hand in hers, I noticed that her eyelids were fluttering. But then, putting her head on one side, looking very serious she said:

'Lucy, you are *sure* about this?'

'Of course,' I said, puzzled. 'Of course yes.'

'I mean, darling—it isn't just possible that you *misunderstood* something? Some—some *action* of his? I mean, he did actually ask? You've not been a little goose, and thought that--' She frowned, bit her lip.

But when, surprised, I assured her that yes, it really was true, then she burst out: 'I *knew* it!' in a triumphant voice.

She leant forward, almost girlish, chin tucked into the palm of her hand. A stream of questions gushed from her; but she was too excited to listen to any answers. A feverish quizzing, barely coherent. 'I knew it,' she kept telling me. 'I had this dream, darling—' She waved the ribbons of the bedjacket about. 'I shall write to Gervase, this *very* afternoon,' she was exclaiming, when a nurse came in. 'You know, it seems incredible I've never met Richard. I feel as if, somehow—'

'But we haven't eaten *at all*,' said the nurse disapprovingly, looking at the tray.

My mother declared joyously: 'My daughter's brought me the most marvellous news.' Excitement was forming beads of sweat on her forehead. 'She's just got engaged!'

'*Isn't* that nice now?' said the nurse. She looked at me over her glasses; then plumping up my mother's pillows behind her, 'And a lovely new bedjacket, too!' she said patronisingly. 'Aren't we spoilt?'

Soon after, I left; but up to the last minute my mother was pouring out excitement, plans, ideas: looking tremblingly, dangerously happy. It was only then when I was halfway down the drive, that I realised there was one question about Richard she hadn't asked: she had never asked me whether I loved him.

Work hadn't started again when I got back to the office. Two of the principals were out, also Mr Jowett. Stella had brought me some egg sandwiches and I ate them while we all looked at Maureen's

Polyfotos of her new boy-friend. We were each to be allowed to choose one: she was cutting them up now with the office scissors.

'It's got a real look of Tyrone Power, has this one, Maureen,' said Stella tactfully, holding it up to the light. They all looked like dark-haired Mickey Rooneys to me.

Suddenly, with a stab of memory—and it was almost as if I'd wilfully forgotten—I realised that I'd still told my father nothing. In the nursing home, he hadn't even been mentioned: yet a mere nurse had been told. Perhaps, I thought, I could ring him at work? Only how to do it without being overheard? how to do it anyway? Feeling torn, indecisive, the edge of my happiness chipped, I imagined the brisk: 'Well—what is it then?' Or, worse: instant mockery. 'That's likely—I'll say!'

But when I got back to Bratherton there was no sign of him, and no message. My grandmother had no telephone. Tired, and rather flat now, I ate a quick supper and about seven, set off for Elizabeth's.

Mrs Horsfall received me coldly. She walked ahead of me along the passage, her uncorseted buttocks in their puce Moygashel seeming to move almost independently of each other. Her presence breathed indignation.

There was no sign of Elizabeth; Mr Horsfall, his shirt sleeves rolled, was sitting peacefully in an armchair. Mrs Horsfall shooed him out. Then, patting the sofa beside her, her expression grim:

'I'll come *straight* to the point,' she said. I sat down hesitantly next to her. 'You know Elizabeth's in Trouble, don't you?' She stared at me.

There was an awkward pause. Foolishly, I hadn't spent any time beforehand thinking what to say: flustered, playing for safety, I said stupidly,

'Isn't she very well at the moment?'

Mrs Horsfall put her hand on my arm; she was shaking with suppressed rage. 'Poorly? Elizabeth's not *poorly*—and that you know.' She looked away from me, 'There's been facts kept back, Lucy—but *Nature* doesn't deceive. All this feeling sick and three times not able to go to work, with no proper explanation—it's not taken *me* long, I can tell you, to put two and two together.' Then as if from some immensely fecund past (for which she had certainly been built), almost triumphantly she added: 'A mother always *knows*, you know.'

She leant forward, adjusting the buckle of her open sandal; the action sent up a wave of her characteristic smell, stronger even than usual in the heat. 'Madam may deny the whole thing,' she went on, 'but I've not lived with her all these years, Lucy, not to know when there's something to hide.' She was still bent over. I could see big white flakes of scurf dotted about the coarse frizz of her hair.

'Lucy—look at me!' It was the same bright red face, looming nearer, that had held me hemmed in corners for so many confidential talks. 'Now, Lucy. Tell me. Which boy is it, that's at the back of this? Which boy?

'Come on,' she said angrily, 'out with it now.'

She sat there, squarely, her broad thighs slightly apart, straining the already creased Moygashel. 'That Andrew now?' She screwed her eyes up suspiciously, 'That Andrew she was so keen on. What of him?'

She had me there; if I said it wasn't Andrew, my 'no' would suggest I knew the real truth. Lack of sleep was catching up with me. I floundered: something about being out of touch.

Getting up suddenly, she went over to the door and shouted up the stairs: 'Elizabeth!' As she came back beside me on the sofa, she announced ominously:

'I'll get that lad's name, Lucy—if we're here all night.'

Elizabeth slipped in quietly. The change in her appearance shocked me. Her high colour had faded, her manner was limp, apologetic; only her hair, fuzzier than ever, stood out nearly horizontally from her face.

She murmured 'Hallo, Lu' without looking at me, then sitting down, she took out a handkerchief and began pulling at it with her teeth.

'Control yourself, Elizabeth!' said Mrs Horsfall, sharply. Then looking at me, her hands planted firmly on her thighs:

'Lucy won't help me at all,' she announced angrily.

'Good old Lu,' said Elizabeth tearfully; she was still chewing the handkerchief. Enraged, Mrs Horsfall shouted:

'Let me tell you, Madam—we're sat here, all of us, till something's out!'

There was silence. No one moved. The room felt very close; a bluebottle buzzed furiously against the window. There was a bowl of cherries on a small table near me; some had gone mouldy and a winey fermented smell rose from them. I thought, feeling trapped, that we might well sit here all night. I couldn't imagine Mr Horsfall daring to come back uninvited.

Elizabeth had begun to sob.

'I'm waiting,' said Mrs Horsfall.

Then, without warning, she leant over suddenly towards her. 'Dirty girl!' she said. Elizabeth put her hand to her mouth. 'Boy mad,' she said, 'you're boy *mad*.'

'Give over!' shouted Elizabeth, 'you just give over.' There was a second's silence; then in an angry, hissing voice:

'George,' she burst out, 'George rotten Turnbull. There's your name for you,' she was pulling the handkerchief this way and that. 'With a wife and a great grown son and daughter, and a business selling gents coms and underpants. He drives a dirty great Rover and all,' she shouted, 'and he took me for a ride—that's what. Took me for a *ride*!'

She stood up quickly, and with a sort of strangled sob she rushed past us and out of the room; I could hear her banging up the stairs; but when I got up to go after her, Mrs Horsfall, obviously shaken, clutched my arm. 'No you *don't*.

'You'd best go home now, Lucy,' she said stiffly as, still holding on to me, she propelled me towards the door:

'I'd counted on you,' she said sadly, almost pushing me from the porch. Her smell was overpowering. I thought that perhaps if I waited she would go, and I could nip upstairs to Elizabeth; but she stood on in the doorway. 'You've let me down. I'll not deny it, Lucy.' Her whole body seemed to be shaking now.

I was more upset than I realised: my legs quivering, my head pounding, I walked the short distance up the hill, back home. There was still no sign of my father. I tidied up a little; then in the sitting-room, wrote to Elizabeth, addressing it to the hotel. I'd never written to her before and it felt strange; she'd never needed my help before either, so that felt odd too. My own news I didn't mention.

Richard rang about ten. I was waiting up, I told him. And yes, I was sure my father would come in any moment. I sat on in a sort of waking dream, the wireless on, the curtains not drawn and moths fluttering and banging against the panes. I listened through Jack Jackson—sometimes hearing, sometimes not.

When the wireless closed down I gave up the wait. Fatigue hit me suddenly, and climbing into bed I fell asleep at once.

I could hear sounds below, when I woke. I thought, I'll get the revelation over quickly, and came down in my dressing-gown. My father was already sitting at the table, reading the paper and pulling at a cigarette. I sat down opposite him and poured myself a glass of milk. But when I tried to speak, nothing happened.

He looked up suddenly. 'It's out,' he said. 'Your secret's out.'

I glanced over; he was staring straight at me. 'What secret?' I said foolishly. My face was flaming; the feeling was one I knew well. Trapped, very much in the wrong, a mere nurse had been told first.

'I couldn't get hold of you yesterday. I did try—'

'Oh—so.' He whistled. 'Well, don't kid yourself that I think you or Winifred give a damn whether I know what's going on or not. Do you?'

I bent my face over the glass of milk.

'And sudden,' he said, 'it's that all right. Not a *hint* of a courtship.' He raised his eyebrows: 'I thought then you'd spurned our local lads?'

I didn't, couldn't answer; I pressed my legs hard against the chair, wishing desperately that the talk would soon be over.

'Don't get me wrong,' he said, 'I'm—pleased enough. I've given my permission. I'm all for *romance*, you know.' He stubbed out his cigarette. 'And from what I could make out last evening, you've nearly given your mother a seizure with joy. Her legacy yielding a hundred per cent, the White Rose in full bloom. Patmore Regained. Or as good as.'

His voice had said that he was pleased; his manner told me that he was angry.

'And I hear it's to be quite soon,' he went on, 'not for the usual reasons I take it?' Then before I could reply, 'I doubt it', he said heavily. 'They're very safe, are Patmore circles. All pressed flowers and purity.'

He took out a fresh packet of cigarettes. 'No doubt I'll be meeting him?'

'Yes, yes of course.' I'd thought I might be going to cry so I'd pulled my face into a sullen, tight expression. 'Of course.'

'Well,' he said, 'if he's like his dad, he's a ruddy bore.' He lit a cigarette, then he looked at me slyly: 'I note he wasn't able to keep your friend Juliet amused?'

'Who told you that?'

He stared at me. 'Who do you think?' he said casually; going out of the room, throwing the newspaper across to me as he went.

Oh Juliet, Juliet who had dared to talk like that in a chance railway conversation. I got up to go, pushing the newspaper aside. As I turned, I saw my father standing in the doorway.

'I'm sorry,' he said. He seemed embarrassed. 'I'm sorry. I shouldn't have said the half of that.' He paused. I glanced at him: the expression on his face was part friendly, part mocking.

'Any road,' he said, 'I wish you *great* happiness.' He ran a finger over his moustache: 'And no regrets, either. I'm not sure I don't wish you that most of all,' he said, going out. 'No regrets.'

Trying to conjure up a memory of Alice Ingleson, I'd managed only a blurred picture: in plum satin, standing in the doorway at the dance. Now, in the flesh, she was more angular, business-like than I'd remembered. Greeting us at the door, dressed this time in button-through, faded green linen, she kissed me briskly, then after saying a couple of times that she'd been very surprised 'and of course delighted, my dear, (Richard tells us nothing)' she, amazingly to me, changed the subject altogether. As we sat, waiting for Richard's father, she chatted in a matter of fact way, of this, that, the other—as if I'd been asked over as the most casual of social acquaintances.

Once, she said: 'Has anyone told Nell?' Richard nodded. 'Good,' she said briskly, going on immediately to remark that there were black weevils in the greenhouse. Some one would have to turn the place out—Richard pulled a face.

Then the telephone rang, the third time already, and while she was dealing with it Richard's father came in. A tall, quiet, dusty man, he reminded me of Nell in the fullness of his features only. His manner was dry: in explanation of the telephone,

'My wife's got this big do on, next month,' he said. 'She's landed

171

herself with organising the teas *and* organising the organisers of all the stalls.' After that, except for saying : 'We're all very happy for you,' and of the wedding, 'Christmas. I hear it's to be Christmas,' he treated my presence there with mild astonishment while managing to suggest at the same time that I was already an old accepted member of the family.

'Remind me sometime,' he said, 'remind me sometime to tell you of a few *certain* methods of discomfiting old Jowett.'

Beforehand, Richard had said, 'We shan't need to stay very long.' Now, nervous, rather restless, he'd already looked at his watch a couple of times,

Juliet had been mentioned only once: 'As Richard knows, I didn't care for her,' Alice Ingleson said, in the tone of voice of someone discussing an item of food. Towards the end of the visit, Richard reminded her about the Foxton-Tukes and Patmore. (It seemed to be the first Bernard Ingleson had heard about the connection.)

'I must look out a few old photographs—when I have a moment. There are a great many, somewhere. Nell may know more about them—she went off to Cambridge with several last summer. A game of spot the relative, I think. Some undergraduate nonsense, at any rate.'

'Well—that's over. And I think, really, it went awfully well.'

Hand in hand, we walked over to Harlow Moor. I was exhausted, shivering as we passed the dreaded reservoirs, the water gleaming darkly in the afternoon sun.

We sat down, on the same bench as two days ago. Richard said: 'I've got something for you. Stupid, and bloody sentimental of me, but I wanted to give it to you up here.'

He took a small box out of his pocket; then watched my face as I opened it. Inside was a ring, antique, a pale ruby set in heavy gold. He said anxiously :

'I feel rather awful. I should have asked—'

'But it's lovely!'

He placed it on my finger. 'It was my aunt's—Mother's sister, Frances. She died just before the War. Her fiancé had been killed at Suvla Bay—she'd wanted it to go to the eldest child. But, you know—if you'd rather choose something yourself?'

I shook my head vigorously. I could hardly speak for happiness.

The weight of the ring on my finger was odd, unaccustomed. Sitting very still now, my head on Richard's shoulder, I could just glimpse the stone. I fancied I had never seen anything more beautiful.

How my mother will love it, I thought suddenly; and as I did so there came over me such a feeling of security as never before or since. Surrounded, enclosed. Richard, Richard's love; Uncle Gervase, Patmore, my mother; Richard's love, Richard. This tight, safe circle.

'Darling, you're *quite* sure?'

'I do. I do love it. I love *you*.'

So secure within: why look without?

Chapter 17

The engagement was to be announced the next week. The evening before it came out, my father, Richard and I all had dinner together.

It seemed that nowadays, I had only to dread an occasion for all to go well. My father was jaunty, his colour high; at first I'd been wary, watchful. But 'Grand,' he said about everything, about all our plans, 'that'll do grand.' Amused, yet pleased, possibly even slightly proud of me.

He talked a lot—although he hardly spoke directly to me at all; but Richard didn't seem to notice this, and I was used to it. That they seemed on the surface anyway, to be getting along well together was good enough for me. After dinner, Richard getting my father onto one of his favourite topics, music halls, said he'd heard how good a mimic he was.

'Well a bit more to drink,' my father said, 'and I'll give you George Formby senior.'

He had another brandy. We were warm, laughing, relaxed.

Afterwards we went back to Bratherton, to the house, and he sang 'Oh Flo', and 'A dark girl dressed in blue' and 'When we went to Brighton on our famous motor car'.

It was a good evening.

My mother had been mentioned only once:

'How do you find her?' my father asked.

'Excited,' I said.

She'd told me yesterday that her breathing was easier, that she felt much better, but 'excited' still described her best. Rapture succeeding rapture. Today, it had been photographs brought by Alice Ingleson (one, oh happy miracle, had been of Patmore).

'And do you know, Lucy,' she'd said incredulously, 'Alice hadn't even looked at these photographs, for over *twenty* years! Can you imagine?'

The ring of course had enchanted her, and she was sure, immediately, that she remembered Frances.

'A rather gawky, dreamy girl, Lucy.' Then, fingering the ring: 'Burmese. That's a Burmese stone, Lucy,' she said authoritatively. 'Pigeon's blood. The *best*, of course.'

I hadn't worn the ring to the office, but the day the announcement appeared I put it on boldly. Stella was delighted: 'I *knew* there was something up—I said to Maureen, didn't I, Maureen?'

Mr Jowett was unimpressed. I'd already had to ask him for two days' leave: Richard and I were to go up to tea at Gunter's, in place of my mother. Now, he blamed the White Rose.

'Fancy training,' he said, again. 'Fancy. Just as I thought—good for getting yourself wed, and nowt else.'

I'd been dreading the announcement, sensing it as the beginning of a complicated ritual which would take me farther and farther away from Richard. He tried to reassure me:

'The sooner everyone's told—the sooner all the fuss is over . . .'

For my mother, however, the fuss couldn't go on long enough. Sitting up in bed with *The Times*, *Telegraph* and *Yorkshire Post*, she read and re-read the insert. The *Yorkshire Post* had carried a small paragraph about Richard—his war service, family, and so on: 'Of course, I regret a *little*, Lucy, that we weren't able to work in anything about the Tinsdales—after all, darling, these *are* the things people want to know. And surely *someone*, Lucy, could have told the editor of the Foxton-Tuke connection?'

But these were mere pinpricks; she was soon distracted by pleasure at the pile of post which the announcement brought me. Most of it I handed to her unread, and she sat up, entranced, surrounded by envelopes. It was as if her own drab, defiant wedding had left her with a great hunger for all the trappings.

'All these exciting, *generous* offers, Lucy!' Half a dozen London photographers wanting to attend the wedding, a dozen makers of this and that wanting to offer discount: she took everything as a personal favour.

'Old Nell's are all still sitting in her room—not opened,' Richard told her.

'Quite incredible,' my mother remarked to me, afterwards. 'To be so *casual*.'

Nell and Quentin came back. There'd been a joint card from them a couple of days before: a 'really?' from Nell and a '*really!*' underneath, from Quentin. I'd dreaded their return. But as soon as Nell saw me:

'Love, we're absolutely thrilled—honestly. God, the excitement. And Richard looks all soft and happy.' She hugged me carelessly. 'Sweetie, it must have been *coup de foudre*. Really. When I think of Q and me, our sober carry on—half a bloody century, and you two take only *days* . . .'

She didn't mention Juliet, as I'd feared. Quentin did however :

'You *have* surprised us, Lucy Locket! I shut up shop for a week, and come back to find Cornwall Road in an uproar. *And* the final rout of Blackett's,' he added (Richard wasn't there), 'that was the best work of all, Locket.' He looked at me, eyebrows raised. His expression was warm, affectionate, but I could have wished he hadn't made the remark.

Letters began to arrive. There was nothing from Elizabeth though, and she hadn't answered my note. Nobody had heard from Juliet; I rather hoped they wouldn't. Jennifer, in an excited scrawl, wrote: 'You dark horse! Ring me up soon, and tell me all about it—we *must* meet.' There was even a letter from Miss Metcalfe. Wishing me every happiness, she still wasn't able to resist an allusion to the White Rose training: I would find, she said, that it would stand me in good stead—in *any* sort of future I might have.

'My God,' said Quentin, reading it, 'imagination boggles.'

'*Yours* doesn't,' said Nell; lovingly.

'Winifred's girl, you know,' said Uncle Gervase to the waitress, his head bobbing from one of us to the other. Then, waving the menu card agitatedly, he began to give a confused order: every few seconds breaking off to congratulate Richard; 'Such splendid news!' or chin jutting out, to ask me anxiously, 'Winifred. Winifred. How *is* my Winifred?' The waitress looked suitably puzzled. Eventually, he finished, only to call after her almost immediately—his voice sounding unnaturally loud:

'I say—could you possibly—also. Some ices?' Richard and I trying to explain that no, really, we didn't want anything more, were unable to stop him; as ever people were turning round to look, but for once—for the first time in fact—I wasn't ashamed. Richard, who didn't seem at all embarrassed, was very gentle with him.

When we'd first come into Gunter's, ourselves five minutes early, Uncle Gervase had already been waiting half an hour; even then he'd seemed very over-excited.

Now, 'This really is absolutely splendid!' he said again, 'tremendous!' The nuns: he'd told the nuns and a Mass was being said. 'Be sure to tell Winifred that.'

He darted from subject to subject: 'Alice, ah yes, Alice. A tomboy. Rather a tomboy. And Charles—' The waitress brought the order: 'This looks *jolly* good ...' Then, 'I think you said Ampleforth —I have this *very* good story about Benedictines. Alice nursed, went to Serbia—it *was* Serbia? Charles was Stonyhurst, you see. My contemporary. A—a superb slip fielder. You couldn't I think have known Charles—' Then, confused, distracted by memory he said again: 'Ampleforth'; his arm shooting out suddenly, narrowly missing the milk jug, 'This story now—I have this story. A Jesuit and a Benedictine—both terrific smokers. And—and they felt it the most enormous hardship, you see, wanting to smoke when they should be praying, so the Benedictine went to his abbot. "Father," he said, "do—do you think that I might be permitted to—to smoke, while I'm meditating?" "*No*," said the abbot at once—he was quite shocked, you see, "I forbid it absolutely." No go. But meanwhile the—the Jesuit has been to *his* superior. "Father," he'd said, "I wonder—would it be in order if—I were to mediate, while I'm smoking?" '

He paused. 'It's rather good, don't you think? I—I get all these stories from the girls, you know.' He flapped his sandwich about: a piece of cucumber dropped into his cup; he seemed quite unaware.

'Now look,' he said suddenly. 'Winifred. Is she getting better? These tests? Is she halfway fit again?' He waited anxiously for our answers; he was looking all about him, and I thought I saw tears in his eyes. But when he spoke again, it was to ask me, very concernedly, about the White Rose.

'This—this White Star place. Was it any *good*? Winifred seemed to think so, you know. Languages. Wasn't it languages? You *liked* it?

'Good, good. That's jolly good.' Helping himself to more sugar, he rattled the tongs against the side of the bowl. Two lumps splashed into his cup.

It was splendid of us to come, he said. All this trouble. He'd put everyone to the most enormous trouble. Suppose, perhaps, the *three* of us were to come to Patmore? A visit. 'It would be awfully jolly, you know, if you could.' But when Richard said: 'Well, we're rather hoping, sir, that *you'll* be able to come to us, for the wedding', this seemed to confuse him. Fussed, he knocked his tea cup, the pale liquid slopping into the saucer.

He would have to see. It depended—on a number of things. Something to do with a gardener. Possibly the nuns could . . . well, you know, if he could be *spared*.

His knobbly fingers, with their enlarged knuckles, drummed on the edge of the table. I was touched by what he obviously felt was his importance in the life of Patmore.

He was still agitated when we parted. He'd bought my mother some chocolates; I'd got her some crystallised violets. 'Does she—does Winifred still like those?' It seemed to jog his memory: 'I wonder, would she? Would Winifred?' Then Richard invited him to dine with us that night, and he was thrown into a fresh panic.

No, no, he said. He assured us excitedly, he was doing something else. Yes, he was *certain* he was. Moving back suddenly, jerkily; stepping off the kerb, almost into the traffic.

We were to spend the night with an aunt of Richard's, in Knightsbridge. She was the widow of his father's brother, so that I couldn't hope this time to be helped by any family resemblances.

But, yet again, all went well. We sat over drinks in the long drawing-room. His aunt smoked a lot, and was very smart, dressed with an expensive carelessness which made me wonder why Juliet had ever impressed me. I felt easy with her at once: more interested in me than the Inglesons had been, she gave the impression that if

Richard had chosen me, then her approval could be taken for granted. She teased him a little: he led a very staid life, she said: 'Incorrigibly upright—like Bernard.'

Now, when I think of those two days in London, it is as an idyll. Elated, in a dream world, I saw all the sights, sounds, scents of that hot, dusty July evening, as part of the glamour.

We were to have dinner at Rules. (Gervase, I thought, would have enjoyed that.) Before, Richard said:

'If there's any sort of place you'd like to go to first—any sort of *name*—just ask. Bentley's for instance? Oysters. There won't be any natives this month, but—if you'd *like* to go there?'

I was dazed with happiness. I felt sometimes that my breath was held, suspended, that I would never breathe again.

Of Rules, I remember almost nothing. The Edwardian atmosphere, the signed photographs, the caricatures, the old theatre bills: an impression of dark plush velvet, of courteously superior waiters— they were all just the backdrop for our enchanted, romantic plan-making.

Over claret, we discussed where to go for the honeymoon. Richard loved travel agents' brochures—he'd go to Cook's, he said: get a great pile of them.

Perhaps, after all, we could get married sooner than January? It was certainly something to think about:

'Because, you see, you're sure. You *are* sure, aren't you?'

'Of *course* I'm sure . . .'

The evening was nearly over. Richard was looking at my ring: my hands cupped round a brandy balloon.

'It won't come off,' I said.

He suggested, a little anxious: 'Shouldn't you try to remove it?' He tugged a little, and I winced.

'It's very simple, you know, to get it enlarged. We can go to the family jeweller—'

'It doesn't matter.' I had in fact worn it several days now, since the announcement. 'Anyway, I feel safer with it on.'

Richard looked puzzled; I wondered too what I could have meant. 'Less likely to *lose* it,' I said hastily, and he laughed.

From Maiden Lane, a taxi home.

'Happy, darling?' In Piccadilly, the lights flashed bewilderingly, beautifully: Richard had wanted me to see them—on again now after nearly ten years. Before the War I'd been too young.

How Elizabeth would have loved them, I thought with a stab of conscience; remembering her now, worrying about her, for the first time that day.

Next morning at King's Cross, I was standing at the door of the train waiting for Richard who'd gone to buy papers and magazines. It was hot weather again; the group of tartan-capped soldiers milling about the entrance hall looked creased, uncomfortable. Richard, coming into view, lifted his free arm in greeting. I waved back.

And at that moment, without any warning, panic overtook me. Immediate, total, suffocating: I could feel it as he came into the compartment, leant towards me, as I smelt the familiar scent of his hair, his skin, his hands. The words came clearly into my head: 'One day—he may not be here,' and I sat, heart drumming in terror at the thought that I might ever be separate from him.

Such strong emotion; surely he would notice?

But he was settling himself, stretching his legs, looking at his watch:

'Shall we risk the coffee?'

Yes, I said, of course.

As far as he could see, he said, British Railways weren't much improvement on the LNER. 'But still—'

Slowly, very gradually, the panic subsided. The train moved out and we settled down. He'd bought me a copy of *Vogue* and prolonging the idyll, relishing the glossy feel of the paper, I began to choose my trousseau—what I would buy if money were no object; then coming upon a menu for a dinner party, and appaulled at the realisation, exclaiming: 'But I can't cook!'

No hurry, Richard said, there was no *hurry*; laughing, tolerant, tender:

'Perhaps though—if we're thinking, you know, of advancing the date, darling—we ought to see about perhaps, winding up your job with the Gnome?'

The air was stifling in the train in spite of all possible windows open. For the last hour or so I slept heavily, waking just before we reached York, feeling refreshed, peaceful. We walked along the platform, Richard carrying the luggage, me the magazines. He said:

'How I used to love—still do—those stairs up to the bridge. Do you know? The ones with tin advertisements under the treads— Fry's cocoa, Mazawattee tea—'

He broke off. 'Hallo, hallo,' he said, laughing, '*There's* a surprise—' I looked over: Alice Ingleson was standing just by the ticket barrier; 'That's not like her. It's Woman's Institute day. What *ever?*'

She'd seen us now and was striding over purposefully: she was wearing an old white linen sun hat pulled well down, and looked hot and distracted.

She kissed us both briefly: 'The car's outside,' she told Richard.

'Okay, I'll drive.'

She had taken hold of my arm : in her grip I felt a sudden return of my panic. When she said, almost at once: 'I have some bad news, I'm afraid—' I knew then that I'd known she had.

In a brisk, antiseptic voice, her face turned away from mine, she told me that my mother had died.

'Very suddenly, my dear. This morning— You and Richard had already left—'

Her hand was still on my arm like a weight. There was the clanking and rattling of a station trolley behind us; we stood back for it. Richard had hold of my other arm:

'All right, darling, all right.'

I couldn't see from the cars outside, which was theirs. 'Which car is it?' I said, twice, 'which car is it?'

Then, I was huddled on the back seat. 'You drive,' Richard was saying to his mother. 'I'll sit with her.' I still had hold of the magazines; my hand released them suddenly and they fell, open and twisted, the pages spreading out on the floor of the car. 'I'm sorry,' I said. 'I'm sorry . . .'

Richard bent to pick them up. I could see, looking at me, a grinning face with cherry lips. Snapping the page shut, he bundled them all to the back.

'Sorry,' I said again. 'I'm sorry.'

I had been used to her ill health for years: hadn't, really, taken it very seriously. Nuisance migraine, nuisance asthma (the darkened room, the Roger's spray): distressing as they were, they weren't killers.

And yet, early that morning, in the midst of such violent happiness, she had had a sudden, very severe asthmatic attack—she'd gone into what they called 'status asthmaticus'. Two hours later, she was dead.

They took me back to Cornwall Road. I remember standing in the hall—the three of us, by the big green vase with a crack in it which served as an umbrella stand; there was a smell of stew coming from above and below the baize door leading to the kitchen.

'I must ring my father,' I said, thinking of him suddenly—the first real thought I'd had since getting into the car; I had an image of him: shocked, desolate, wanting me at once.

Alice Ingleson said something to Richard in a low voice.

'Okay then. You deal with it.'

He brought me through into the drawing-room, sat me on the sofa, then bringing me a glass of brandy, sat down beside me, his arm round my shoulders. I had begun to shiver: 'Try some. Drink a bit, darling.' I sipped: tonight it was bitter, medicinal. I drank all of it, very quickly; Richard, stroking my face, my hair, said, 'I know, I know.' Out in the hall, I could hear Alice Ingleson on the telephone. He said: 'She's told Jowett you won't be in tomorrow.'

She came back into the room: I was to stay the night with them, she said; her voice had a gentle edge to its efficiency. My father would come to see me early the next morning.

I sat on—it must have been half an hour or more; I was frozen inside, could feel the hard lump of ice, solid, pressing, painful. Bernard Ingleson came home, and I saw his wife take him aside. Then he was back in the room—the air full of murmured condolences. At supper, conversation was restrained, tactful, solicitous; I stared at my stew with its irrelevant greasy colours, unappetising in the heat. Someone said: 'Try and eat a little.'

After the meal—it was still only half past eight—Alice Ingleson looked out a play on the wireless. We all sat politely and listened. Billed as a comedy, it wasn't I remember, very suitable: there were a lot of jokes of the 'bumping old so and so off' and 'you're better off dead' variety. But after it, they let me go to bed.

I was to have Nell's room, as the guest room wasn't aired. I hadn't been in there since the dance: Nell's belongings were everywhere; Alice Ingleson, coming in with a hot drink and some sleeping pills apologised for the untidiness: 'Quentin is welcome to put up with it.'

Richard, holding me close, asked: 'Shall I stay with you—sit here, till the pills work?'

I shook my head: I would be all right, truly.

At first I lay between the sheets quite rigid; stabs of feeling coming and going; little cracks in the ice; but I still couldn't cry.

Then after a while I got out of bed and going over to the suitcase, took out the crystallised violets. What to do with them? Alongside, lay the chocolates Gervase had bought her. What to do with *those*? The problem struck me suddenly as enormous, the possibilities endless. Perhaps they should be destroyed, or hidden; buried with her, sent back to Gervase, donated to a hospital? Perhaps this, perhaps that, perhaps the other?

I was still worrying at it, when what seemed hours later, I fell at last into a drugged, dreamless sleep.

My father came the next morning; I'd been hovering around waiting and let him in before he rang the bell. Alice Ingleson had already gone out to keep an appointment, the housekeeper was nowhere about, and a woman I'd never seen before was banging the Hoover round the drawing-room: too nervous to ask if we could go in there, I took him instead into the small study where, in December, Quentin had upbraided me over the Italian dress.

We stood and looked at each other.

'They've a big place here,' he remarked awkwardly. 'Bigger than you'd think from the outside.'

His face was very drawn, and that he should be so pale shocked me. His eyes were tired, bloodshot, his hair uncombed, and there was a long shaving cut on his chin. Looking away from me, he sat down suddenly in the swivel chair and taking out a packet of cigarettes, lit up at once. There was an alabaster ashtray on the desk—I pushed it towards him, and noticed that his hand holding the cigarette was trembling. I wondered suddenly, against all hope, if perhaps by some miracle he had really loved her all along?

Crushing in his other hand the packet of Gold Flake, he launched straightaway into practicalities: the plans for the funeral, what they'd said at the nursing home, what Dr Varley had said.

He made some remark about Bratherton church and I said:

'Isn't there—wasn't there—something about being buried at Patmore?'

'No—there wasn't,' he said shortly.

We were both silent for a moment. Then, without looking at me, and as if talking to himself: 'What a rotten, ruddy *mess*,' he said explosively. 'What a marriage! What do you *blame* for a muck-up like that, eh?' When I said nothing: 'A marriage that was dodgy from the start—*and* before.' His hand was still trembling. Stubbing out his cigarette he took another; it was almost flattened. He tried to coax it back into shape:

'I'll tell you something,' he said suddenly, looking at me directly now. 'I knew it was no go. Right from when she ran off, cocked a snook at Patmore, I knew it. Knew it in my stomach. And I could have got out then. If she'd turned up in the flesh at Patmore, they'd have had her back right enough. Only there was no telling me anything those days. Twenty, and stuffed with romantic notions. Stuffed with them from here to here, and a sucker for anything that wasn't blood or mud or death. That was me. Patmore—the flowers that bloom in the spring. They bloomed at Patmore all right—'

He was talking very fast; I wondered if perhaps he'd been drinking. But there was no smell of alcohol. He seemed more shocked than anything: looking at some point beyond me, through me.

'I've been a fool, *and* a knave,' he said. 'Lately though—' he paused. 'Lately—mostly knave.'

I must have looked puzzled because:

'I'll tell you something,' he said, his face working. 'Last month, the month before last—'

184

There was a knock on the door; he started.

It was the housekeeper with a tray of coffee. Taking it shakily from her, 'This is Mrs Johnson,' I said.

She hadn't heard the bell, she told us. We should have gone in the drawing-room; would we like to move in there now?

My father, looking hurriedly at his watch said that it wasn't worth it. He'd be gone soon.

Then at once, after she'd left, his voice rather shaky, 'We'd best get back to practical matters,' he said, 'I've not much time.'

I poured him a cup of coffee; although he didn't take sugar he stirred the spoon roughly round the cup. 'You'll have to take my word for it, about the grave,' he said. 'It'd be a difficult business anyway—even with cremation; and for Catholics it's not on, isn't cremation. I'd a quick word with Father Casey last night.'

'I see,' I said.

He looked at his watch again: 'I'll deal with Ma Pickering. And anything else like that. Meantime—you'd best stop here—if it can be arranged.'

I said that I was sure it could.

'Good.' He stood up, drinking his coffee hastily, then rattled the cup down onto the tray, wiped his moustache. His face looked foxy—in its pallor almost that of a stranger—so that I wondered suddenly: what is he doing in this house?

'I'll ring later, when I've more arranged.'

I followed him out into the hall. We stood there awkwardly: I thought, imagined for one moment that he was going to kiss me: I moved forward. 'Don't give yourself the trouble,' he said. 'I'll let myself out.'

Later that morning I tried to write to Gervase. It proved horribly difficult. Alice Ingleson, back again now, produced writing paper and an envelope— If I preferred, *she* could do it? But I sat at her desk with its bulging pigeon holes and struggled with the awkward phrases; my language came out formal and cold. Still shocked myself, I was setting about shocking someone else, and when I'd finished I felt drained.

After lunch, she insisted that I lie down upstairs. 'Grief is exhausting,' she said in a matter of fact tone, as if discussing the after effects of 'flu. 'If you can't rest though, try and read something light.' She handed me a pile of detective novels, pre-war Penguins with large print: 'You won't find anything suitable in Nell's room.'

The idea was repugnant, terrifying: I couldn't just lie up there for the afternoon. But when I said: 'I ought to go over to Bratherton really,' remembering that I'd packed for two days only and that we'd just arranged, an hour or two ago, an indefinite stay, she answered firmly:

'Richard's seen to all that, my dear. He'll drive you over this evening.'

She left shortly after for a sale of work, which she told me ended at six; I waited upstairs till she'd been gone a few minutes, then got up and leaving a note in the hall, set out for Bratherton.

A headache which had been growing all day hit me as I came out into the baked air. Then, in sight of the house, I wished I hadn't come. I went in by the back way : on the quince tree growing up the wall, there were already half a dozen fruit, wooden, furry. Inside, lavender polish and scouring powder hung in the air; Mrs Pickering must have been in. There were no signs of my father having been about. Standing in the hall I shivered: my head was aching relentlessly now, fiery cramps at the base of my skull. Because it was the thing I feared most, I went straight upstairs to my mother's room—pushing open the door, willing everything to be all right.

The window was shut and it was very hot; two flies buzzed angrily on the sill. Standing in front of the dressing-table I thought I had only to screw up my eyes and I would see her—dressing excitedly for Gunter's, bending a little forward at the glass, pushing her hair under her hat, pulling on her gloves.

I felt dizzy and the room whirled: to recover I sat down on the edge of the bed. I thought that probably I should take the letters from the workbasket—now, at once. When I tried the drawer, I thought for a moment that she had locked it, but it was only a little sticky, and when I looked they were lying there the same as ever, right under the tangle of wools and silks, the odds and ends of material. I didn't look at them at all, but carrying them into my room found a large envelope and crammed them into it. Too painful to read, impossible to destroy—they were to remain there for many years.

I was packing, when the doorbell rang. I leapt up terrified, rushed onto the landing. I didn't for some reason think of Richard, so that when trembling I opened the door and saw him on the step, I couldn't at first say anything.

'Are you sure you're all right?' he said at once, anxiously. 'I found your note. I was through early today—There wasn't much on and old Barraclough wanted to see the client I had booked.' He looked at me closely:

'You're—not all right. You shouldn't have come alone,' he said reproachfully, 'I'd have brought you over, darling.'

'I'm ill,' I said, realising as I said it that it was true; not just unhappy, but ill.

He felt my forehead; his hand was damp, but cool and soothing and so large it banded my brow.

'It might just be the weather,' he said. 'This damned heat is rather too much of a good thing—'

My legs and back were aching intolerably now. He made us some tea while I finished packing; we talked, carefully, about my father's visit.

'It's good that you're staying on. I mean, not just because it's wonderful for me—but trying to cope here, mostly alone, it would be pretty difficult for you—don't you think?'

I wondered if it mattered really very much *where* I stayed.

He held me in his arms: I felt nothing. I really am ill, I thought.

That evening my temperature was a hundred and two. The next day, a hundred and three. Semi-delirious, I lay in Nell's bed, my mind full of images of decay.

My temperature stayed up. Several times a night I would wake up, my nightdress soaked through; I moved on to wearing Nell's now, then old ones of Alice Ingleson's. Their family doctor, sounding my chest, muttered asides about infections in hot weather, overstrained condition etcetera. Nell, back from spending the weekend with a school friend, insisted that I stay on in her room: 'Unless you *want* to move out, love.'

The day of my mother's funeral came and went; I had had to miss it of course. But a couple of nights later I dreamt that I'd been there after all. It was a confused scene—yet with all the curious rightness of dreams. My mother was there, which seemed quite natural;

G

standing about, laughing and talking with everyone. She was dressed as for tea at Gunter's, and looked very happy. Only Richard, who was standing quite alone, looked sad. I wanted to go over to him but I thought: I can do that later.

The coffin was standing in the middle of the room. 'Don't you want to look in it?' said my mother; I turned away. 'Silly,' she said, laughing. 'There's nothing to be frightened of. It's only *Peter* in there—'

I began to laugh too. Then everything became suddenly mixed up with my grandfather's funeral; my laughter went on and on—a loud frightening sound; there seemed no way to stop it. When at last, I woke up, my hand was over my mouth.

Chapter 19

I was up again; I felt very weak and didn't want to do anything but sit about the house. I'd lost a lot of weight; and my ring slid off with ease now. I moved into the guest room. It was large and dark and, even in the heat of the day, felt chill. 'God, isn't it depressing', said Nell, massing flowers round it; begonias, fuchsia, late overblown roses.

The second day up, I mentioned something about Mr Jowett, and found to my surprise that while I'd been in bed, Alice Ingleson had wound up the job for me. 'I hope you're not going to be silly about money,' she said briskly, handing me a cheque. Richard, when I mentioned it, seemed embarrassed. 'God, she's bossy—I should have told you she'd done it.' Kissing me: 'Would you like me to try and get it fixed up again?'

But I couldn't have been bothered.

Surprised that I should have seemed surprised, Alice Ingleson explained that once Nell's wedding was over I would find myself very busy. 'Richard tells me you thought *October?*'

Oddly enough, her high-handed gesture hadn't really upset me: it seemed that the energy even to feel angry was wanting. But the consequent blank in my days I found appalling.

At first it wasn't too bad. There were things to do, even if they were unpleasant. Letters of condolence to answer, for instance; although I was shocked at how few: being the Duchess of Bratherton had obviously not been the way to win friends and influence people.

Gervase's letter had come while I was in bed. 'This is terrible, *terrible*,' he wrote, 'how are we to go on? What *shall I do?*' And then, about the funeral: he was dreadfully sorry, but he couldn't possibly attend. It was a terrible thing, but he couldn't. In his shaky, spidery hand he added a postscript, a long involved explanation, about how the convent garden party was on just that day, and how the nuns counted on him, *absolutely*, to preside over 'guess the weight of the cake'. It wouldn't do at all to let them down ... I did see, didn't I?

'Poor old chap,' said Richard, who'd written to him while I was ill. I found it though, a very difficult letter to answer; for I, too, had been unable to face the funeral.

After the letters there were my mother's effects to go through. Mrs Pickering, crying a lot of the time, helped me with these, so did Richard. My father had collected everything from the nursing home:

'You'll want this,' he said, pushing the Memory Box towards me.

He seemed still very tense and edgy, and was smoking, not perhaps more than usual, but with greater ferocity. For the time being, he'd moved over to my grandmother's. He thought, though, that he might go off for his holidays soon. 'You're right enough where you are, so I shan't worry. I might spend it in Town—I've three weeks due.' He was awkward with me—not so much irritated by me as uncomfortable, embarrassed in my presence. And weak, lank-haired, convalescent, I didn't see how I could be anything but depressing company.

I was alone a lot in the house in Cornwall Road. After her one interfering gesture, Alice Ingleson seemed to have time for no more; apart from making a few polite enquiries as to how I was going to spend each day she showed little interest, and made no suggestions—other than recommending me to rest. 'I hope you're getting plenty of rest,' she would say on her way out and then on her way in again; seemingly firmly convinced, like many people who are never still themselves, that rest was the remedy for everything.

As I'd suspected, Nell didn't get on with her mother. They squabbled frequently—often noisily. 'Girls, *girls*, Pax,' Bernard Ingleson would say, raising his hand; removing himself with a dry comment from the scene.

When she was alone with me, Nell would often unburden herself. 'Oh God,' she would say, 'I hope it won't be like this for you.' Once she said: 'Mother's excelling herself these days—all these *ghastly* decisions about nothing. God, it's wearing. Richard's bloody lucky; he never gets across her at all. Not that he'd give a damn anyway—I remember he used to sing to himself, hum, whenever she rowed him. God, it made her furious! But that was years and years ago—now, love, he just gets treated like a rather nice guest.' She paused. 'And *you'll* be all right I think, honestly. She's so damn thankful you're not Juliet.' Then she added: 'Aren't we all, though? The sort of unspeakable relief that it's not going to be her walking down the aisle—and really it did look like it at one stage. He's my own brother but he can be bloody stupid. I mean I'm fairly easy going, love, but she would have been *hell*. That stupid petty business of the dress. And God, Rome—you've no idea what *that* was like. Richard absolutely shattered and la belle dame just smiling away to herself. Murder. I expect like some flowers she blooms in the right climate but as far as I'm concerned, she's tat.'

Another time she said: 'It's probably all my bloody fault, but if I can't get away ...' Then she added, 'I'm a virgin—would you believe it? and it's hell. I can't think why I've lost the religion and kept the rules. But there it is. I think though I'll just have to go away again. Q says he's seen the banquet laid out just once too often—'

Her talk, the aura of the wedding, my living in the same house with Richard, surely, I thought, they should arouse in me the most intolerable desire? But I felt nothing. It was as if I had died too.

Already the wedding had been put back to December. Almost daily Richard reassured me, telling me that soon, very soon, I would feel better. It was just a matter of time.

Meanwhile, he felt terribly guilty about the Gnome. 'Are you sure you don't want me to try and get you a job? You must get awfully bored ...' But I said no; and he seemed relieved.

He was very understanding, almost too much so. We went out continually—whenever he was free. Sometimes Quentin and Nell joined us, but mostly we were alone. 'It's a chance to get to know each other.' We went for drinks, for walks, to films, to the theatre, to horse shows, flower shows, to a pony something or other. We drove up into the Dales, went away for the weekend with friends, visited Robin Hood's Bay because I had once said I'd like to, and met what seemed to be an unending stream of Ingleson acquaintances. I talked, and smiled, all with a curious feeling of deadness. Sometimes, I would get sudden attacks of terror, precisely because no one had noticed.

Then, sometimes, as he touched me, I would come alive for a while: little threads of memory: the picnic, the proposal, a remembered scent, feel; for a moment, I would believe that all was well.

My father, I saw little of. He told me that he'd postponed his holiday. Perhaps he would go abroad, France maybe; anyway it'd be September if he did. And he'd want me to keep an eye on my grandmother—who by the way, was really beginning to look up.

Nell had asked me to be a bridesmaid—to cheer me up, I supposed; she had already three or four of them and a couple of pages. 'It's your last chance, love,' she said, 'I should take it. You don't want to get a useless yen when you're a bulging matron ...' I couldn't really imagine wanting to be either bridesmaid or bride but I had duly gone for a first fitting, pinned round in lemon tulle.

We were well into August now. For the last few weeks, I'd given barely a thought to Elizabeth. Once or twice, feeling guilty, I'd wanted to tell Richard about her, ask if we could see her, then feeling suddenly overwhelmingly tired I'd put it off for another day. She'd never answered either of my letters and now from worrying about her, I'd moved on to thinking that her silence must mean it had all been a false alarm.

Then one afternoon as I came back in from collecting some raffle money for Alice Ingleson, Mrs Johnson called out: 'Lucy, you've a visitor'; and going into the drawing-room I saw her sitting there, legs sprawled over an armchair, discarded *Fields* and *Country Lifes* lying all about her.

'You old beggar, Lu!' she said, jumping up. Her colour wasn't as high as usual and she was a bit fuller in the face, but otherwise it was the same old Elizabeth. She was wearing her old gaberdine mac, so that I couldn't see if she'd filled out anywhere else.

I felt unbelievably glad to see her.

'That was an awful thing, Lu,' she said, 'about your mam. I've only just heard. Dad got it from someone at work. Honest, I'm ever so sorry, Lu.'

She'd sat down again now: she gave a great stretch, then pushing her sandals off she began massaging her toes.

'Now—about *you*,' she said. 'You beggar. You never let on. I never knew a thing about any wedding till I rang that place where you worked—and then I thought they were having me on— Yesterday it was. You are a *one*, Lu. Heck—sitting with me that time, and never letting on—'

She hesitated a moment, then: 'Hey,' she said, frowning, 'did *she* arrange it? Your mam, I mean. Was it, you know, a sort of *family* thing like?'

'Of course not.'

'Because I thought when I heard—well, it's the sort of boy she'd have *chosen*. They do that in Spain, you know, Lu. I read it in *Picture Post*.'

She stood up again. 'Give us a dekko, Lu,' she said, taking hold of my ring. I tried to pull it off for her, but I must have fattened up again a little, because it wouldn't come.

'Heck, it's *big*, isn't it?' she said admiringly. 'Is it ruby?' She prodded at it: 'Go on with you, really, Lu! You of all people. What'd I say, about that hair?'

For a bit, she quizzed me: asking me my plans and not listening to the answers—the same as ever. It was strangely comforting. Then she sighed and gave a great yawn, showing her big white teeth.

'Eh, but I'm empty,' she said with a shudder. 'Sort of sick like. Lu—you couldn't get me some biscuits? And pop? If they've some pop—'

There was no one in the kitchen. I put some biscuits on a plate, but I couldn't find any pop so I filled a glass from the soda syphon in the dining-room. When I came back in she was looking at the photograph of Richard which stood on the grand piano. It was very dated, and must have been taken just before he went in the Army.

'Phew!' she said, 'he's all right, Lu—not kidding. Reminds me a bit of Andrew—not much, but a bit. Andrew was more film star, like.'

She'd put the photograph back and was munching a biscuit wolfishly. She hadn't said anything yet about herself. She wrinkled her nose up at the soda water: 'What's this?' She tried a bit: 'Does it settle you? I wouldn't want to throw . . .'

She seemed the same, and yet not the same. I wanted to ask for her news but wasn't sure where to begin. To get her started, I said:

'Look—that row with your mother, that evening. I'd meant to stay—'

'You'd have been daft,' she said, with her mouth full of biscuit. She gulped down the rest of the soda water, pulling a face. 'She gave me a real night of it after. Shouting—and calling me dirty this and that—it was like nothing, Lu.' She belched loudly. 'I scraped my eyes out. And then—when I thought she'd done—she had Dad come in and ask me for the name all over again. Then she went downstairs and she rang him up—rang George up, just like that. Turned midnight and all.' She paused: 'Only, she wouldn't tell me what she'd said. And I was that bad by then, I'd have done anything, Lu— Even, you know, *taken* things. I'd my eye on the gin bottle at the hotel, only I didn't know like how much it'd need ... But then come the next Saturday, she had me up the doctor's. You know—Dr Varley. I never felt so daft. The way she talked it was more like I'd been raped. "Just taken, Doctor," she kept saying, "just *taken*."

'But he wasn't bad, really. He told us like it was a bit early to be sure, but the signs were mostly pointing, and we'd do best to make plans. She told him then, she'd got money off George, "Quite a bit," she said, "there ought to be a law." Honest—she's not bad, you know, Lu—when it's not you she's after ... Then, that night, she rang him again. It was good, Lu. I heard her. She really gave it him. "I could finish you," she said. "I could *finish* you. A girl young enough to be your daughter. Where's your shame then?" And I don't know what *he* said but she got back at him: "You should be thankful, Mr *Turnbull*, it's only brass you're losing. Elizabeth's lost a lot more than that ..." '

She pushed the empty plate and glass into the fireplace. 'I'll be glad to be gone, though,' she said, massaging her toes again. 'If she's said it to me *once*—"you've let me down, you've let me down"— it's a dozen times. I'll be daft with it yet.'

'But—where will you *go?*'

'Another hotel. It's all arranged. For when we know it's certain— when he gives a kick like—I'm going to my Uncle Harry's. Uncle Harry and Auntie Iris. They've a pub, Windermere way. It'll not be too bad, Lu, I'll help, you know—serve in the bar. And they said I've to wear a wedding ring, and look sad like. He got killed in a motor bike accident, Lu.'

'But the baby, what about the baby?'

'Oh, *him!*' she said airily. 'He's to be adopted. And when the season starts—May or so—I'll be back, and I'll either get another job this way—or if they'll let me, I'll get one miles from all of them. Heck, I dunno, Lu.' She yawned again. 'I could *kick* myself—I mean, when you think, Lu, of folk trying every night. Then there goes George—once in and out. I mean, well it's daft, isn't it?'

The clock in the room struck four and she jumped up: 'I'm on this evening, Lu. I'll have to get a bus from station.

'Heck,' she said prancing about the room, 'I don't *feel* different.' Then, 'Know this?' she asked, beginning to hum. 'Twelfth Street Rag—' She looked around: 'Got any records here, Lu? I wanted "Twelfth Street Rag," Peewee Hunt.' Jerking her hips from side to side, 'do whack a do, whack a do,' she sang, her head going up and down: 'do whack a do, whack a do...

'You ought to look a bit more cheerful, you know,' she said suddenly. 'Really you ought, Lu. Heck, how'd you like to be me, eh?'

The hot weather continued. I would find myself thinking suddenly of my mother—with her bursts of reminiscence; her string of endless cloudless summers which never ever could have been. The sink full of plates, Pugin's scraps dried and going off, lapsing into a croquet dream—eighty in the shade and home-made lemonade.

'Then there was this smell, this *scent*—when you came into the cool, from outside. Perhaps it was only flowers, beeswax—but I've never smelt it again, anywhere else, *ever* ...'

Often now, brought up in this furry world where past and present were so often not separated, so deliberately blurred, I felt I was in a strange country. The Ingleson household was full of immediacy. They spoke mostly of brisk arrangements—of what old so and so had said, or done, or should do, or would do. Polite with each other, they were so in a remote way; almost as if, I thought sometimes, they didn't care enough to quarrel.

Only Nell kept up her irritated, argumentative state of war with her mother. It was a new thing, she told me; 'I never used to bother. *She* never used to bother,' In the end, after a blazing row on the stairs – Alice Ingleson striding past me, face flushed, 'you think of *no one* but yourself, my dear!'—she went to stay with friends in Dublin for ten days. She would be back just over a week before the wedding.

'And for God's sake leave well alone. *Everything's arranged*—and

I'll write non-stop thank yous when I get back, and Oh God yes I'll go to bed early, every night—'

The days dragged on. One evening, with the car parked in the Tewit Well Road, I wept in Richard's arms. He told me:

'Look—you will feel better, I promise you. Soon.' Caressing me: 'Are you sure you wouldn't perhaps—what do you think—like to move the wedding *forward* again? It could be awfully quiet—as quiet as you like, darling. And it isn't as if, you know, by then, we won't have somewhere to live—'

For the last few weeks we'd been looking at houses. It was the new pastime. There were tours of likely double cottages, vicarages, town houses: 'Because you do agree, don't you darling, about having somewhere fairly large at once?' (Already I'd agreed that of course—but of course—we wanted a baby right away); viewing large dark kitchens, never once seeing myself in any of them, I listened to talk about dry rot, damp course, freehold and leasehold, conversion ('Now, the best chap for *that* would be . . .').

All the time it felt like a game: a preliminary to playing houses.

Then one morning Alice Ingleson said, giving me a list of errands: 'You might call in at Quentin's place. There should be a brass fender he's picking up for us. With Nell away—he's impossible.'

I agreed to go of course; but I didn't want to: I felt certain he'd mock me in some way. Although he was kind enough when I saw him these days, I had the memory of the dress still, and didn't want to see him alone.

The first thing to frighten me was the bell in his shop, which went on clanging and clanging long after I'd shut the door; there was so much about too, such a sheer quantity of bric-à-brac, that I was afraid of moving in case I bumped into something and began a fearful chain of destruction. Brightly coloured stuffed birds in glass cases—some in wicker (Miss Lister, oh horror)—heaped-up Victorian jewellery, china stacked to perilous heights, a piano with ranged along it a row of waxed dolls, lolling in faded cream silk.

'Lucy Locket!' exclaimed Quentin, coming through from somewhere at the back, 'lovely Lucy.' He hugged me warmly. 'Come on in—this fearful place. Into my office.'

Then the shop bell rang and almost at once he disappeared again.

Still apprehensive, I sat down to wait for him, huddled up in the corner of an old leather sofa, horsehair curling out of one of its arms. The room was small and dark and slightly damp: piles of books lay on the floor, collections of old periodicals tied up with string, bound *Girl's Owns* and *Punches*; against one wall were several paintings in great heavy frames.

Coming back, he opened a cupboard and took out two patterned china cups, unmatched, and a tin, marked Fortnum and Mason. 'Coffee, Locket? Too coarse for café filtre this, so we'll have to use a rather grubby percolator, tasting unforgivably of metal I'm afraid.

'All right then,' he said, when he'd fetched out sugar, milk. 'Tell me all about it. How's Cornwall Road—I haven't been up for days. How's *Alice?*'

Very busy I told him, describing the atmosphere. 'She's sent me about a fender . . .'

'Ah *yes*. Well I have it, actually, but I fear me it isn't going to be to her taste. Richard pronounced against it yesterday—'

The shop bell rang again; he wasn't gone long this time. Back, he said at once: '*Now* tell me, Locket—how's the fairy tale?'

'All right, everything's all right.' I shifted uneasily on the sofa : 'Why call it that?'

He looked at me curiously, lifting his eyebrows. 'Oh, but it *is*,' he said, smiling. He'd sat down opposite me, sunk deep in an old chair bucketed by its broken springs. 'It really is, you know—once upon a time. La Belle Dame sans (well, sans anything but the spurious charm she wields so well), with Richard in tow, or thrall if you like. Then just when everything goes amiss—along comes the princess. Round and soft and full of sympathy, and just a hint of Cinderella too. She thinks *him* Prince Charming, and —you know the rest. All in the best fairy tale tradition. All you have to do now is live happily ever after, Locket.'

The coffee spluttered in the glass lid; he bent to turn the gas flame down. 'I'm sorry, I'm mocking. I'm incurable. What I don't understand, I laugh at—'

He poured out the coffee, 'Very much in love?'

I nodded. I supposed that I must be; my feelings only buried, not gone; they would come back, gloriously, to prove that I spoke the truth.

He shrugged his shoulders suddenly: 'Enough'. Then, changing the subject:

'Doris Hirst was in here last week. I can't recall what after—'

Vigilance relaxed I listened then to a couple of stories about Juliet's behaviour in Rome ('Richard besotted or no—we really were bloody fools to invite her—'). So that I was taken quite unawares when, a moment later, he asked:

'Lucy—what does your father think of all this? Richard sweeping you off your feet, his being left alone, your being so young—what does he think?'

'He's pleased about it,' I said hurriedly.

Quentin took my cup:

'Good. Coffee again? The off flavour's novel if nothing else. Fortnum's, we *cannot* blame—'

He handed me the cup, and without any warning I began to cry: great slow scalding tears—I saw one splosh onto the leather. He leant forward at once, his face concerned:

'Locket love—what is it?'

'Everything—' The tears were gushing out now. 'Nothing—I mean nothing's the matter.' I was crying into the coffee. He took the cup from me:

'It's not Richard, is it?'

I shook my head, and then in a firm but for him surprisingly gentle voice, he said:

'Could we talk then—do you think?'

There was silence for a moment. And then as if unleashed by the tears, out they tumbled—a profusion, a confusion of thoughts, comments, reactions.

'But Locket,' he protested, 'steady on.' He raised his hands in bewilderment, 'I'm *lost*—'

Once begun though I couldn't stop: gulping, swallowing, I babbled on, confusion piled on confusion. 'They *did* get on, or they thought they did—only by the first time I remember—I had to take sides you see, when there's a war on you have to take sides, and first it was him and me, then—Oh God, I can't stop *crying*—then I moved over to the enemy—I mean, then I changed over to my mother's side, and later there were the letters. I found these letters, you see—'

He held up his hand, stopped me.

'This is rather awful,' he said, 'and calls for a drink.' He went back to the cupboard and taking out a bottle of manzanilla, poured two glasses. Then he went through to the shop; I heard the outer door bolted.

Coming back, 'Shut for lunch,' he said, sitting down. Then, very patiently, he tried to make sense of it all. For the next half hour, calming down gradually I talked, and sipped, and talked. At intervals, I apologised:

'Nonsense—Nell has wept on me, you know. Many many times—'

About Elizabeth, about Patmore, Gervase, the tea-parties: I can't think in retrospect that he said anything particularly wise, or particularly helpful for that matter, but he did listen, and listen well.

Once he remarked:

'You do talk to Richard don't you? You *can* talk to him?'

'Yes, yes,' I said, remembering. Then I added; 'It's just that, since I lived there—'

'That I *can* understand.'

When eventually, and very late for Alice Ingleson's errands, I left, he said:

'I take it as a compliment— Having a *crise de nerfs* on my premises, Locket. Come again, if you'd like. Life's enormously dull, with my Nell chased out of Harrogate—'

'The fender though. What am I to say about the fender?'

'Anything,' he said. 'Tell her anything.'

Surprisingly, it was better, I was better, all the rest of that day. The warmth I felt towards Quentin, towards Richard, towards everybody was the first I'd felt about anything for what seemed to me a very long time.

That evening Richard and I went out to dinner—it had been arranged a few days before, and accepted, apathetically by me. But I knew that I was getting better, because as we drove back again afterwards, warm and relaxed, through the summer evening, it was desire, and not its pale ghost, that sprang up again.

I did go back to see Quentin, a few days later. I'd had a letter from Gervase, even more confused than usual, which had upset me.

Richard had already left for work when it arrived, and after I'd walked what seemed twice round Harrogate for Alice Ingleson, collecting and delivering shoes, dry cleaning, electrical gadgets, I found myself just near Quentin's shop, with the letter in my handbag.

'Do you think he's all right?'

'Show.'

I handed him the letter. Shaky writing sloping downwards over three black-edged sheets of writing paper, it was a strange mixture of conventional phrases of mourning, and cries of pain, as if suddenly, Gervase had *realised*:

'She has gone to a happier place, but we, how are we to go *on*? "For peace her soul was yearning, And now peace laps her round—" Where is my last link with the life that was, *where*? "Her cabin'd ample spirit, It flutter'd and fail'd for breath. Tonight it doth inherit The vasty hall of death." She has pierced the veil—how is it with her? How is life on the other side? ". . . the woman I loved, Needs help in her grave, and finds none near"—there is only the past left, that's all. I had so *little* of it, so little of her. All that I can remember, so quickly gone. Summer lightning. I *never reproached her* though, she will tell you that. Never, never—' Desperately, tailing off without a signature, he wrote, "O my whole life that ends today, The woman is dead that was *none of his* . . ." '

'Browning *and* Arnold,' said Quentin, handing me back the letter. He asked: 'Who takes care of him?'

I explained about the nuns. 'They'd notice I'm sure, if he got really bad. It's just that—'

'I know.'

Outside in the shop the bell rang.

'I wonder,' he said, coming back, 'I wonder how angry he was— really? His girl being pinched like that yet *never* a cross word. It's quite remarkable. Tell me—was Richard good with him? I should think exceptionally so—'

Very good, I said; very, very good.

We decided then that I'd discuss it all with him this evening. If we were worried, we could perhaps write to the Reverend Mother?

'And now a drink,' Quentin said. 'It'll have to be a short one today, I've a crate of magazines to sort by lunchtime.' When he'd poured out two glasses, Campari this time, he said: 'Tell me something amusing, Locket. Some of the *lighter* part of your saga . . .'

I told him about Miss Lister. 'But Locket,' he exclaimed in delight, 'I never knew such *excitements* went on in the Cold Bath Road—'

'She was awful,' I said, 'and anyway she didn't get rid of my accent. Looking back, for my mother's sake, I'd have liked to get rid of it—for her. And also,' I said hesitantly, 'sometimes, you know, with you all—with the Inglesons—I wonder if they don't mind?'

'Love, that you *can* forget. They never notice anything.'

He collected up my glass. 'I'm outrageously rude about them. Often. But members of the snobocracy they definitely are not. And anyway where should I be if they were? Jewish blood, for a start. Then—school okay, regiment okay—but, imperfectly anglicised, a Wop for all that. If niggers begin at Calais, Locket, how can Rome hope to escape?

'Reassured?' he asked. He looked at his watch:

'Locket—that crate.'

I stayed behind to help. We sorted the magazines into three piles, saleable, reparable, and rubbish. Inevitably, we dipped.

'Nell will go wild over these,' he said. 'Just listen. *Girl's Own*, 1888. "To *Grumpy*: there are surgical instrument makers in London who might supply a finger, as well as a whole hand—"'

'Locket,' he said, 'imagination boggles, what *could* she have asked?'

That evening my father telephoned. I hadn't seen him for a fortnight, since we'd met last at my grandmother's. He'd meant to get over to see me, he said, or at least to meet me somewhere. He'd been trying, he said now, to decide what to do about the house.

'It'll have to wait though. I'm off to London tomorrow.' He said something else, his voice sounding as if he'd taken his mouth from the receiver.

'What's that?'

'I said, I might go abroad . . .'

The line was crackling badly. There was an awkward pause, and then, his voice sounding warily friendly: 'I hear you're house hunting,' he said, 'any luck?'

Yes, well, there was one place, I told him, 'It needs a lot of doing up though.'

He asked where it was; the name; some comment. But the line had worsened and I couldn't hear him at all.

'What did you say?'

'I'll write,' he shouted. His voice came as through cotton wool. 'I said, I'll write.'

The next morning, I had a present from him. A suitcase: bright red with a great assortment of straps and an enormous handle, and quite unlike any suitcase I would have bought for myself. There was a note with it too: he'd never given me an engagement present, he said. Here was a 'going away' suitcase.

I was overwhelmed by the present—and by the note. When had he last written to me, unless to say 'milk gone off' or 'sleeping in Harrogate' or 'quarter streaky bacon ration in brown dish in larder'? Sitting up in the guest room I read and re-read it: between gazing at and touching the suitcase.

In my mind's eye, I filled in 'Mrs Richard Ingleson' on the label holder. We would begin again, I thought. Myself, metamorphosed by marriage: his friend, not his daughter. (For it had been all right, had it not, that dinner after the engagement, when we'd gone back to the house, and he'd sung 'Oh Flo' and 'A dark girl dressed in blue' and 'When we went to Brighton'?)

'Darling,' Richard said in the evening. 'You'll stop the traffic with that.'

'I tried to thank him,' I said, 'but he's already left—'

'When he's back, though. Then, another dinner would be awfully nice, don't you think?'

Fourth finger, left hand, sore now with the ring which had stuck obstinately, inflaming the skin. It was the day of Nell's return and in the morning Alice Ingleson had a coffee party. Several concerned, elderly women tried to remove it for me (it was interesting, was it not, how much *larger* the modern gel's hand was?); there were complicated and painful assays with string, but all without success.

That afternoon I took it down to the family jewellers: it was recognised, removed, admired and promised for Saturday.

I came out of the shop; the weather, still very hot had a September richness to it. Standing in the sun waiting to cross the street, I looked down at my finger : its bareness seemed odd, the sensation of lightness, of freedom, almost frightening.

There was a break in the traffic. I was about to move when I saw coming towards me—blonde head, curls tossing, ungainly walk that was almost a waddle—Jennifer.

She saw me; there was a piercing, delighted, 'Lucy!'

'You dark horse,' she said over and over again, then: 'how *lovely* to see you! I feel awful—I wrote you and I did mean to follow it up. *You* didn't do anything about it either—you bad thing . . .'

We stood there, blocking the pavement at the crossing. 'Look,' she said, 'why don't we have tea somewhere?' She was on holiday : tomorrow they were all off to Whitby, the whole family, plus three cousins and two uncles.

We sat in Fuller's, and thirsty in the heat drank our way through three pots of tea. Our table looked down onto the street: it was next but one to the table I'd sat at that first time when Juliet had brought me to meet Richard and Quentin, all those years and years ago.

'It's so *exciting*,' Jennifer kept saying, 'fancy you being the first of all of us to get married. I don't think anyone else is honestly—I've looked carefully every day. What about *Juliet* though? Remember Juliet? Do you ever see her? And Marjorie, do you remember poor Marjorie? I saw her last week—at a gymkhana. She's doing jolly well. She's sort of second in command at some riding stables—the person's quite old, and I think Marjorie's meant to take over one day. She looked really *happy*, Lucy . . .'

We tortured ourselves with memories of the White Rose: 'Wasn't it absolutely *awful*? And *do* you remember—that promise about shorthand? I used to worry for weeks after, Lucy. I thought she'd appear sort of from nowhere and ask, "Have you done your daily shorthand?" Awful, embarrassing, like constipation things. *Have* you done your daily duty? Honestly it was weeks and weeks before I felt free of that place . . .'

After tea, we went window shopping. Had I got all my trousseau? Jennifer asked, and when I said I hadn't begun: 'Let's start looking *now*.' She'd like to buy me something for it too, 'No, but really. I've lots saved up.'

We went into the lingerie department of one of the big stores.

There, the giggles began again. Jennifer pointed to a shapeless, pink sateen nightdress: 'Can't you just imagine Miss M in that? Why are they *always* that sort of pink? she'd look just like a salmon, Lucy ... Then those *knickers*—e t b's or directory something—didn't she, aren't you *sure* she had those on underneath? Lucy, if we'd only *thought* of that—we'd never have needed to be so scared. I mean ...' There was another burst of giggling; we were overcome with our silliness. An assistant asked coldly if she could help us? and Jennifer surprised her by buying me on the spot a blue and white petticoat, with three layers of frills and a wasp waist.

On impulse, I asked her to be my bridesmaid. She'd love to, absolutely *love* to.

At the corner of James Street we parted.

'As soon as we're back from Whitby you must bring him over—we'll all get together. Lucy, it's going to be such *fun* ...'

I walked back slowly through the Valley Gardens, then on over Harlow Moor; some of the leaves were turning already, reddish-gold. By the time I let myself into the Inglesons' house it must have been nearly six. No one was about. Lying on the Benares brass dish in the hall was a yellow envelope: I looked at it idly, and was surprised to see my own name. I'd never had a telegram in my life: my first thought was, 'Something has happened to my mother.'

The absurdity of this made my hand shake as I tore open the envelope. Unfolding the form, I learnt that my father and Juliet had married, earlier that morning. They were leaving tonight for France.

'Regret so sudden. Letter follows,' my father said. They both sent their love.

Chapter 20

I sat, I don't know for how long, on the upright chair in the hall. After a while, my arms clasped tightly I began to rock to and fro. I felt that my face had gone very stiff: when a little later Richard came back from work, I found it hard to speak.

'Good God,' he said, as he read the telegram. 'Christ, what a thing.' He had gone very white, 'Look, darling—are you *all right?*'

I have a memory of his holding me, of our standing in the hall: 'Shock. It's just that you've had a shock, darling. We—we'll sort it out, in a bit. Find out *more.*'

Then I was on the sofa in the drawing-room again, once more trying to sip brandy through stiff lips. There seemed to be a lot of talking going on round me; Bernard Ingleson, back home now was sitting in a chair: Richard was saying something to him in a low voice. Alice Ingleson, her hat still on was walking up and down the room in distracted busyness, talking all the while in a loud voice, tossing off remark after remark—many of them unfortunate. 'My dear, I'm *sorry,*' she kept saying. And at one point: 'Richard, you were *well* out of it.' Then realising I suppose that this remark could have been better phrased, she added hastily: 'Well, as they say up here so often—there's nowt so queer as folk—'

In a tight, strangled voice I burst out: 'I've brought doom to this house—this is the second death. I'm a bad omen here—'

'But darling,' Richard said quickly, 'no one's *died.* God, I know it's upsetting for you—but no one's *dead,* darling.' He looked puzzled: coming back across the room, sitting beside me again, his arm round my shoulders.

'More brandy, I think,' Bernard Ingleson suggested, reaching across for the decanter.

An hour later, we sat in the dining-room. It was Mrs Johnson's half day: Alice Ingleson had cooked the meal. We ate grouse shot by Bernard Ingleson and Cecil Barraclough. It tasted of nothing. My mouth was dry and ashy and sitting there, I had the familiar blank non-feeling I'd experienced after my mother's death; but added to it now was a sensation of vivid, swirling nightmare.

The telephone rang: Richard went out to answer it. Alice Ingleson, heaping my plate with summer pudding said: 'Nell, I expect. Quentin said they might ring from Liverpool.'

But Richard putting his head round the door said: 'It's Doris Hirst. Can she come over here—in about half an hour?'

Back again, he was immediately concerned for me. They were all concerned. Wouldn't I rather be out while she was there? Richard could easily drive me somewhere, sit with me somewhere; I'd only to say—

'She sounds pretty agitated,' he said. 'She and Ronald have just got in. Apparently there was a letter in the afternoon post—'

I looked at the bread on my plate, oozing deep crimson juice. Unable even to contemplate eating it: 'No, no it's all right,' I said; I wanted to stay. I hoped, I think, against all reason, that when she came, she would somehow prove it all a mistake.

But her entry, fifteen minutes later, dismissed this folly at once. We were drinking coffee in the drawing-room when, escorted by Bernard Ingleson, she bustled in, trailing agitation. Without looking about her, talking non-stop, she gave Richard and me only a nod as if she hadn't really noticed we were there. Receiving a brandy :

'Ronald wouldn't come,' she was saying. 'He's *far* too upset— she's shocked him to the core, Bernard!' Her voice, shriller than I remembered had a tremolo to it now : 'And the *deceit*—that's what her Daddy can't get over.' She sipped at the brandy: 'Behind our backs—all of it. And he was a married man, a married man, Alice, when it began you know. The letter—'

Richard, turning to me whispered: 'Come on out, darling.' But I shook my head, sitting there obstinately. Doris Hirst's voice rose:

'The age difference—it's disgusting. Twenty-five years, Bernard. And what *is* he? A clerk—an insurance broker's clerk! A nobody, for my Juliet—'

To try and stop her, Alice Ingleson had come forward: she muttered something to her. Doris Hirst, reaching for her brandy said wildly:

'Lucy, dear, I didn't see you. I'm *beside* myself this evening. And Richard, dear—' she put down her glass, wringing her hands. The action and the word 'wring' sent me back suddenly to the hotel cloakroom that evening in June when, all her rings laid on the sill, she'd talked of her naughty Juliet, while I, glowing, had waited to go back to Richard. My eye caught my own bare fourth finger.

'How *you* must feel, dear,' she was saying now, 'what *you* must think.' Overdoing it in her embarrassment: 'You *poor* girl. The whole affair—I can't think. And your poor mother. Barely two months since she passed on—'

Richard had enclosed my ringless hand in his: he made now as if to pull me up from the sofa. 'But two months dead' I thought. It came back to me 'But two months dead . . . the funeral baked meats Did coldly furnish forth the marriage tables . . .', thumbing the glossary in my School Certificate *Hamlet*—Elizabeth underlining in red every bawdy reference. The baked meats had been plaster food for a doll's house—of the kind I had once coveted. I'd seen them always as that. Bright pink hams, crimson jellies, beige cottage loaves all eternally fixed to their dishes; apt foods—never stale because never fresh, they would keep for the next ceremony. Another funeral, a wedding, a birth.

She was fumbling in her handbag now. 'I *have* the letter . . .' Getting out her reading glasses, snapping shut their case. On her knee, I saw lying half a dozen sheets of big, sprawling writing:

'Look here, Doris!' said Richard urgently; he let go of my hand. Alice Ingleson who had been out for more coffee came back into the room. Suddenly Doris Hirst began to cry: little hysterical sobs, and Bernard Ingleson came forward, putting a friendly arm about her shoulders.

'There, there,' he said in a soothing voice. 'Some more of the brandy.' She finished it in a sobbing gulp. Almost choking, she went on:

'They're after her money. They've all been after her money. We *wanted* her married—you know that, Bernard,' the reading glasses slipped forward on her nose; she pulled them off impatiently: 'Ronald would have done anything for her, anything. He'd have got her *any man* she wanted. He was silly about her, was her Daddy.' She got out a lace handkerchief and screwing it up, dabbed at her eyes. 'She should have married *Richard* of course. I said at the time, "Why don't you marry Richard? He *loves* you . . ." '

Bernard Ingleson had poured her some more brandy. 'The War,' she said, 'the War is the only explanation. It was the WRNS that changed her. There was a married man *then*—'

I saw two pages of the letter slip to the floor. Outside, the front door banged loudly.

'Hitler has a lot to answer for,' she said, beginning to sob again. 'Disturbing people—making them grow up unsettled, upsetting their lives.'

'Look, we *must* go,' Richard said, getting up: as he took my hand, the door of the room was flung open noisily.

Nell, surprised, stood looking from one person to another:

'What*ever* is up? Richard, Lucy—what's *wrong?*'

For a second or two no one moved. As she stood there, Quentin's blazer flung over her shoulders, her face flushed, questioning, there emanated from her such an aura of happiness that I was frightened. She had brought the scent of it into the room. Huddled on the sofa, I could feel coming from my every pore the sour smell of misery.

Quickly, concisely, Alice Ingleson explained.

'Oh God,' Nell exclaimed, '*poor Lucy!*' Coming across the room, she kissed me impulsively, the blazer slipping to the floor, then I heard her say to Richard: 'Poor love. *You* must be pretty shook—'

'Catch her,' I thought Richard said: as suddenly overwhelmingly dizzy, I blacked out.

When I came round, I was in the guest room. Only Nell was there.

'Just lie still,' she said. 'Richard'll be up in a moment. He's gone to get you a drink—and to see what else he can hear. You fainted, and I'm not surprised. It was damn stupid keeping you in there—Richard's in a bit of a state, of course—but the *parents* should have shown more sense . . .

'You might as well get into bed,' she said. 'I'll keep cave if you're used to being modest.' While I undressed, she talked, sitting sprawled in the armchair. She looked tired beneath her happiness.

'I haven't thanked you for cheering Q up. He's a miserable old thing when I'm gone.'

I'd begun to shiver: 'I wasn't *very* cheerful,' I said. 'In fact, honestly, I was rather weepy—'

'What the hell. He enjoyed it anyway. He's madly avuncular—though he'd die rather than admit it.' She stretched luxuriously. Then:

'Look, love,' she said 'do you want to talk about this drama? Because if you want to open your mouth and scream—call her any filthy names—just go ahead. I mean, I don't know the story—but if *she's* involved . . .'

I shook my head. 'I liked her,' I began. 'I never—' Then hearing footsteps along the corridor, I stopped: Richard came into the room:

'Gone,' he said. 'At last. Although she *says* she has more to say.'

He'd brought me some hot milk: it looked revolting, steaming, a thin skin already formed; I remembered how my mother had hated the thick skin over the tapioca, when I'd visited her at the nursing home.

'What did she say this time, though? Lucy'll want to know—won't you, love?'

'Not that much really,' he said; his voice which he must have meant to be easy, sounding thick, 'she insisted on reading great chunks out of that letter—' Putting the drink beside me he sat down on the bed; Nell getting up, came over and sat on the other side, and for a while we all talked.

It was an odd conversation: everyone trying to preserve everyone else from hurt, fumbling for words, mis-aiming. And although the centre of their attention, I felt at the same time as if I were speaking to strangers—sometimes even, for a few terrible moments, strangers who'd been sent to plead my father's, Juliet's cause. Yet when I asked, timidly, for facts it was plain that they were both of them very angry indeed that I'd been told nothing, had been prepared in no way.

'After all, he could have told you. Or warned you or something. Even if the Hirsts were kept in the dark—'

I commented at one point, 'Well—it's a free world—' feebly using an expression which belonged more properly to Elizabeth. ('It's a free world, isn't it?' she would say cockily: to bus conductors, librarians, cinema usherettes, park attendants—)

'Not in this context, love, it isn't,' said Nell. She picked up the cup : 'Drink that milk up, I should. He's put brandy in it.'

I didn't expect to go to sleep after they'd left, and lightheaded with the brandy and not much to eat I lay between waking and sleeping: not wanting or daring to think.

Richard—in what I suspected had been an edited version—had given us more excerpts from Juliet's letter. Much of it I already knew. I knew of course that they had met on the Pullman going up to London; but not that they had spent that evening together—and the next, and the next. He'd managed to get up to see her again too, only a few weeks later. (The weekend of the picnic, of course.)

'Juliet's words and Doris's comments, they tended to get a bit mixed. But sometimes it was just obviously Juliet. A lot of waffle—stuff about the "impossibility of meeting up here". Natural enough—and "You can't expect me to explain—I just knew this was *it*." Then she bloody well glossed over the real problem—what they'd been going to do about it all—and went straight onto the wedding. Which wasn't in fact so awfully sudden. They'd had it all planned, this last month or so—'

Nell had said slowly, 'Hell, are you thinking what I'm thinking? That there's a babe?'

Richard reddened. 'Well, Doris was on about that, too.' He tried to mimic, ' "She assures me, Bernard, she assures me there's no *need* to get married." ' Her and her bloody euphemisms,' he'd said angrily.

'Let's leave the subject. Lucy's had enough.'

Richard had asked tenderly: 'Are you sure you'll sleep, darling?' And Nell had said, vigorously, that I'd have to do it alone. 'Mother's on the warpath.'

Then for a second, as he'd held me in his arms, as my cheek brushed aganst his—rough with evening—I'd felt my skin suddenly shrivel with terror: his touch, the smell of his flesh, at once repugnant, frightening.

Now, alone in the room, I trembled still. I thought I wished them both back again. Out on the landing I could hear Alice Ingleson arguing with Nell, and feared she might come in to me. Gradually the house grew quiet: doors being locked, windows rattling as they were opened—then silence. All I could hear was a steady, thumping sound. It was a while before I realised that it was my heart.

Then I must have drifted off.

I woke suddenly. The grandfather clock down in the hall was

striking two o'clock; at first I couldn't think where I was. Then in seconds, everything was back. Memory; yesterday, last night; my father, Juliet.

Completely wide awake I lay rigid, cold in this strange room that had always obscurely depressed me. Out in the garden an owl hooted eerily. Moonlight piercing thinly through the gap in the curtains lit up the edge of the chintzy bedspread, made weird shapes of my clothes heaped on the chair. The whole room, as I gazed, seemed slowly to grow lighter. I heard myself say, out loud, suddenly: 'He has betrayed my mother.' I said it over several times: 'He has betrayed my mother, betrayed my mother, betrayed my mother.'

I couldn't bear to name him at all. Then: 'But *she* is my mother,' I thought, with a sort of cold horror. 'My stepmother Juliet. Juliet, my wicked stepmother. My stepmother, wicked Juliet. Wicked Juliet . . .' I muttered, mumbled, repeated the words over and over again, an incantation, a charm. Somewhere, beneath the black ice I could sense emotion moving. stirring; cracking painfully the surface. I shut my eyes: not to think, not to know.

But it was too late. I thought, very calmly, that if I had a straw effigy of Juliet, I would set it on fire; a waxen image, and I would jab it with pins. From the real flesh and blood Juliet I shied away. Feeling, terrifyingly, at my finger-tips, the strength that could crush her tiny bones. Then, gradually, I admitted that too; and for a long while I lay there, secure in anger. I thought only of her. Who else, after all, was there to be angry with?

During the next few days, everyone was very kind. To keep my mind off everything, I was made particularly busy: with Nell and Quentin's wedding so near it wasn't hard to find errands for me. I went for the last fitting but one for my bridesmaid's dress. I should also have gone for my ring, but I forgot to collect it.

I waited for a letter from France. 'Letter follows' had been the wording. I wanted to look at the telegram again but no one had seen it; I searched, surreptitiously, through four waste-paper baskets, and later a dustbin buzzing with flies, before giving up.

On the Sunday, Richard went with me to see my grandmother. He felt very bad, he said, that we hadn't thought of her before. I, too, worried. On the way, he said: 'Will she live with them—or what do you think? I can't see, I must say, Juliet coping—'

I said that I thought since money wasn't a problem (and even as I spoke remembering suddenly my mother's remarks—at the height of her anger. 'I came to realise, Lucy, that he'd expected me to bring *money* out of Patmore. I was to be *worth* something.' Evident in their untruth. Ironic now.) they'd find a comfortable way round. He was always devoted, I said—although I wouldn't have called her possessive. Most of her fussing had been over my grandfather.

The few times Richard had seen her he'd got on well with her; I felt ashamed now that it was he who had thought of her, and worried how she might have taken the news—if indeed, she had heard it.

She received us in the front room: since the first time I'd brought Richard she'd insisted on using it even when, as today, we'd plainly not been expected. Wearing a polka dot dark brown dress, her hair looking newly washed, she surprised me by her spry, alert manner.

Yes, she'd certainly had the news. That she had . . . 'Fancy!' she kept exclaiming, 'fancy Peter playing a trick like that on me. Springing surprises on me, at my age!' She seemed excited, beside herself.

'She'll give him a son, that's what,' she said at one point. 'Happen, she'll give him a son—' Her voice was a little shaky: 'I wrote Arnold,' she said. 'I've told your Uncle Arnold.' Going over to the window she adjusted the net curtains; sunlight sprang in momentarily. 'I've heard said—she's quite a catch.'

Richard, trying to change the subject began talking, rather desperately, about some building he'd noticed—a gutting and complete restoration of a house three or four doors down.

But she answered with vague politeness, as if from far away. Temporarily the conversation dried up; then looking about her—as if trying to catch again what it was that had preoccupied her—she put her hand to her forehead:

'He should 've asked Alfred,' she said in a tone of surprise. 'He never asked Alfred, you know.' She looked first at Richard then at me: 'Shouldn't he have?'

I said nothing. And Richard, carefully, to humour her, something like: 'Well . . . if . . .', shrugging his shoulders. She laughed. She looked almost witchlike, her face caught in the light: neat features, exaggerated now by age, were my father's, mine.

'Damn it,' Richard said, walking back with me through the Valley Gardens, up to Cornwall Road, as concerned as I was. 'Damn it. I wonder whose problem that's going to be?'

We went out for a drive together afterwards. He was very understanding about my inability to feel anything, my reluctance to touch, to be touched.

'You've had a rather frantic three months, you know. Good *and* bad. That, and the shock—'

But sitting beside him, as now, physically frozen, hearing the voice I had worshipped sounding harsh and grating (as indeed were so many sounds now) I would try—and fail—to come to life again. The evening before, he had held me in his arms: I had stood rigid, returning the gestures mechanically; moving gradually away; stealthily, in frantic fear that touching my breasts, my lips, my thighs he might discover that now I was made of wood.

It was Monday again. I felt certain that today a letter would come, and I was first downstairs. But though I turned and turned again everything from the fat pile on the doormat, none was from him.

At breakfast, Richard—late because he was a heavy sleeper— asked me had I remembered we had a party tonight? 'And the ring. If you could collect that, darling?'

Nell wasn't down yet. Alice Ingleson, reminding me that today was the last fitting for my bridesmaid's dress, said:

'Nell will have to pull herself together today. No sitting around canoodling at the back of Quentin's shop.'

The weekend had been one of sunshine. Today it was close, heavy; even indoors, a sticky thundery heat oppressed the air. Bernard Ingleson, going out, thrust a ten shilling note into my hand. 'Get your hair done for tonight,' he said. 'Always cheers a woman, a hair-do.'

By ten o'clock the house was empty. Nell had gone to help

Quentin. 'Why don't you come too, love?' Mrs Johnson had left at nine for her thrice-weekly shopping expedition. I waited now until I had seen Alice Ingleson go out of sight down the road, bound for a meeting and coffee morning in nearby Brunswick Drive; then I went upstairs and packed my old suitcase—placing reverently at the bottom my mother's letters, and carefully and quietly let myself out of the house.

Outside the air was still heavy; there were thunderbugs everywhere. As I came through the garden I felt them settle on my skin, my hair. Standing at the bus stop—keeping a wary lookout for familiar faces—I saw them dotted black all over my hands: minute irritants.

At the station, I asked about trains to London. There was one in two hours' time, and leaving my suitcase in the left luggage, I went up to the nearest post office where I took ten pounds—my all—out of my savings book. Back at the station, I bought a third-class ticket to King's Cross.

Nearly two hours to fill. I walked along James Street, past the War Memorial and the windy corner, down the hill and into the Valley Gardens; as I went through the gateway, the first drops of rain were falling, heavy, sluggish. I turned into the Sun Colonnade, and in one of the inner rooms, sat down to wait.

The smell of chrysanthemums in the small space was heady, strong; shaggy orange, bronze, yellow blooms; beads of water on their leaves. Outside, of a sudden, the rain was released: like some tropical downpour it cascaded from a sky full of it, coursing relentlessly in torrents down the glass.

I had no idea, no sensation of time passing. It grew very close inside; condensation from the steamy heat ran down the windows in droplets. Then somewhere far away, a clock struck the half hour; I leaped up: terrified now that I might miss the train.

But without my noticing the rain must have eased, because when I turned to walk back down the colonnade, it had stopped completely; the air fresh again, the gardens nearly deserted.

I walked straight to the station. I didn't see anyone that I knew on the way there, or on the journey itself. At King's Cross, I read a notice about a YWCA hostel. I spent the night there, and in the morning set out to look for a secretarial job.

214

The White Rose diploma was quite a help, and by afternoon I was fixed up. Later, in the evening, I wrote to Richard.

They came after me of course. There was immediate, enormous concern for me. I was under age, my father could have ordered me back. But I had by that time found a bedsitter; and my calm, frighteningly controlled manner deceived and persuaded them sufficiently to leave me alone.

Within the year, Richard had married; very suitably. He has two daughters, both of them grown up now. One is a very successful show jumper locally.

Elizabeth's baby was a boy. She married, very soon after the birth, a Canadian she'd met at her uncle's hotel. She lives in Winnipeg now.

Nell and Quentin surprised everyone by having six children, and thriving on it. Quentin has grown very plump.

My father and Juliet live in an old vicarage outside Leeds. They have an Italian villa also, on Lake Orta. I have a twenty-one-year-old stepsister—very beautiful: I saw her once in an old copy of the *Yorkshire Tatler*; Juliet worries about her constantly, I'm told.

Jennifer gives me all my information. She got in touch three or four years ago after seeing my picture in a newspaper article about my husband. She is married to a doctor and has three boys, and hasn't changed at all.

Gervase died in 1953; suddenly and very peacefully. The day before, he'd spent repairing the scenery for the convent's Nativity play : I had a long letter about him from Sister Xavier.

And me: in 1956, after seven lean years in which I expected and received nothing, I met a Hungarian, a pianist who'd come over after the uprising. We married in 1958 but have no children. We live nowhere permanently, and are very happy.

I have never been back to see my father. I used to worry, those first years, that he might be happy. Now, I worry only that he might not.

I am reproached nightly, for after more than twenty years I've begun to dream of Gunter's again. My mother, Uncle Gervase, my young self—we are all there; even my father—who was never there—sits with us now. But his back is turned, and he never speaks.

Gervase, worried and confused, would like to tell me something. I am a little goose, my mother says, her head on one side: 'Don't you think, Lucy, you may perhaps have got it *wrong*?'

Certainly. But what to do—except dream the dreams out?

Or, I could go and see my father. Easy enough, God knows: all I need is a train ticket, King's Cross to Leeds. I could do it this year or next year: sometime; never?

But nothing less will do, that is certain. He's not a ghost—yet.